Mule

A NOVEL OF MOVING WEIGHT

TONY D'SOUZA

A Mariner Original · Mariner Books · Houghton Mifflin Harcourt
BOSTON   NEW YORK   2011

For information about permission to reproduce selections from this book,
write to Permissions, Houghton Mifflin Harcourt Publishing Company,
215 Park Avenue South, New York, New York 10003.

www.hmhbooks.com

Library of Congress Cataloging-in-Publication Data
D'Souza, Tony.
Mule : a novel of moving weight / Tony D'Souza.
p. cm.
"A Mariner original."
ISBN 978-0-547-57671-8
1. Drug traffic—Fiction. I. Title.
PS3604.S66M85 2011
813'.6—dc22   2011016050

Book design by Brian Moore

Printed in the United States of America

DOC 10 9 8 7 6 5 4 3 2 1

For my beloved Jess,
sexy, strong & constant

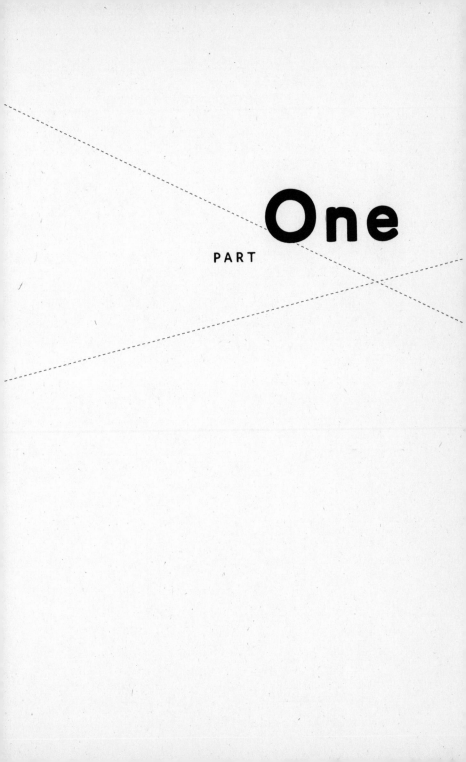

PART **One**

1

Birth of a Mule

BY THE MIDDLE OF 2006, years of hard work were paying off for me. I'd made the leap from writing for local rags to selling feature articles to the national magazines. I'd landed myself in the pages of *Esquire*. I'd even been published in the mighty *New Yorker*. Travel had come to me, attention, publicity, parties, all of it. At thirty, I was suddenly making and spending money in a way I never had. Wild and lusty Austin, my adopted hometown, was the perfect place for the mood I was in; the arrogance of my new success was a giant that followed me through the nightlife everywhere. And why shouldn't it? I was a normal guy enjoying what I'd earned. When *Playboy* ran my byline on a story about the backstage scene at City Limits, a Chamber of Commerce rep started giving me VIP passes to all the big events. Soon after, at a private rooftop party at the Belmont on 6th, I found myself at the end of the bar, drunk, well dressed, grinning. It was late October, the weather was mild, the stars were out, and at long last I was somebody. Standing before me was a beautiful girl.

"What's your name?" I asked her.

"Kate," she said.

"Here with anybody?"

"Not yet."

I snatched her arm, claiming my prize.

First it was sex everywhere, in the dressing rooms at her store, in my truck outside the bars. But by just a few weeks later, it was becoming something else.

"Can I ask you something real, James?" Kate said to me in bed one night. "How many people have you slept with?"

I laughed in the dark. I told her, "Don't you know you're the only one?"

She elbowed me in the ribs. She laughed, too, and said, "Don't lie to me. Nothing will ever matter as long as you don't lie."

We lived in that dream, breathing it, eating it. After more than a decade working in department stores, Kate had just been promoted to general manager of the downtown Metropolitan Apparel. She was twenty-seven, pulling in double anything she ever made in retail, feeling as big about things as I was. We were always together in the restaurants and clubs, celebrating our success like an endless coronation. All the loud people around us were doing the same thing.

One night, everyone else in the world asleep, I lit a cigarette beside her on the couch on her porch while she smoked a joint. I said quietly, "Kate? What's really going on with us?"

She said, "Do you mean, When is this going to end?"

"It's always ended for me," I nodded and told her.

She said, "Don't you know I'm scared, too?"

Should we be cautious? But the future felt enormous, everything possible, and carelessness took control. Shopping at Whole Foods a few days before Christmas, Kate caught a whiff of the salmon in the seafood section, ran outside, and vomited.

We rang in New Year's 2007 leafing through baby books in Kate's bed, because I'd given up my apartment to move in with her and we were pregnant. We were nervous, happy, and soon we had the first sonogram pictures taped to the bathroom mirror. In the pictures, the fetus was a tadpole attached to the yolk sac. We nicknamed the baby Peanut.

Six weeks later, we'd lost our jobs, and both of our careers were gone. We never considered not keeping our child.

The end of our life in Austin is the same story almost everyone in the country can tell now. Metropolitan terminated Kate for "inability to manage employees effectively," right after she told them she was pregnant, even though she'd never been written up for ineffective management, or anything else. She came home in tears. Of course they didn't want a pregnant girl running their trendy store. Of course they wanted to cut her inflated housing-bubble salary—her sales associates let her know she'd been replaced for less than a third her pay.

We immediately filed a discrimination case with the Equal Employment Opportunity Commission, which Metro contested, and then the EEOC informed us that although our case had merit, there weren't the resources to pursue it. We didn't have the money to risk taking on the corporation on our own. Kate's COBRA coverage began a steady destruction of our slim savings. I sold my beloved Ranger for next to nothing on Craigslist to pay for engine repairs on Kate's twelve-year-old Forester. Kate had been fired; she had to be on the phone day after day with the Texas Workforce Commission, explaining what had actually happened, begging for unemployment benefits. But before we could celebrate the commission's letter finally granting them to her, every editor I'd ever worked with let me know that not only was there no work for me now, there wouldn't be anytime soon: subscriptions and ad revenues were way down, and they were having to lay off their in-house people. I'd always loved freelancing for the guts and freedom of it. Now I was paying the dues of that freedom. I didn't even qualify to apply for unemployment.

I continued pitching story ideas everywhere, but the rejections came in like an endless wave. I sent my résumé to every print outlet I could think of, and didn't hear back from any of them. Then I tried for anything I thought would offer a livable wage—substitute teaching, marketing, paralegal—and never got called from any of those either. Even the temp agencies said they didn't have anything right now for someone with my qualifications. I kept asking myself, How could this have happened to me, with the byline I've worked so hard to build? Kate and I would rub each other's shoulders in the night, saying to each other on the verge of panic, "Everything will be fine if we just keep trying."

We were among the first to get hit by the downturn, didn't even know there was one yet. We felt alone, ashamed, humiliated. We avoided all our working friends, knew they didn't want to hear our embarrassing sob story. Once Kate's $370-per-week unemployment payments started coming in and we saw that we could just scrape by on them if we squeezed out every penny, we breathed a little, tried to make the best of it. We told each other we were lucky that Kate didn't have to work while she was pregnant, that something in my field would turn up soon. With nothing else to do but pray for a callback, we swam in the pool of our complex in the middle of the day, and in the evenings we drove across town to hang out with Mason.

Kate had met Mason through a girl at Metro when she was new in town and looking for a weed hookup. Mason was a longhaired born-over-here Korean kid with a thick Gulf Coast accent. The only thing really Asian about him was a samurai sword on his wall he'd purchased off TV. He pushed cell phones at Sprint for his day job, sold pot on the side to make ends meet. His wife, Emma, was a waitress at Kerbey Lane, and together they had a two-year-old daughter named Bayleigh.

Mason and Emma were evacuees from Biloxi, had lost their house in Katrina, were still waiting for an insurance settlement eighteen months later. Unlike the people we usually spent time with, Mason and Emma never tried to pretend to be upbeat. They told stories about the hellhole the city had put them in when they'd first been relocated from the FEMA trailers, how the door of that apartment had been kicked in three times while they'd been sleeping, how they'd bought their own television over and over again from the pawnshop every time it was stolen.

But Bayleigh made them happy. She had pigtails, was always bouncing around the room and saying, "Watch me jump, Mom! Watch me jump, Dad!" like everything in the world was just fine. Kate and I would go over at her bedtime, and she would say, "Watch me jump, guys!" to us, too. Then Emma would tuck her into bed, come back out, and tie on her apron for work. She'd narrow her eyes at Mason from the door and tell him, "Try not to pass out, in case she needs you." He'd shout back, "You think I'd ever pass out on my own kid?"

None of us were in the mood to say much, so we didn't. Mason and Kate would smoke a blunt. I'd drink beer. We'd kill the evening together staring at the TV. Kate had the kind of morning sickness that went on all day. The weed calmed her stomach enough so she could keep down food; Mason knew our situation, didn't charge us anything. Kate had printed out a study done on Jamaican women that said pot had no effect on their babies. Still, sometimes when we'd drive home, she'd whisper to herself, "What if I'm hurting my child?" I didn't like that she was getting high, told her so, but felt as helpless about it as everything else. It was only once a day; she promised to quit soon. How could I begrudge her what she needed to cope with all the shitty things that were happening?

When Mason was stoned, his eyes would get really narrow, he'd grind his teeth, smack his hand on his knee, and shout out of the blue, "Man, we're never going to recover from the fucking hurricane." Then he'd notice we were there and his voice would soften. "I'm sorry, you guys, I know what you're going through. You have each other. Everything is going to be okay."

With no calls for interviews, and no options left except menial labor and minimum wage, I became depressed, stopped shaving. Then I noticed my beard was falling out. I saw it in the bathroom mirror the first time, small bare patches under my chin like crop circles in a field. I looked it up on the Internet: alopecia areata barbae. There was no known treatment or cure; it was caused by stress. Kate noticed it one day when we were showering, and to lighten the mood she called me Captain Patchy. The Internet said that sometimes the lost hair would grow back quickly, but in other cases it never did.

Kate would usually fall asleep on Mason's couch after they'd finished their blunt, her hands on her belly, her long black hair splayed across her cheek. She seemed so tragically beautiful to me at those times, like a weary woman in a Rembrandt painting. When she was sleeping, Mason and I would go outside to smoke cigarettes on his balcony. His apartment was one in a stack, the view from the balcony of only the parking lot below. That life could be this terrifying was something I'd never imagined, and I'd worry my beard patches, say as much to him. Mason would tell me, "I know what you mean. And to ask us to bring our kids in on top of it? Who makes this shit up?"

When our lease ran out in May, we gave up on Austin, used our security deposit and the last of our savings to move. Mason came over to help us pack our U-Haul. It didn't take long, because we didn't have much and the rest of it we were leaving behind. Then we sat on boxes in our emptied living room and ate a bucket of Kentucky Fried Chicken together. Mason and Kate smoked a blunt. Mason said at last, "You guys have become such good friends, if you ever need anything, please just ask. We're all we're ever going to have in this life, you know? Each other and our kids and that's it."

My mother had told us to come to Florida, that we could stay in her spare bedroom until we figured things out. But Kate wanted to have the baby where she was from in Northern California, where she said we could get by on almost nothing. She told me again on our drive across the Great Southwest that her part of California was like no other part of the state. That there were mountains and trees were everywhere. That the snow sometimes fell six feet deep in the winter. That the border of Oregon was only an hour away and there were lions and bears in the woods. "And the people," she said, her hair tied back in a blue bandana like she'd started wearing it, "are a mountain people. They're rough and hard, and there's a part of me that's like that, too."

Where she took me was Dunsmuir, a tiny mountain town in a rugged canyon that once thrived on the railroad and logging. Her parents had found a place for us there, a rundown cedar-shingled one-bedroom cabin on the Upper Sacramento River that a guy they knew owned. When we pulled up to it, I expected a frontier family to come out onto the porch and stare at us like, "What do you people think you're doing here?" The cabin was off the road in a stand of cedars; the rent was

$375 a month, water and a two-burner Coleman included; there was no electricity; we'd have to buy wood for the stove to heat the place in winter.

I put on a brave face about it, still couldn't believe all of this was happening. Kate's scrawny father had been an itinerant timber faller, her tough mother had driven a forklift in the McCloud sawmill before it had closed. When I met them for the first time, I could see they were worn-out drunks. They were supposed to help us move in, but they sat on the porch and drank can after can of Coors. Kate didn't have much to say to them as we carried in our things, so I didn't either. I could tell right away we hadn't come here because of them.

The air was crisp and clean; everywhere were lakes and streams, everywhere high forested ridges. The water that flowed down from there fed the great agriculture fields of California. Kate took me driving through the timber up old logging roads to look at the snow-covered height of Mount Shasta. "People dream of the mountain," Kate told me one evening as we sat on a blanket in a field of lupine, six thousand feet up. "The Indians did. Some of the Gold Rush miners did, too. Then in the sixties it started calling the hippies, a white mountain every night in their dreams. They rode the rails, came in beat-up cars, raised their families in camps in the woods. Now it calls the odds and ends. People show up with just the clothes on their backs. Somehow they make their way here and never leave again."

"So why did you leave, Kate?"

She thought about it. She said, "I guess I wanted other things out of life then, James. A mountain just didn't seem like enough to me at the time."

A few weeks after we moved in, Kate's mother came by one evening with a pot of pork and beans, sat for a while and rubbed Kate's belly, and then asked Kate for money. I was lying on the bed in the backroom to give them some time together; of course I was also listening in on what they had to say. What her mother said was "If you have any spare change, you know we could use it. You must have saved something out there in the world. Isn't that why you went there? God knows this cabin isn't spendy."

First Kate said, "Don't you know that's why we're living in it?" Then she said, "Is it going to be the same old shit after all this time?"

Later, when Kate came to bed, she took my hand to feel the baby. There it was like always, kick kick kick.

"A boy or a girl this time?" she asked.

"A boy this time," I said.

"You still want to name him Evan?"

"My old man would have liked that."

We were quiet in the evening's cool, the cabin quiet around us. At last I said to Kate, "Did she really ask you for money?"

"It was only a matter of time."

"Don't they think about us and the baby at all?"

"They know the baby will survive on my milk."

There wasn't any work up there to look for, so I didn't. Discussions about what we were going to do next we put off for now. We were getting by on the little we had, growing closer together. Sometimes it felt like nothing was wrong.

That long summer in the mountains, I'd never seen anything so lovely as my pregnant Kate. Inch by inch her belly grew, and with it our baby inside her. She spent more time in the mornings brushing her hair because the hormones had made it thicker. She headed out early for walks, coming home with her bandana full of wild blackberries she'd gathered from the bushes by the tracks. "Do you think you could live here forever, James?" she asked me one afternoon.

I'd caught two rainbow trout from the river, was gutting them in the sink. I'd spent a little extra money on a couple cheap poles; all I ever did anymore was fish. "Live here forever? Maybe if there was any work. The air's clean. It's safe. It's the most beautiful place I've ever been."

"But in a place like this, it would be just you and me. No big distractions and not a ton of friends. Just you and me and the kid. Would that be enough for you?"

The trout were fat and fleshy, and had appeared on my line like miracles. That I'd reeled them in for our dinner had made me glad all day. Outside the window, the Steller's Jays were blue dashes in the boughs of our cedars. I said to her, "What did all of that mean anyway? If we could pay for it, I'd live anywhere in the world with just you."

Mason called at the end of August: he and Emma were fighting. Of course they would work it out, but could he come and see us for a while? Kate called up someone she knew from high school, a guy named Darren, who she knew could hook her up with some weed. I worried about the cost, but she said she wasn't going to ask him for much, probably wouldn't even have to pay for it. It was the least she could do for Mason, she told me, after everything he did for us before we left Austin.

When I came back the three and a half hours from the Sacramento airport with Mason in the car, still reeling in my head from the busy city, Kate had a neat blunt rolled for him and they got stoned on the porch right away. All the two of them did, as they smoked under our tall trees, was laugh like a pair of old hyenas. When I asked them what they were laughing about, Mason grinned at me and said, "Poor James doesn't even know. It's because this kush is so fucking good."

"Look at you now," he said to me, "a mountain man and all. In a motherfucking flannel jacket just like a goddamn lumberjack."

I crossed my arms where I stood in the yard and beamed at him.

"How much do you pay for an eighth of this?" Mason asked Kate. Kate batted her eyes at him and said, "Man, don't you know I grew up out here? I get this shit for free."

He said, "You have any idea the money I could make with a pound of this in Austin?"

It was great to have Mason at the cabin, a friend from the life we'd lived before, seeing us grown into this different place. I'd become proud of the mountains and how beautiful they were, wanted to impress him with our life in them. Mason mostly slept all day, which Kate said was because of the altitude, and when he'd rub his eyes open at last, it was all I could do not to drag him from the couch and down to the river. By the time he'd come to Dunsmuir, I knew a dozen foaming riffles that consistently produced big trout.

Fishing the bend at Sweetbriar one afternoon, Mason said to me, above the roar of the water, "I've got this idea. I've got this money saved. I'm going to go to Korea to see my uncle and buy as many knockoff cell phones as I can. I'm going to bring them back and sell them out of the back of the store. I'll double my money easy."

It was another one of Mason's schemes. He always had a bunch: to buy a camera and start a real estate video business, to buy a mixing board and turn his living room into a recording studio, to buy a home silk-screening machine and sell T-shirts on eBay. They excited him for a time, but they frustrated Emma, who would always point out the catches. "Plenty of people already have real estate video businesses," she'd say and roll her eyes. "How are we going to compete with them?" Or "Who'll want to record their crappy albums in our dirty living room or buy T-shirts you haven't even designed yet, Mason?" Knockoff cell phones from Korea seemed to me like something in that same vein. Instead of saying so, I asked him, "How much do you have saved?"

"Four thousand dollars."

A year ago, that wouldn't have seemed like that much money to me. Now it did. I built a driftwood fire on the bank, and we lay beside it in the grass and charred the fish we'd caught on a spit I'd rigged up with sticks. In the almost four months I'd been up there, I'd figured out how to do such things. As we gazed at the empty sky, I said, "You really think this cell phone thing will work out?"

Mason took a long drag from his cigarette, thought about it. "You know what, James? Sometimes life feels like an endless pile of shit."

Kate and I got married the last day Mason was with us, down the mountain in Redding at the Shasta County Clerk's Office. Kate wore a white maternity dress she'd grabbed off the rack, was really showing. I wore a jacket and tie. She changed in the bathroom before the service, our rings were from the mall. When we said our vows, the secretaries stood up at their desks around us to watch. Kate started crying; I wiped my face and I was crying, too. Then the marriage official introduced us to Mason as Mr. and Mrs. Lasseter, and we all laughed at the sound of that. We had Chinese food at a buffet restaurant afterward, and people in the surrounding booths congratulated us and wished us well for the baby. It wasn't the kind of wedding we'd ever imagined having. At the same time, it was private, sweet, and what we could afford, and our lives were what they were now, no matter how we wanted them to be.

Mason took a few buds of weed home with him on the plane when he left, wrapped in cellophane and hidden in his underwear. Then he called us from Austin to tell us that he and Emma were stoned already.

"It was so good to be with you guys. You guys will have the happiest baby. When you come through Austin, bring us some of that Siskiyou kush. We'd make a killing, I promise you that. I mean, I know you really can't, but you know what I mean. Thanks for having me as the best man at your wedding. Thanks for the fishing and everything."

One night in bed, Kate said to me, "Why did I give my life to those people? Why did I let them treat me the way they did?" It was quiet, cool in the cabin, and there was nothing I could say. Kate said, "Why didn't I think I was worth more than that? Why did I let myself get so hurt by it?"

We got a crib from the secondhand place down the mountain and Kate turned the corner of our room into a nest. And if we were going to make it through the winter, she told me, it was time to hurry up and start putting in firewood. We'd need at least eight cords, a pile as big as the house.

I shaved off my beard patches, went to the bar in town, gave them my name. Guys started coming to pick me up at the cabin in the mornings, and I'd spend the day with them wild-catting pine off the Forest Service concessions. I knew what we were doing was stealing, but it was the way people lived. We'd labor until nightfall, covered in dust from the saws, then haul the wood back to town with the trucks' headlights off so the rangers wouldn't see us. The few times I made the mistake of trying to talk to those guys about the baby coming and being out of work, they laughed—their whole lives had been like this.

Then I started cutting wood for Kate's high school friend Darren Rudd, a thin and rangy blond man with a hard and quiet edge to him, younger than I was, focused and serious. Unlike everyone else up there, Darren barely drank, didn't chew tobacco. The land we were working was on the back side of McCloud, and it wasn't Forest Service land but his own. He wore a sidearm on his hip, I didn't ask why. When I asked him how much land he had, he said, "Which piece?"

Something in me knew to be wary of Darren. Still, I liked him. He knew the world, alluded to adventures he'd had in India and Thailand. He told me that he wished he'd gone to college as I had, that in another time and place he would have liked to have been a writer, too. When I got up the nerve to ask him where his money came from, he cut the motor on his chainsaw, shrugged, and said, "Oh, you know. Here and there. SoCal, Vegas, Denver, Phoenix. Sometimes it comes from as far away as Florida."

I wiped my brow, felt the grit on it. I said, "My mother lives out in Florida."

Without looking at me, Darren said, "A smart guy can put up big numbers in Florida if he's interested."

In bed that night, I asked Kate about Darren's money. She told me, "The Rudds have always been pot growers. They've been doing it for generations. When we were kids, his parents would get raided and the boys would all get taken away. Then suddenly they'd all be back, half the time without any shoes. When we were young, it made them surly. They were the meanest kids in school. Darren has real money now, a hell of a lot of it. I guess all that meanness finally did some good for him."

When I'd talk to Mason in Austin, from the ridge where our cell phone worked, he'd always say to me, "Man, what I could do with a pound of that Siskiyou weed." When I'd talk to my mother in Florida, she'd say, "You know, I'd love to have you guys here."

One day working with Darren, I finally asked him, "How much would a guy have to pay for a pound of Siskiyou weed?"

"If the guy was a friend, he'd probably have to pay two and a half," Darren said.

"Thousand?" I said.

"Yeah, thousand."

"And how much could a guy get in Florida for it?"

"A guy could drop it in Florida for five or six."

"Thousand?"

"Yeah, thousand."

The idea of something became planted in me. I didn't know exactly what the idea was or what I would do about it, just that something could be had here in the mountains for a price you couldn't get it for anywhere else, and that I could buy it for that price and take it somewhere else and sell it for more than I'd paid. When I thought about it, I saw money, money we needed. I put thoughts of risk and danger away. I was already living in so much fear: that my child would go without, that I'd drag my family through poverty. More than anything else, I felt like I'd failed Kate in how our lives were supposed to be.

I called Mason two nights later. "You know that present Kate had waiting for you and it made you laugh and laugh?"

"Yeah, I know what you're talking about, James," Mason said cautiously.

"How about instead of going to Korea with that money, you stayed in Austin and I brought some of it to you?"

He was quiet for a moment. Then he said, "I'll tell you what. If it's the same stuff Kate had, that's what everybody here wants and can't get. If you brought it to me, I could get rid of it with just a few phone calls. It'd disappear around here like *poof.*"

"How much could you get for it?"

"Sixty-five an eighth. Maybe more if we came up with a good name."

"How much would that be on a big one?"

"A big one?" Mason said.

"Yeah, a big one. You know, like how you buy meat at the deli."

"Meat at the deli? What the fuck are you talking about?"

"By the pound, Mason. Jesus Christ."

"Let me get my calculator."

I knew the basics of the weed trade from when I smoked it in college, but what I didn't know as I waited for Mason was soon I'd be able to reel off the numbers in my sleep. Eighths in a pound? 128 of course. Quarters? 64. Halfs? 32. Dimes in an eighth? 3.5. Nickels? 7 or 8, depending on how greedy you were and what you thought you could get away with. A single pound of Siskiyou kush could be rolled into a thousand thin spliffs. The potential existed for a guy with a primary source to more than quadruple his money.

Mason came back on the phone. He said, "At sixty-five, I'd net eight. At eighty, it would be over ten."

"Thousand?"

"Oh yeah, James. Thousand."

I didn't hesitate. I said, "What if I could get it to you for five?"

Chopping wood was brutal labor. I was splitting the rounds I'd earned and gathered in our yard evening after evening. My body hardened; soon the widening pile was higher than my shoulders. Still, when Kate would come out onto the porch wrapped in her blanket, she'd shake her head and say, "We aren't going to make it." When the first frost came and we fired up the stove, I figured out right away what she meant. The stove was a glutton, ate wood like a beast, just a week of it chewed a hole in the pile big enough to lie in. Kate said, "When it gets really cold, we'll have to run it all the time. Because if we don't, we could freeze to death in our sleep." When she saw the look on my face, she smiled and added, "Well, we might not die, but we are going to have a little baby to keep warm."

Even in that hardest of our times, we hadn't been completely abandoned by the state. Kate had qualified for the WIC food program, and Medi-Cal would cover the cost of the birth. Despite all the humiliating phone calls and hoops we had to jump through to get it, we were grateful for the help. Still, every part of government assistance just reminded us that our lives as we'd known them were gone.

Kate said to me in the dark one night, "Can you remember anymore who we used to be?"

She was warm in my arms, her belly swollen, the baby kicking insistently against my hand. I said, "I remember I thought I was such hot shit."

She said, "I remember how the money made me feel. The partying. The friends. I had no idea it could end as suddenly as it did."

I was quiet a moment. Then I said, "Are you worried about the baby, Kate?"

"I think about her all the time."

"Are you afraid it's going to hurt?"

"I only want her to be well."

"So she's a girl this time?"

"Tonight she feels like a girl."

"What do you want to name her?"

Kate thought about it. "I've always dreamed I'd make it to Europe one day. To Rome. And I've always liked the name Roman because it sounds so strong. We can add an *a* at the end and make it pretty: Romana."

"Did you ever have any idea how strong you were going to have to be?"

"Not until they fired me."

"And now?"

"Part of me will always be angry."

The baby stopped kicking in Kate's belly. Then it was just the two of us. I said, "You ever worry that we rushed into this?"

"Sometimes I do. But mostly I'm glad about everything that's happened. Sometimes I'm even grateful. They forced me to stop working; life slowed down. I've been able to really feel this baby grow. You're at home with us all the time and you've been able to feel the baby. As long as I focus on things like that, everything seems fine. We'll have a little more time before the unemployment runs out when we can just lie in bed and be with her."

"And then?"

"And then something will have to happen for us."

"What if something doesn't happen?"

"I don't know."

Kate went into labor the second Friday in October, two weeks overdue, and her water broke in bed. It had snowed during the night, and it took me an hour to shovel us out to the road as she waited on the porch in her coat and boots. "Why'd you let it get so deep, dummy?" she kept shouting at me between contractions.

The storm had closed the pass; we had to go south to Redding. The icy drive down the mountain took two and a half hours. Kate's labor quickened in the car. She began to scream every few minutes as if being killed right beside me, and it was all I could do to keep us on the road. At the hospital when they rushed us in, she was already dilated past eight and a half centimeters, too late for an epidural. The looks we got from the nurses let us know they saw us as crazy mountain people.

In the birthing room I found out things I didn't know: my wife has a primal strength in her, and the world as we've constructed it is a joke. Just before the end, dripping with sweat, Kate looked up at me from the bed with this stricken face and whispered, "I can't do it, I can't do it." I knew right then she was going to die. My wife and my baby were both going to die. I knew I'd never love anything again as much as I loved them. I knew my heart would be broken and I would have to die there, too.

Then someone said, "Dad, we've got a baby girl!" and someone else took my hand and put surgical scissors in it and someone else guided my hand and I watched the scissors cut a milky plastic tube with dark lines in it. And I understood that the tube was the umbilical cord, and then I understood I was holding my daughter in the palms of my hands. She was covered all over in stork bites and blood clots and vernix. All this relief poured out of me as she began a long, loud squall. I knew right then I'd do anything for her.

When we'd gaze at our baby asleep in her crib, Kate would whisper, "How could I have had no idea I would love someone so much?" For my part, I was constantly checking Romana's breathing. Kate's parents brought us TV dinners. My mother flew in, made her camp up the road at the Acorn Motel. She'd been upset that we'd married without her having met Kate or even being invited; the baby's birth made her forgive all that. "It would be a lot warmer for you guys in Florida," she kept saying and shaking her head as she shivered by the fire and knitted a blanket for her granddaughter.

My mother took me aside before she left, told me, "What's

happening to the country is frightening, but people don't just starve and die. Your beard doesn't have to fall out, and you don't have to go on hiding up here. Maybe life won't turn out the way you thought. So what? That baby doesn't care about any of that."

Mason called from Austin to congratulate us. "In a year you'll say, How did she get so big? Then one day she'll stand up in her crib and go, Hey, old man, wake your ass up! Get me my goddamn bottle."

I went out on the porch, asked him, "Are we doing this, Mason?"

He said, "Yeah, we're doing this."

"How are we doing this?"

"We're going to figure that out."

But the next time he called, he didn't want to do it anymore. He said, "What if you get pulled over out there, James? I couldn't live with that."

He was right, I had too much to lose now. So I let the whole thing drop like the dumb idea it had always been.

Two days later, I got a text from him: "lets do it."

I called him, asked, "Can you send me the money in advance?" I could see him shaking his head as he said back, "You know Emma would never let me."

My family was middle class, and when I was in high school, my father had died of a heart attack. There'd been a modest life insurance policy. I'd spent most of my share on my bachelor's degree, hadn't let myself look at the remainder in the ten years since. Kate knew about it; we called it the baby's college money. Even after we'd lost our jobs, we'd promised each other to treat that money like we didn't even have it, to do everything we could never to touch her future.

Now I called MetLife. The woman on the phone told me my current balance was $22,031. If I wanted to write checks on it, she'd have blank checks sent; if I wanted to leave it alone, it would keep on growing at four percent interest. "Something really must be happening out there," the woman told me. "Lots and lots of people are tapping into their accounts right now."

One morning, I woke up to find Kate wrapped in her blanket and staring out the window at the latest round of snow.

Without looking back at me, she said, "Florida."

Taking a pound of weed to Mason wasn't a real thing to me yet, was still just an idea. Then Darren Rudd came over to congratulate us on the baby. He brought us oranges from a ranch he had down in Santa Cruz, was driving a new cherry-red F-150 Ford pickup I hadn't seen before. He'd had a haircut and his nose was tanned. When I asked if he'd been to the beach, he shrugged and said, "Yeah, in Phuket."

Darren liked the baby, held her. She was three weeks old and spit up on the shoulder of his calfskin jacket. When he told Kate she was looking slim again, she smiled at him and said, "You've always been such a liar." Then she took the baby to nurse, and Darren and I stepped out onto the porch to give her privacy. He had some kind of grain alcohol from Bangkok with a scorpion in the bottom of the bottle, and we took a couple sips from it standing up in the cold, dark night.

"What were you doing in Thailand, Darren?"

"R and R. Having some fun with the ladies."

"Work been treating you good?"

He nodded. "Things are changing. If they legalize, we'll have a few more things to figure out. But figuring things out is the nature of the business. There are always problems cropping up that need to be solved." He patted the place beneath his jacket where I knew he wore his gun. "In fact, I just had to figure something out over in Humboldt. Those inbreds over there can be such thieving idiots sometimes. Now I'll be heading back to Chiang Rai for a while, up in northern Thailand. I've got land there, too. I'm putting in a working organic farm, sustainable agriculture, doing my part to solve the world's problems. I'd do it here, but it's too expensive. You can't beat the cost of that cheap Thai labor.

"So I've got my dreams," Darren said, "and unlike you right now, I also have the means to pursue them."

I let the comment roll off me. After all, things really were like that. Then I said, "Remember when I asked you how much a guy would have to pay for a pound of Siskiyou weed?"

"I remember I told you if the guy was a friend, he could get it for two and a half."

"How would he have to pay for it?"

"In cash, like everyone else."

"No advances for a pal?"

He patted the place where he kept his gun. "There aren't any pals like that at my level of the business, James."

I worried my beard patches. I said, "Kate and I have been talking about going to Florida; there's a guy in Texas I've been thinking of taking some to if we do. He's got the money waiting for me there. So I'd have to write you a check."

Darren squinted hard at me as if trying to figure something out. He said, "A check'll work this one time. After that, it's cash. Are you sure you can trust your guy in Texas to pay you when you get there? Things can get messy in a hurry if you're not careful. This business isn't as easy as people think. Not just anyone in the world can be successful at it. But if you can, it can reward you like you wouldn't fucking believe. Think you can handle stress? Hold yourself together under pressure? If you have that in you, you can completely change your life." He grinned at me. "It seems like you're under a lot of pressure already."

I hadn't shaved in a few days; I knew he could see my beard patches. I dropped my hand away from my face.

"There's another thing about it, James. Once you start, it's hard to stop. You sure you want to mess around with this?"

The MetLife checks arrived in our PO box in town; Kate didn't see them. Then we spent a night at the Mount Shasta medical center, because she had mastitis in both breasts. The doctor put her on an antibiotic drip, and that was the end of the breastfeeding. When she asked the doctor what she did wrong, he said things like that just happened sometimes.

Romana was on formula now, so I had more time with her. When she'd cry in the night, I'd warm a bottle on the stove and feed her while Kate went on sleeping. That life could be as simple and satisfying as this, I'd never known. But there were other parts to life, too.

When we'd talk about it, Kate would say, "Who knows? Maybe we'll find work out there in Florida." I'd tell her back, "We're going to have to live with my mother, you know."

We didn't have Internet at the cabin; I started spending afternoons on the one working computer at the tiny Dunsmuir library. I was Googling "drug trafficking" and "interstate drug trafficking." I was reading about the marijuana laws and the protocols for highway stops and searches. I soon learned all about the Fourth Amendment: that you should never leave anything in plain sight in the car that would give the police a "reasonable suspicion" to search it; that if you were pulled over, you should never consent to a search; that you had a legal right to refuse, and if you did refuse, the clock was ticking on them and they could not detain you for more than twenty minutes without a stated reason. On the drive home from the library, I'd sit in the car and talk myself through a stop.

"Sir, I pulled you over for speeding. Will you let me search your car?"

"I'm sorry I was speeding, officer. Please write me a ticket, but I do not consent to a search. If I am not under arrest, I would like to go on my way."

"Sir, if you're not breaking any laws, why won't you consent to a search?"

"Because I believe in my right to privacy under the Fourth Amendment. If you're not going to write me a ticket, may I please go?"

If the officer asked me to step out of the car, I should lock it and put my keys in my pocket. At no time should I answer any questions. The police would have to prove "reasonable suspicion" to a judge in order to justify a search. If they went ahead and searched without it, a good lawyer could get my charges dismissed.

On the website of the Office of National Drug Control Policy, I read about the High Intensity Drug Trafficking Area program in force on certain highways, and studied pdf's of police manuals on how to profile drug couriers. I learned that empty fast-food wrappers in the car were a sign of someone traveling across the country quickly, that a windshield splattered with bugs was a sign, that maps were a sign. That transporting pounds of drugs was called "muling," "moving," or "carrying weight." That the average smuggler was a thirty-two-year-old male, unemployed, often with license and registration conflicts, driving a vehicle that didn't belong to him. That when questioned, the courier usually told a confusing story about his route and reason for traveling. That any perfume or other odor in the car was a sign of a smuggler masking the scent of weed. That most smugglers were high and nervous.

But I understood the drug interdiction police would not be looking for me; they were out there profiling blacks and Hispanics, especially non-English-speaking Hispanics. Just being white would be my best protection. The fact that I'd be driving my own car would help if I was pulled over. That I was articulate, with no criminal history and a perfect diving record, would help even more.

Still, there were the drug dogs. If I got pulled over and refused a search, the cops would try to get a K-9 unit to the location as quickly as possible, run the dog around the car. If the dog barked or scratched or indicated drugs in any way, it would give the police the reasonable suspicion they needed to search. It was clear from my reading there was no way to beat a dog. Dogs could smell drugs buried in coffee grounds, in grease, in gas tanks, anything. Even if the dog didn't indicate drugs, the handler could jerk the leash in a secret way to make the dog do it. The dogs were so infallible, their searches always stood up in court. If they ran a dog on you, you were done.

I plotted the route to Austin, Googled each stretch of highway for interdiction activity. The NORML website had a detailed interdiction map, and I saw I would have to avoid all of the I-10 along the Mexican border, where the Border Patrol operated checkpoints and the Fourth Amendment didn't seem to apply. I saw, too, that the I-40 through Flagstaff was a High Intensity Drug Trafficking Area, as was the Texas-Oklahoma border.

I read stories about people who'd been busted. I learned never to drive at night, to check that all my lights were working every time I stopped for gas, to stay with the flow of traffic. If a cop started to tail me, I would have to be cool. If I got pulled over, I'd have to control any nervous tics. And the punishments? If caught with a pound in Arizona, I'd face a year and a half behind bars and a $150,000 fine. In New Mexico, eighteen months; in Texas, two years. I'd have a felony on my record and mountainous legal expenses. Forever after, I'd have trouble getting any kind of legitimate work. At the same time, there wasn't any kind of legitimate work to get right now, was there?

The one thing I shouldn't have watched was the videos on YouTube of the police making highway busts. The cops popped the trunk, saw the bales of weed, pulled their guns, tackled the drivers to the pavement. Then they posed with the captured dope like hunters with their deer. But I wouldn't get caught, I'd tell myself on the drive back to the cabin; I'd be just another car on the highway like thousands and thousands of others. It would work best if I forgot I had the weed with me. Even the police websites admitted they barely caught anyone. My one pound would be hidden in the fifty-billion-dollar annual U.S. pot trade. And if I did get caught, I'd explain to the judge that we'd lost our jobs, I couldn't find work, we had a new baby, I'd done it for the money. Not a single thing I'd tell him wouldn't be the truth.

Darren Rudd drove up in a silver Malibu the day before Christmas while Kate was at her folks' with the baby. He was grinning when he met me on the porch; under his arm was a Christmas present. He handed it to me, and it was lighter than I'd imagined it would be, the length of two footballs wrapped end to end. I gave him the MetLife check. He put it in his pocket without looking at it. Then my heart began racing.

"You want to weigh it?" he asked me.

"I have to trust you," I told him.

"What you have to do is drive fast and swerve a lot."

Drive fast and swerve a lot? After everything I'd read?

As he turned to leave, Darren said, "Take it easy, James. It's just a thing we say around here when we're wishing each other luck."

Kate and I had lopped the top off a fir tree below the Castle Crags the week before, our first real outing with the baby. We'd

set it in a stand in the corner of the cabin. It was the prettiest
tree of my life. Under it were our few Christmas presents: a
bronzed pinecone ornament I'd bought for Kate as a memento
of our time in the mountains, things from our parents for the
baby. In an envelope was an airplane ticket, our decision made
at last, Kate and the baby's one-way trip to Florida, our savings
spent again. The girls were leaving on New Year's Day; I'd be
following behind in the car. Now I'd have a pound of weed
with me. I hid Darren's present among the boxes.

I cracked my knuckles, cracked my neck, went outside and
smoked. Long icicles hung from the eaves over the porch, and
suddenly I was more worried. I didn't really know Darren, did
I? What if he'd ripped me off? I couldn't help myself: I hurried inside, peeled the tape, opened the present. It was a thick,
vacuum-packed plastic bag stuffed with weed. The ends of the
bag were mechanically sealed, the buds inside as dense as cat-
tails, hairy with threads, covered with crystals like they'd been
dusted with sugar. I quickly wrapped it up. It was obviously
incredible weed.

When Kate came home, I took the baby from her, pointed
under the tree at the present. She made a face, went and picked
it up, carried it to the table.

"Where did you get this, James?" she said quietly when she
opened it.

"Darren brought it up."

"What are you going to do with it?"

"I'm dropping it off at Mason's on my way to Florida."

Kate touched the bag with her finger as if trying to understand what it meant. Then she sat on the couch and stared at
the fire dancing in the stove.

"How was it at your parents'?" I asked, just to say something.

"You know my parents were drunk."

"Did you get anything to eat over there?"

"I drank a little wine with them."

I sat down beside her. Romana was swaddled and sleeping in my arms. The cabin was quiet around us with the crackling of the fire. The tinsel-covered tree was a festive thing. Kate said, "What gave you the idea to do this?"

"Do you even have to ask?"

"What do we do if you get caught?"

I shook my head at her. "I've got it all mapped out. I'm not going to get caught."

Kate said, "Couldn't you have bothered to tell me first?"

"I knew you'd say no."

"I asked you never to lie to me."

"I had to do this, Kate."

We went to bed with our backs turned; neither one of us was sleeping. At midnight Romana cried and I got up and fed her. When I finished, Kate was standing behind me in the firelight.

"How much are you going to make?"

"Twenty-five hundred dollars."

"Where'd you get the money to pay for it?"

"I used the baby's money."

She nodded. The bag had been on the table all of that time, and now we approached it like sleepwalkers. Kate broke a hole in it and the stink immediately filled the room. She fished out a bud with her finger, held it up in the firelight for me to see. She said softly, "See how it's white where it's been cut? That means it's organic. Lots of growers use chemicals; they show up as dark rings in the stem. This bud's all natural. Darren's done a really good job with it."

She broke off a piece, crumbled it on a blunt wrapper, rolled and licked the wrapper shut. Then we went out onto the porch in our coats. There were stars in the sky, the moon on the snow. I knew that soon we'd be giving these things up. When Kate was halfway through her smoke, I asked her, "Is any it good?" She said, "It's a fantastic body high."

"I'm sorry I didn't ask you first."

"What do we have left if we don't have trust?"

We went inside and looked at Romana in her crib, our beautiful sleeping baby. Just before we turned to sleep, Kate said, "I knew I shouldn't have let you get involved with Darren."

Kate told me, "You have to call me from every stop, and you can't take any chances. You drive the speed limit and stick to your plan. You stop at night and get enough rest, and then you come home to your wife and daughter."

I promised her all of those things.

"You make Mason pay you what you guys agreed. Don't let him change the deal once you get there, you hear me?"

"Yes, Kate."

"You want to know something, James?"

"What?"

"I've never seen so much weed in my life."

I took the girls to the Redding airport the next day, New Year's 2008, said goodbye to them for the very first time. Kate held up the baby and I kissed them both through the security glass. Then their flight was called.

Up at the cabin, I dismantled the crib, put the pieces in the back of the car. There were bags of clothes to pack as well, the diaper pail. I thought about leaving the spare tire behind, hiding the weed in the wheel well. But that would be the first place the cops would look. I sealed the package with clear packing tape, left it wrapped as a present in the back window.

Why not? I thought as I smoked in the night. It's the gift-giving time of year. Who won't be traveling with gifts in their car? Who won't be on their way to visit people? By midnight I'd worked my way through a six-pack of stout; even then I couldn't calm my nerves. Why had we been so stupid as to open the package? I took it out of the car, smelled it; there wasn't any odor. Orion's belt was bright in the sky, the stars gleaming everywhere. I said out loud to them, "Am I going to get caught out there?" There was nothing but my breath in the air.

I went inside and sat by the fire and picked up my daughter's teddy bear. It was a small stuffed toy with an embroidered heart on the belly. When I pressed the heart, the electronic piece inside said, "I love you." Kate had handed it to me at the last moment at the airport; it was covered with the milky smell of my daughter. I smelled it now, pressed the heart, and the bear told me, "I love you."

I named the bear JoJo that night; I don't know why, I was drunk. I said to him, "Keep me safe, JoJo, and I'll bring you back to the baby. I know you know the baby loves you. I know you want to be with her again."

In the morning, I put the key under the mat on the porch, took a last look at the cabin. Despite everything, we'd been happy here. I stopped at Kate's folks' place for a final goodbye, then pulled onto the I-5. It felt like a cop was waiting behind every bend, and for the first fifty miles I drove in terror. But JoJo Bear sat in the passenger seat and kept me company, told me "I love you" every time I needed it. Down in the valley the traffic picked up, and I calmed down and got lost amid the cars.

Sacramento wasn't a long way from our cabin, about three and a half hours, but I'd started late because of everything I'd had to do. When I phoned Kate from a gas station just north of the city, she told me to call her friend Rita, ask if I could crash at her place for the night.

"We're at your mom's. We're missing you," Kate told me in her quiet voice. "Is everything going okay out there?"

"Don't worry, Kate. I'm being careful. Everything's going just fine."

Kate had worked at Macy's in Sacramento when she'd left the mountains after high school. She'd lived in an apartment downtown, near the nightlife; Rita had been her roommate. Now Rita lived on the south side of town, in a simple duplex in an urban neighborhood with her two young boys. She was attractive like Kate, still in retail. She gave me her couch while she put the boys to bed. When she came back downstairs, she asked if I wanted to smoke.

I tapped the bottle of Alleycat I'd brought in with me. "Haven't touched it since college. Never liked it. Now I know enough to stick to beer."

"Drinkers and smokers," she said and laughed. "Isn't that the way?"

Rita sat in an armchair, looking tired from work, rolling a joint on a little wooden cutting board on her lap and telling me about Kate in the old days. "So you married Kate Sisson? Isn't she so pretty? Man, all we ever did back then was spend our money. God, did we have some fun."

It was quiet, and I felt safe. The fear I'd had on the road was gone. I liked Rita, would have hit on her in my past life. Should I tell her about the weed? Should I not? What would she think of me if I did? At last I said, "Rita? Can you keep a big secret?"

She knitted her brow, looked at me suspiciously. Then she said softly, "Sure."

I hurried out to the parking lot, didn't want to leave the weed out there all night anyway—it was worth more than the car. I grabbed the package, brought it back to the house, unwrapped it on her kitchen table. The place was silent, the children asleep. Rita took one look at all that weed, covered her mouth with her hands, and said, "Man, are you totally insane?"

She immediately called her brother Henry, who came over with a friend, Jerome. Jerome had a digital scale. He zeroed a small Tupperware bowl on it, began fishing out big buds. Rita grabbed one, smelled it, passed it to Henry. They nodded their heads. I got nervous among those strangers, and said to Jerome, "How much are you taking out?"

"An ounce."

I mulled my lip. "How much does an ounce weigh?"

He shot me a confused look. He said, "Dude, do you even know what the fuck you're doing?"

They took turns running out to an ATM, bought three ounces, $1,200 cash. Not six hours into it, I'd already made half our money back. Rita wanted the biggest buds for herself, so did Henry and Jerome. When they passed around a bowl of it, Henry closed his eyes and said, "Chronic."

Henry was a third-grade teacher, Jerome a teller at a bank. Both of them looked like their jobs. Henry said to me, "If you stay over another day, you'll get all of this sold, most of it at four hundred an O.Z. Nobody wants to go through a dealer. It would be between you and our friends."

Could I stay? Hustle back up to Dunsmuir, grab another pound from Darren? But Kate and the baby were waiting for me in Florida. Jerome said, "Dude, this shit you got is the real kush. Wherever you take it, they're gonna be blown away. Call us anytime you're passing through. We'll always score a few ounces off you."

Later, lying awake on the couch, I thought about the evening, how excited they'd been. I'd had no idea about that part of it. Hadn't that made me feel good, like I hadn't in a while? Hadn't that been why I'd done it? The roll of money was thick in my pocket. I knew Mason would understand why I'd started selling it.

Just before Rita had gone up to bed, I'd said to her, "Am I taking this money from your kids?"

She'd grinned at me and said, "I still have a job, don't worry about me. And don't you have a kid now, too?"

I left in the morning before they got up. The yellow dawn was breaking over the dirty city and there were already cars on the road.

I stopped that evening in Needles, California, in the Mojave. Kate and I had done that road eight months before, and as I retraced our journey, I thought about all the things that had happened in the meantime. The warmth of the summer and catching my first trout, the tall trees around us in their evergreen coats. The baby kicking in my wife's belly, our quiet evenings together. Splitting wood in the falling snow, the firelight in the cabin. The awful drive down the mountain, the birth of my little girl.

When I called Kate from a truck stop outside Los Banos, the girls three time zones ahead, Kate told me she and the baby had gone to the beach already, she was feeling good about things today. When I told her I'd showed the weed to Rita, she said, "Why would you have risked that, James?" I explained the money I'd made, and Kate said she was proud of me for selling some of it myself, that though I shouldn't show it to anyone again, it was okay this once because Rita was trustworthy. Kate said, "Did she tell you at all how we used to be?"

"She said you guys had a lot of fun back then."

"Did she say anything embarrassing about me?"

"She said you liked to spend your money."

I crossed the desert, mountains, plains, quickly learned the art of driving flawlessly so as not to be pulled over. Every moment in the car was a moment when something could go wrong, every second behind the wheel was real work. Speeders stood out from the crowd as targets for the police, of course, but so did people driving too slow. Staying in the middle of a pack of cars was the best thing to do, no matter what the speed. I constantly scanned the road ahead for cops parked in speed traps in the brush, obsessively checked the rearview for cruisers coming up on my tail. Every time I changed lanes, I signaled; at no time did I ever tailgate. I did my utmost to drive perfectly every inch of the way, never give a cop a reason to hurry up behind me, flip on his lights and siren.

I didn't listen to the radio, didn't talk on the phone. As I burned down a tank of gas, four or five hours without stopping, Kate worried about me all of that long silence. "How am I supposed to know you're okay out there?" she'd ask when I'd finally call from a gas station.

"No news is good news. I'll text you if I get pulled over."

In northern Arizona, the highway was bustling with cops. In Albuquerque, my left taillight went out, and I stashed the weed under the bed in my motel room, bought a replacement bulb from Pep Boys, read the car's manual, fixed it myself. I took the I-40 all the way to Amarillo, then dropped down through the heart of Texas. I drove each day from dawn to dusk, peeing at rest stops and eating cheeseburgers. The car still had Texas plates on it because Kate and I hadn't wanted to pay the exorbitant California registration fee. Once I left the Golden State, I saw that Texas plates were common everywhere.

I saw so many things out there I hadn't noticed before.

Some cars simply looked like they were hauling drugs, the windows tinted, the hubcaps spinning, the plates from out of state—they might as well have had neon signs in their back windows flashing "Pull Me Over! Pull Me Over!" I'd always been a standalone speeder, zooming down the road all by myself and exposed, but now I didn't leave the safety of other cars, which mostly drove the limit—I'd had no idea most people didn't speed. There were so many different types of vehicles on the road, any one of them could be carrying weed. When I'd come alongside an old guy in an RV and he'd nod his head at me, I'd think, He could have two hundred pounds in there.

Every fifty miles or so, somebody really was pulled over. Sometimes the driver would be sitting on the side of the road while the cop looked through the trunk, most times not. They weren't the kinds of scenes you'd notice unless you were thinking about them, blurred images passing at seventy miles an hour. But all along that drive I was hyperalert, taking note of everything I saw.

On the third day, south of Lubbock, the rain came down and I pressed on through the night. Something about the rain made me feel safe, that I was in Texas with Texas plates, even safer.

Mason ran downstairs to the parking lot when I called at two A.M. It was the same old longhaired Mason. "Thank God you made it," he said and hugged me. When I handed him the Christmas present, his eyes lit up. He said, "Is this really here?"

We ran up the stairs to his apartment. Emma was passed out on the couch. Mason unwrapped the present at his kitchen counter: the buds were really there. He shook his head as he stared at all that weed. He said, "We have to do this again."

What I learned in Austin was that people in this business could be flaky. Mason didn't have the money that night; he hadn't even taken it out of the bank. When I asked him why not, he said Emma hadn't let him. "We didn't want it lying around the house, you know? Plus, I've got to make some sales first."

When I said, "What about Kate's and my money?" he said, "I promise you're going to get it." When I said, "What about the risks I took?" he gave me a sorrowful look and said, "I know, I know, and I'm sorry."

I spent the day in Austin with nothing to do while Mason drove around town selling weed. I ate fish tacos at Trudy's, walked around in Zilker Park, watched *Cops* on mute at the Nomad Bar. Wasn't it weird to watch other people get arrested? A relief in a way? Mason called me every other hour to check in; just then he was way up in Round Rock, waiting for some guy to finish playing Frisbee golf.

"Frisbee golf?" I said.

Mason said, "I know. I know."

Toward evening, Mason hadn't met the guy yet; he was out drinking at the time. Dollar-beer night at Cain & Abel's—how was he supposed to miss out on that? the guy had said.

What could I do but shrug it off? It wasn't like I could get rid of the weed on my own.

I drove to where Kate and I used to live, off 183, went past the apartment complex where we'd conceived our baby. They'd changed the code on the security gate, so I parked at the curb and smoked a cigarette. There were stars in the sky, the lights of the city. A plane rose from the airport nearby. What a strange place the complex seemed now. Had we ever really lived there?

Back at the apartment, I watched Emma feed Bayleigh mac and cheese. Emma shook her head at me and said, "What was it like out there, James? Weren't you terrified?"

I told her, "It felt good to be in control of something."

Mason was exhausted when he got home. He microwaved a plate of hot dogs, ate them standing up in the kitchen. Then he smoked a joint, washed his face, and gave me the money. It was a roll as big as my fist, all rumpled tens and twenties. Mason said, "Count it if you want, but it's all there. I rounded it up a few hundred bucks to cover your motels and gas."

I counted it out on the kitchen table: $4,300. Added to what I'd made in Sacramento, I'd more than doubled our money. There was one ounce left to take home to Kate. I'd never made money as easily as that.

When we went out onto the porch and lit cigarettes, Mason told me, "That Frisbee golf guy's in law school. What's he got to worry about? He's so fucking inconsiderate, sometimes I want to kill him.

"I've been doing this my whole life," Mason said, "and I've never had an opportunity like this. This kind of weed? At this kind of price? With everything that's going on out there? This could be real for us, James. This could be what we've been praying for."

Houston traffic was a snarled mess, the worst three hours of the trip. Louisiana was a five-hour breeze, Mississippi and Alabama one-hour jaunts. When I went through the tunnel at Mobile, I knew I'd reached the East. The forested Florida panhandle never seemed to end, then I turned south into the peninsula. All I had left was that one little ounce, stuffed under my seat with the bankroll. After driving the pound across the great western span of the country, it didn't even feel like I was breaking the law. When I filled up in Ocala, palm trees stood at the side of the gas station. I pointed them out to JoJo Bear.

"We made it," I said to JoJo.

JoJo said back, "I love you."

My legs were numb the last miles to Sarasota. I'd been in

the saddle for a week. I adjusted my driving to the slower city speeds, and then I was at my mother's.

My mother had wind chimes in the live oaks in front of her little house; they swayed and glittered in the sun. They made it sound like a Buddhist temple, like the world was at peace.

"Is it really you?" Kate said on the phone when I called.

"I'm sitting outside in the car."

The front door opened. There was Kate, the baby in the crook of her arm. We met in the middle of the driveway. No one else was around.

Kate said, "You look different."

"So do you."

"Did you really miss me?"

"Of course I did."

We kissed as though for the very first time. Then she handed me my baby. Romana was awake with her dark eyes. When she saw me, she began to cry.

"She doesn't remember who I am."

"You've been away a long time."

"I thought she'd always remember me."

The adventure had come to an end. I showed the money to Kate in our room, and when I slid the cash under our mattress, she said, "Thank God that worked out, and thank God it's over. I don't ever want to have to do that again. Your mother's been wonderful, but can you imagine how stressful it's been for me? Every day to be worried like that, to have to act like everything's fine? Your mom kept telling me I need to get more sleep. I kept telling her it's just the time change."

Then Kate grinned and said, "Did you bring me any weed?"

2

The Mule's Handbook

SARASOTA WAS A BUSY little retirement city. The half near the water had a ton of money; my mother's house wasn't in that half. She was east of the Tamiami Trail, had a little Florida block house with two bedrooms, one on either side. She was always dressed and coiffed, an upbeat older lady living on a grade school teacher's pension. She said to me, the second day I was there, and every following day, "What about work, James? Isn't it time you started looking?" I'd take a long swallow from the orange juice carton in her fridge, shake my rumpled head at her, and say, "Tomorrow." Then she'd say in a quieter voice, "What about Kate?"

"Tomorrow for Kate, too."

"Is something the matter with you guys?"

"Nothing's the matter, Ma."

"You aren't fighting in there, are you?"

"Kate and I are just fine."

What Kate and I were doing was lying in bed with our baby, watching her discover her hands. The last of Kate's unemployment checks was coming in at the end of the month. We'd laze in bed long into the day, exhausted by all the shitty things we knew were going to have to come next.

When my mother finally asked for copies of my résumé so she could take them around for me, I showered, shaved off my beard patches, put on a clean shirt, and drove on the Trail downtown. The *Herald-Tribune* building was tall and new, a beautiful boom-time structure in glass. Sarasota had gotten drunk on the speculation, but was now getting slammed. Foreclosures were on every block, all the strip malls had vacant stores. Construction on a dozen residential developments had completely stopped. There were rumors that the billion-dollar multitower condominium project near the center of town was about to fail. As I drove past all that economic wreckage, I didn't have any illusions the *Herald-Tribune* would hire me.

Instead of looking for work, I went to Siesta Beach, swam in the warm water of the Gulf, watched the pelicans coast by on their outstretched wings. Then I'd lie on the sand and try to figure out how to get ten pounds of Darren Rudd's kush to the guy named Eric I'd met in Tallahassee.

That last day on the road, I could have made it to Sarasota, but instead I'd stopped at an old friend's place and spent the night with him. I'd known Roger Sholtis since college. At our little liberal arts school in Kenosha, Wisconsin, we were reporters on the student paper. But we were also different. He lived in a study dorm, I joined a party frat. He'd always told me we'd have to go to graduate school to get ahead in the world, but when the time came to apply, he was the one who did. While I'd migrated down to Austin, he'd stayed home in our native Chicago, earned his master's at Northwestern, worked for a foreign policy journal in D.C., covered Haiti, and published a couple of university press books on the subject. Now he had a teaching gig at Florida State University.

I called him when I crossed the Florida border; he was happy to hear from me. How was married life treating me? he wanted to know on the phone. And was it true I'd recently had a baby?

The first thing that humbled me was Roger's house: old, traditional, in a leafy neighborhood near the capitol. There was a swing on the porch, a white picket fence around the yard. Inside, there were polished wood floors, upholstered furniture, colorful paintings from Haiti of black voodoo goddesses. There was a huge handmade chest of drawers he'd brought back from China, hardcovers in his bookcases. All of it was much better than how either of us had grown up—his dad had sold tires, mine had sold insulation.

Roger said, "You chose freelance, I took this. You got to go to the Playboy mansion, so I don't want to hear you complain."

I laughed and said, "You know they didn't invite me to the mansion, Roger."

Roger had a beard, glasses. He'd put on weight, had a softness to him that I didn't have yet. Some graduate students were coming over later, he explained, a getting-to-know-you party he threw at the beginning of the semester. But first we could have a drink and talk about old times.

"How's freelancing these days, James?" Roger said from his armchair as we drank his expensive claret.

"Honestly, Roger? It doesn't feel like it exists as a profession any longer. At least not for me. I got so discouraged I just gave up. Now they're saying they don't even know if they're going to be around next year."

"The newspapers, right?"

"The magazines, too."

"What are you going to do?"

"I have no idea."

"What about the Internet?"

"Doesn't pay."

"Going to keep writing?"

"How can I afford it?"

Roger rubbed his beard. He said, "Didn't I warn you to get a graduate degree?"

What could I say to that?

The graduate students, I learned when they came over, were serious people in their mid-twenties. The conversation was like that, too. Roger introduced me as his friend who had made it as a freelancer, an actual grunt from the field, successfully published in the national glossies. I wanted to correct him about all of that, but didn't.

I felt strange there, out of place, wished I hadn't come. I escaped into the backyard to smoke a cigarette. Through the living room window, I could see Roger, the students arrayed around him like he was the lord of the manor. Which he was. Was this something I could have had? Was everything that was happening to me my own fault?

Two men came out, asked to borrow my lighter, lit cigarettes with it, and moved several feet away. "Awful party," the clean-cut one whispered.

The hairy one whispered, "What'd you expect?"

"Why are they such arrogant pricks?"

"They give them tenure and they can be."

"He's going to bang that stuttering chick."

"Maybe the big brunette, too."

"You could not pay me enough."

"I bet it seems like good stuff to him."

The clean-cut guy turned to me and said, "You guys were buddies in college?"

"We worked at the student paper together."

"Is this how he was back then?"

"He's happier now."

"You published something in *Playboy*?"

"A year and a half ago I did."

"Did you get to go to the mansion?"

I shook my head.

The hairy guy took out a joint and whispered, "Let's smoke some weed, Eric."

Eric said to me, "How's the money in freelance?"

"There isn't any money in freelance."

"Yeah, I had no idea about the money. It would have been nice if somebody had bothered to explain that part of it to me before I went into the program."

"Then you wouldn't be paying to be in the program," the hairy guy said, and lit the joint off his cigarette.

"You smoke?" the Eric guy asked me, holding up the joint. I shook my head. The whole time at the party, I'd been feeling this intense humiliation. Now I heard myself say to them, "You guys want to try some kush?"

They spun around and looked at me as though for the first time.

I hurried around to the car and fished out a bud from the baggie under the driver's seat, from the ounce I'd saved for Kate. Back in the darkness of the yard, they took turns smelling it. The hairy guy said, "Where'd you get dank like this?" Before I could answer, the Eric guy said, "He got it in Cali."

"You drove this across the country, didn't you?" Eric said to me.

I said, "I took some to a friend in Texas."

"Did you make any money off that?"

"Of course I did."

He took a step closer to me. He said, "You know people out there?"

"My wife grew up with a grower."

Eric laughed. "A guy like you has a source in Cali? You've got to be fucking kidding me."

The hairy guy had papers and he broke off a piece, quickly rolled a spliff. Soon after they started to smoke it, he was giggling. He said, "Am I drooling? Am I drooling? I can't feel my fucking jaw."

Eric said to him, "Go inside, Reggie."

Reggie said, "Are you crazy? I can't go inside there like this."

Reggie looked at Eric to see if he was serious. Eric stared hard at him. Then Reggie shrugged and was gone. Eric touched his finger to my chest. He said, "What kind of sign are we standing under tonight? Let me tell you something. I'm the man in Tallahassee people would kill to meet. I flip ten pounds a week, bring it straight up from Miami. Half the campus is high on my shit."

He said, "Want to make some money? I'll hand you five grand a bag for ten pounds of this. You won't even have to wait. All you'd have to do is mule it and I'd have the cash ready. Nobody else in town can put up cash like that. How do you like it, that our paths crossed like this?"

I said to him, "You know what it's like to drive it?"

"Twice a month, heavy weight."

"How do you manage your speed?"

"Always with traffic."

"You like doing it?"

"No."

"It's pretty goddamned stressful."

"That's what it's like."

I considered him now. He was handsome, fit, his teeth gleamed white like they were capped. His linen shirt was new; he looked like he had money. I said, "What are you doing at Roger's party?"

He said, "I was in Iraq. Marines. Then I came here and earned my degree. I thought I'd stay and do the grad program, write a book about what I saw."

"What'd you see?"

"Invasion force. Combat. What the fuck do you think I saw?"

Eric said, "What about your quality? Can you always come through with this? How about your people? Do they have the production?

"This is for real," he said softly. "Ten pounds, fifty Gs."

We looked through the window at the party. Everything I'd been feeling about it fell away. Eric wanted the rest of the bud in my pocket, and I gave it to him. When he asked what the name of it was, I told him, "I didn't even ask."

"Let's call it Voodoo Kush," he told me. "If you bring me the weight, I'll give you the money."

When the graduate students went home, the big brunette was still on the couch, her long legs folded beneath her, leafing through one of Roger's books. When Roger walked me down the stairs to the basement's spare bed, his mouth was wet with drunken happiness. "You should have got that grad degree." He patted my shoulder. "She's twenty-three or twenty-four. Hopefully, she's not crazy.

"Life has turned out good, hasn't it?" Roger said as he pulled back the bedcovers for me. There was another painting of a voodoo goddess on the wall down here.

I asked him, "What's with the paintings?"

"They're Haitian goddesses of love. Of protection, luck, and money. I got them for next to nothing down there. This one I got in exchange for a meal."

I looked at the goddess before I slept; she was holding an infant child. Around her in the night sky were blood-red hearts; her white eyes seemed to bear down on me. Upstairs, the sound of the girl's laughter rang long into the night. At dawn, I was on the road.

Kate looked for work, and her résumé was soon on file all over town. When she'd come home at noon and it was my turn to go out, I'd drive to the beach and go swimming. I'd dive to the bottom of the clear, warm water, sit on the sand, think. How was I going to tell Kate about this?

I called Darren Rudd from Siesta Beach.

"How was your trip, James?"

"Piece of cake."

"Did you drive fast and swerve a lot?"

"That's exactly what I did."

"How are Kate and the baby?"

"Everybody here is fine."

"How did you like making that money?"

"You know how I liked it, Darren."

A line of pelicans coasted past, the beach was otherwise empty. I said to him, "My friend in Texas was happy. People I stopped and saw in Sacramento were happy, too. I had no idea how excited people would get. Now there's a guy here who wants to do it."

"That's how these things get started," Darren said. "Then they just get crazy."

Darren asked me, "Who's this guy?"

"A friend of a good friend."

"How much does he want to do?"

"Ten pounds."

Darren whistled. "How are the numbers?"

"The numbers are great."

"I told you about those Florida numbers, didn't I?" Darren said. "Nobody here would have any problem doing ten times what we already did, as many times as you'd need. That's what we do. We're good at it."

"Would the price be the same?"

"It would be for now."

"I'd have to convince Kate."

"Just tell her about the money."

My mother had women friends who came over to the house, all of them retired. They sat in the living room and played mahjong. "Have they found any work yet, Lynne?" we'd hear them whisper. "Are they still sleeping in all day? What are they doing in that room? They're depressed about the economy, you know."

When we'd come out at last and make an appearance with Romana, they'd assault Kate with advice. Why wasn't the baby wearing a hat? She could freeze in the air conditioning. Why did she never have on mittens? She could scratch out her eyes, the poor little dear.

Lying in bed at night, Kate would say to me, "I can't take this anymore."

I knew about mothers and daughters-in-law, hoped it wouldn't happen to us. I loved my mother and I loved Kate—couldn't they get along?

They didn't. My mother felt that the baby should begin eating rice porridge, that solid food would help her sleep, but Kate read that Romana should have only formula until she was six months old. "It's not the right thing for her, Lynne," Kate would say as the discussion ground on. My mother would say back, "Well, that's not how we did it."

"Well, this is my baby and this is how I'm doing it."

"Well, I'm sorry I give any advice at all."

The slamming doors, the mediations. God, what a wretched time.

We should go out for a meal, I told Kate, spend some of the

money we'd made. We'd taken a big chance — why not enjoy it a little?

We dressed up the way we used to when we first met, left the baby with my mother. We ate tapas at Sangria on Main Street, danced at the Gator Club, and at the end of the night we went to Siesta Beach. The stars shone above the dark expanse of the Gulf. No one else was there. I put my arm around my wife as we sat by the surf, held her against the wind.

"Do you love me?" I asked.

"Of course I do," she said.

"There's something I've been meaning to talk to you about."

"There's something I have to tell you, too."

"A guy at Roger's place offered me fifty thousand dollars to bring him ten pounds of Darren's weed."

"Fifty thousand dollars?"

"Yes."

Kate looked at the stars. She shook her head and finally said, "You've known about this all of this time?"

"I have."

"And you've already decided to do it, haven't you?"

"Yeah."

Kate looked at the dark water. "How much would we make out of that?"

"Twenty-five thousand dollars."

"Do you really think you could do it?"

"It would be the same drive as before."

Kate asked, "Couldn't we buckle down even more?"

I didn't say anything.

Then she said, "Did you talk to Darren? What did Darren say?"

"Darren wants to do it."

"How do you know you can trust this guy?"

"He's one of Roger's students."

Kate made a face. "What's a student going to do with ten pounds of weed?"

"He's a graduate student. He's been there for years. He says he moves it through the frats."

"It sounds too good to be true."

"Let's find out if it is."

She whispered, "Twenty-five thousand dollars."

"We could start our lives again."

For a long time, Kate didn't speak. Then she told me, "You have to be careful and check this guy out. If anything feels strange, don't do it. You listen to Darren and make a good plan and then you stick to it. No more showing it off to people, no more telling anybody about it. You talk to Mason and see what he wants, too. Then you come home to us."

Kate said, "We're going to be careful with the money. We're going to make it last. We'll get our own place as soon as you get back and we won't ever do it again."

"Yes, Kate."

"James," she said, "do you remember those two times in the cabin at the end when we didn't have a condom and we did it anyway?"

"I remember."

"We're having another baby."

Three weeks after I'd met him at Roger's, I finally called Eric. I was excited, nervous. I was worried I'd waited too long, that the opportunity had passed. The call went to his voice mail. "You've reached the Superstar. Yeah, you know it. Leave me a message." Beep.

"It's James, who you met at Roger's. Sorry I haven't been in touch. I talked to my friends, everything's a go. Call me when you get a chance."

I walked along the beach, drove around town. By the evening, Eric hadn't called, and there was nothing I could do but go home. In our room, the baby was sleeping, and Kate was reading the local community college catalogue in bed. If I really did manage to get that twenty-five grand, she wanted to go to school, something she'd never been able to afford. She'd study business, maybe get an MBA. "I want to be the one in control this time," she told me. She was wearing her reading glasses, looking studious already. She said, "Did you get a hold of him?"

"Voice mail."

"What time was that at?"

"Noon."

She was quiet, her face flat. She let the catalogue fall to her lap. Then she said, "At least we won't get in any trouble now, I guess."

We went outside on the patio. The moon was a scimitar in the sky. Kate crossed her arms as I smoked and said, "Why didn't you tell me about him right away?"

"I was afraid of what you would say."

"What is it with you being afraid of me?"

"What can I do if you say no?"

When we went inside, my phone was vibrating.

"James, my man, I'm glad to connect with you." From the sound of it, he was at a party. I pointed at the phone to let Kate know. She watched me from the bed.

"The Superstar," I said.

"You know it," Eric said.

"Sorry I couldn't call sooner."

"No worries, my man. I've been busy, too. God, it would be nice to deal with someone besides the motherfuckers in Miami. It would be really, really nice to get my hands on that voodoo you had."

"Everything's good with the people on my end."

"So when are you coming through?"

"We have to figure out the money."

"We can't do that on the phone, my man."

"Can you swing by here on your way to Miami?"

"I have a guy doing that for me right now."

"Then how about you pay us a visit down here and we'll talk?"

"No way. You're the one who has to come up here."

My hand on the phone was cold and wet. I said to him, "It's hard for me to get away, with my kid."

"No worries, my man. Another time. Call me when you come through."

"Wait," I said. "When do you want to meet?"

"Tomorrow. Outside the theater at the Governor's Square Mall at three."

When I was done on the phone, I looked at Kate. Her face was as white as I knew mine was.

"You're going up there?"

"Tomorrow. I have to."

"You'd better be careful."

"I will."

We didn't know Eric, didn't know a thing about him. Could I check up on him with Roger? I knew it wouldn't make any sense to Roger if I did. I sat beside my wife, set my hands in my lap. Kate said, "You're going to have to get that money."

"That's what I'm going up there to do." I looked at her; from the way she sat there I knew she was thinking about the new baby.

After our talk at the beach, we'd driven to Wal-Mart and bought a pregnancy kit. When we did the test at home, the two pink lines appeared in the window right away, just like they had for Kate when she'd tested herself a couple of days before. Then we'd talked about it all through the night.

Were we happy about it? we'd asked each other. The room

had been dark and quiet. The baby we already had was sleeping in her crib. It would be nice to have the children be close in age, we'd agreed; they were going to be Irish twins. Wouldn't that be a funny thing to try to explain?

Now I put my hand on Kate's belly. "Can you feel anything in there yet?"

Kate put her hand on top of mine. "Not yet. But my body feels the way it did when I was first pregnant with Romana."

"You're going to start getting sick again."

"Then you'll have to bring me some more weed."

"My beard isn't ever going to grow back, is it?"

"You look fine without it, Captain Patchy."

I told my mother I had an interview, turned down her offer of gas money at the door. I knew she was underwater on her house, as worried about things as anyone, even if she wouldn't admit it. "Thanks for letting us stay here," I said to her. She said, "Don't ever thank me for things like that."

The drive to Tallahassee was long and dull, five hours in the car. I was nervous the whole way. What if it was a sting? What would my story be? I was wearing the same flannel jacket and beat-up Levi's I had on my drive from California. They'd gotten me across the country safely and I thought of them as lucky now.

In the lot outside the movie theater at the Governor's Square Mall, I was talking to Kate on the phone when Eric coasted past in his car. I sat up in my seat with a start. In the middle of our conversation I whispered to her, "He's here."

"You know we love you."

"You know I love you, too."

His car was a black Mercedes, long and sleek. He looked as clean-cut in it as he had at Roger's. He cruised by again, circled, came back. When I winked my headlights at him, he grinned at me. I started the old Forester, followed him. There was a Marine Corps sticker on the bumper of his car. At the stoplight when I caught up to him, I could see that under the Marine Corps insignia the sticker read, "Iraq War Vet." Downtown Tallahassee was busy with traffic, congested around the capitol. Eric switched lanes at every opportunity as though trying to shake me. Why was he doing that?

We entered a residential neighborhood; the people here had real money. He pulled into a long and curving cobbled driveway. The large house at the end of it was Bavarian, all dark beams and eaves—foreboding. When he stepped out of his car, he was dressed in white, even his shoes. I took slow, deep breaths as he came striding across his long lawn to meet me. He held out his hand, pulled me in close, then yanked up my shirt. He ran his hand around my waist, cocked his chin at my car, and said, "How many miles you got on that piece of shit?"

As we walked up the flagstone pathway, Eric said, "James, I'm really glad you made it. I've been thinking a hell of a lot about you. The Cubans have been killing me, you have no idea the shit they make me eat. We can't do too much because we can't have them notice, but we can still do plenty. Ten pounds here, ten pounds there, everybody stays safe and happy. I mean, their stuff's indo, it's good haze, but it's nothing like your kush. And with the kind of margins you're giving me, there's no way we both won't get rich."

"What kind of margins do you get from the Cubans?"

"Six. Six point two. Five and a half when they're really glutted. Come inside," Eric said, unlocking the heavy front door. "My humble abode is yours. Want a smoke? Want a snort? Want a drink? Want a bitch? Let's see who's freeloading on my couch today."

"I should have told you six," I said as I followed him in.

"Then we wouldn't be talking."

The carpeted front rooms we passed through were dark and empty. It felt like nobody lived there. Then we entered a bright modern kitchen. Lying on the center island was an assault rifle, ventilated barrel, compact stock. Eric opened the tall steel fridge. He said, "I got Stella, I got Beck's."

I shook my head and said, "Got to drive home after this." I should have turned around as soon as I saw that gun.

Eric leaned his hip against the island like the weapon wasn't there. He was excited, started talking with his hands. He said, "God, how I've wanted to hook up with Cali. But how are you supposed to do it? Fly out to Humboldt? Hold up a sign? Do you have any idea how happy I was when you showed up?"

He beckoned me down a long white hallway. He said, "The landlady came snooping around here once. Nearly got herself capped—she didn't know that. You'd think three and half Gs a month would get you some privacy, but I guess not."

We went into a dark, wood-paneled den. There were two guys sitting on a leather couch, shooting up Liberty City on a projection TV. The room was furnished like an MTV set: a tank full of tropical fish built into a long brass bar, neon beer signs, posters of Phish and the Dead. On the coffee table were half a dozen bongs, so much ash that the table seemed covered in snow. There were loose buds on the shag carpet, loose buds on the table, the air smelled like they'd all just smoked. Eric said, "The fat one is my crazy brother, Eddie. He got the defective genes in our family. The Mexican one is Manuel. He was my gunner in Iraq. Now he's my adopted orphan."

They were greasy and bloated, Eddie pasty-skinned and bearded in a food-stained white T-shirt, Manuel's face pockmarked with acne scars. Neither of them looked at me.

Eric took me across the room to a framed picture on the

wall. In it, a dozen heavily armed soldiers stood before a tank, making gang signs with their free hands. Beside the picture was a diploma: *Florida State University, Political Science, Eric L. Deveny.*

Deveny, Deveny, Deveny.

The soldiers were outfitted for desert combat. The landscape behind them was a flat and endless yellow pan.

"Which one are you?"

"Third from the left."

He'd been heavier then, a chubby, childlike version of the sculpted person he was now. Eric pointed his finger like a gun at the faces in the picture, shot each one in turn as he said, "This guy is dead. Armor-piercing IED. This guy lost his leg below the knee. This is Manuel. We ended up running heroin over there with these three guys and a local sheik. This is the motherfucker who ratted and got us discharged. I've got his address in Utah. One of these days I'm going to go out there and kill him.

"Fucked-up shit," Eric said to end it. "But a lot of good times, too. I wouldn't have joined, but I needed the money. Not a day goes by that I don't think of that."

Eric beckoned me up a carpeted flight of stairs at the side of the den. As we climbed them, he looked back over his shoulder at me, grinned, and said, "Nobody gets to come up here, my man. This is where it all goes down."

It was a kind of loft, a small windowless space, an FSU banner of the Seminole taking up all of one wall, a computer workstation in the corner. There was a king-size bed with rumpled sheets on it, heavy dumbbells on the floor, two armchairs and a coffee table on a red Persian rug. On the coffee table was an orange Nike shoebox packed with row after row of banded money.

We sat in the chairs. Was there a recording device behind the Seminole flag? Video camera? The way we sat there felt like an interview. Or a haggling session.

Eric ran his hand over the money. He said, "Fifty Gs, my man. Bring me the weed, you go home with this."

I looked at the money, held together with simple rubber bands, each folded set in the rows a thick bundle of bills.

"Those twenty-dollar bills?"

"Tens and twenties," he said.

"You have to give me half up front."

Eric made a face. He said, "Are you fucking crazy? It doesn't work like that. You show up with the shit, you go away with the money. That's the only way it's ever going to be."

I knew right then I was going to use the baby's college money.

"How am I supposed to pay for it?"

"You have to figure that part out."

"Then you have to give me some earnest money."

"Why would I give you that?"

"How else will I know you'll pay me when I get here?"

"You're looking at the cash, aren't you? Why else did you come up here?"

"I came up to get half."

"Well, you're not getting that."

"Well, you have to give me something."

Eric touched his forefinger to his temple. He was quiet for a while. Then he said, "How long will the trip take you?"

"I figure I'll be back in two weeks."

"I can't let my money sit out there for two weeks. I've got shit coming up from Miami. I need this money here working for me."

We both sat back in the chairs.

"I thought you just wanted to see it," he said.

"I thought you were going to give it to me."

Defeat washed through me. Eric flipped the lid closed on the box. He said, "This isn't going to work out, is it?"

I'd come this far. The money was right there. I said, "We're smart guys. Let's just relax and think about it."

We went back downstairs, through the den, out a sliding glass door, onto a high wraparound wooden deck. The yard was huge, sloped down to a creek. No other houses could be seen through the trees. The place was beautiful, anyone's dream. When we lit cigarettes at the rail, I noticed my fingers were trembling.

Eric said, "You don't have any clue what I've put together up here. I've worked so fucking hard at it. A million guys would want what I have. But I'm the one who took it."

I said, "I want to make this happen. More than you know."

"Don't see how it can be done, my man."

"Maybe I could do some driving for you."

"I already have a guy doing that."

We were quiet, thinking as we smoked; at least I was. I would use the baby's college money to buy the ten pounds of weed from Darren. What if this guy didn't pay me when I got back?

We went upstairs. He opened the shoebox to let me look at the money again, then shut it. He shook his head and said, "Do you know the kind of hard-ons I've been having about this?"

God, how I wanted that money. I said to him, "Just give me something so I know you're in it."

"I'll give you two grand."

"Give me three."

"How do I know I haven't just bought you and your wife a trip to Vegas?"

"Because of Roger. You can always get to me through him."

Eric looked at the money, shrugged. Then he offered me

his hand. "Sold. Sold, my man, for three thousand dollars." He opened the lid, took out three bundles, began to hand them to me. When I snatched at them, he pulled them back. He winked and said, "Really want it that bad?" Then he flipped them to me and I slipped them in the pocket of my jacket.

"I dropped that guy's class, by the way," Eric told me. "I'll figure out how to write my book on my own."

When he walked me out, we looked around at the evening. There were no cars going by, no listening van, nothing like that, no one else there. "I need to get stoned," Eric said at last.

"I need something, too."

"Call me from the road."

"I will."

In the car, I smelled like sweat, like stress, like I'd had a long day, which was true. It was past midnight when I got home to Sarasota. The girls were already sleeping.

I crawled into bed beside Kate, held her. "Made it home safe," I whispered.

"That's great, baby," she murmured. "Did you manage to get the money?"

Now the clock was ticking. I'd been naïve, had the idea that getting ten pounds of weed from California to Florida was a thing you just went out and did. I had no clue how the money worked, the paper trail, all the things I'd eventually have to use: the cell phones, laptops, Internet, post office, credit cards; the cash, of course, always the cash; the planes, rental cars, motels; I had to eat sometimes, too; the timing and coordination of the handoffs—everything you had to do to get something like this done. Again and again in the coming days I would stop and think, Impossible. Then I'd take a deep breath, turn my mind to the project, make myself find the solution.

My research into the police became a constant thing. I dried out my eyes scanning news reports on my laptop. Where had the recent busts taken place? How had the couriers been busted? Had they made mistakes with their driving? Speeding? Following too close? Or had they been profiled? On what stretch of highway had the bust gone down? Had the cops run a dog? How about traffic? Would there be more cars on the road during a particular period of time, making it easier to hide in—a holiday weekend, say, or a rodeo congesting a certain area? Or were rising gas prices emptying the roads, leaving me the only idiot out there?

All of that didn't come into play during that first big run, but a lot of it did. Even the first time, I risked an immediate federal interstate drug trafficking offense: huge fine, long sentence, permanently ruined record. Kate pitched in, always would: she kept my mother occupied, took care of the baby, worried for me. The work would always be intense for her, too.

I couldn't sleep that night I came home from Eric's; the stress had already begun. It would get worse and worse until reaching its crescendo the night before the run in the panicked racing of my heart. Was I going to get stopped at the interdiction choke point at Flagstaff? Were they going to nail me in Sulphur, Louisiana? On the Internet it said that the cops in Sulphur paid gas station attendants who reported suspicious activity a cash percentage of any takedown. Wasn't that cheating? But I also knew, as I held my wife in bed that night, that I now had money that belonged to a former combat Marine who kept an assault rifle in his kitchen. And if everything went right, I'd make $25,000.

At dawn, I was up and pacing the room. First I had to call Darren, then I'd know what to do next. But I couldn't call him yet because of the time zones; it was still the middle of the night in California. When Romana cried out, I fed her a bottle. Soon Kate was awake, and she asked, "What was it like up there?"

"Big place, expensive wheels. His last name is Deveny."

We Googled his name together on the laptop. There was a William Deveny at an address in Miami. Eric's father? There was a Norman Deveny in Jacksonville who had an automotive repair business. We tried Ric Deveny, Rick Deveny, and Ricky Deveny. No hits. We tried "US Marines heroin trafficking" and "US Marines implicated in heroin trafficking." These only returned articles about Marines rounding up poppy growers in Afghanistan.

Then we tried Facebook. Deveny, Eric. There he was. Kate and I both sat up in bed. In his profile picture he was holding his chin, a glamour shot, his hair the way he wore it, looking like a young Tom Cruise. The few other pictures he had were of him partying with attractive college-age women: a toothy blonde, a pair of Italian-looking girls who could have been twins, all at bars and holding drinks, the women wasted and draped over him. There were a couple of him with guys from his unit when he was fighting in Iraq. He hadn't logged on to Facebook in over six months. The posts on his Wall were from people asking him, "Where are you, Superstar? Where have you been?"

"Could he be a narc?" Kate said.

I said, "This guy isn't a narc."

"What else happened up there?"

"Nothing else happened. We talked, had a cigarette, figured things out."

"Did he seem dangerous?"

I thought about the assault rifle. I shook my head and said, "I kind of liked him."

"What was there to like about him?"

"He knows what he's doing."

I called Darren from Siesta Beach.

Darren picked up, yawned. He said, "You get it squared away with your guy?"

"He wants to do ten."

"Did you get the money?"

"He wouldn't give it to me."

Darren said, "You can't play if you can't pay. That's the way life works."

"I do have the money, Darren. It's in this account. I'm going to have to write you a check off it."

"No checks this time, James."

"Wire transfer?"

"Cash, or it doesn't go."

I thought about it. I said, "How am I supposed to take that much cash out of the bank?"

"I wish I could come and explain it all to you," Darren said, "but I have to go to Thailand. I'll e-mail you a bunch of phone numbers before I go. Get up on Skype, you'll be able to contact me. My guy Billy will finish up everything on this end and meet you when you get here. Billy's worked for me forever. If you have any questions, he'll sit down and walk you through them. It'll be a lot better when you're here, because then you can just talk, you know?

"As far as getting cash out of the bank, it's your money, right? You can withdraw as much as you want. But the thing here is planning for the future, laying a good foundation to protect yourself and your business. You have to manage the paper trail, and you have to start now. Like I say, I wish I could come out there and explain it all to you. But you don't want to do anything they can follow up on. You don't want to do anything that will connect you to anyone else. So no checks, no money transfers, even money orders are a hassle. If you buy three grand in money orders at a single place, you cross a threshold and they have to file a report on you. If you buy two grand in a single go, you cross a different kind of threshold and they have to file something else. So don't do money orders, and if you do, keep it under two Gs and drive to different places. You don't want to trigger those thresholds and give the bad guys any reason to look at you."

I'd Google it all as soon as I got home, learn about money laundering, the Bank Secrecy Act, Monetary Instrument Logs, and everything else.

Darren said, "Let's say you want to buy a car and the seller wants cash. The bank's going to tell you that you shouldn't deal in cash, that it's probably a scam. You tell them you know the guy, you're not worried about dealing in cash with him. Everybody knows he wants to do it to hide something, but that's his concern, you don't care. But here's the thing. When you deal with a bank, you leave a paper trail, and when you move ten grand or more, you leave behind a special paper trail. They are going to file a Currency Transaction Report on you. They have to: ten thousand is the trigger for the bank. At casinos, it's a smaller amount, five thousand. At money order places, two thousand. You have to remember that. Now, you could take out the money little by little so you'd never reach the ten thousand trigger, but you don't have the time for that. And anyway, you'd need six months or more, because if you kept going to the bank and taking out two grand here, three grand there, it would be even worse, because it's something called structuring. It's a huge trigger, and the bad guys can build a money-laundering case against you. So you have to stay in cash once this is done, find a safe place to keep it. Especially if anyone around you figures out you're in the business, they're going to

know you have a lot of cash. That's why there're as many rob-
beries as there are. Don't worry about that for now."

There were people on the beach around me, teenagers playing volleyball, a guy running along the surf with his black Lab.
I was sitting in the sand listening to this.

"So this one time you're going to take out a big amount and
they'll file the CTR on you. They'll always have that on file,
there's nothing you can do about it. But you can't do anything
else to draw attention to yourself. You're taking out the money
to buy a car, you know they have to file a report. It's going to
be the only time you'll register on their system. You have to
concede them that one thing.

"Get a receipt, keep it. Because if you get pulled over when
you are bringing the money out here to buy your car, the bad
guys are going to take that money away from you and hold it
until you can prove it's legally yours. You know the bad guys
are out there on the roads trying to get the money, don't you?
The whole thing is about the money, that's all they really want.
Half the time they just steal it from us, and the rest of the
time they're allowed to keep eighty percent of whatever they
take—it's how they buy their equipment. It's a bitch to get the
money back if they seize it. Most people don't even try. It's a
civil case, no arrest, people are glad to just walk away and let
the money go. Usually, nobody has a way to prove it's theirs
in the first place. But you will, James. You'll have that receipt
from the bank."

"I don't have time to drive out there, Darren. I'm planning
on getting on a plane, coming back in a rental car."

Darren was quiet for a moment. He said, "That's not a good
idea. The one thing's driven out, the money's driven back. It's
a continuous loop, and that's the way it's done. Building that
loop is everyone's goal. Think about everything being moved

out there on the roads. Now think about how much money is coming back. That's what you have to do. Two parts to the drive. Four days across, four days back. You celebrate a day or two at the end, and then you do it again."

"I'm not doing it that way. I don't have time for that."

"You'd better not let them see the money at the airport. They can 'civil forfeiture' it from you there, too."

"Civil forfeiture?"

"They figure anyone with that kind of cash is up to something. They wrote the forfeiture laws to let them take large amounts. If they take your money, you'll spend months in court trying to get it back. So figure out a way to get it on the plane without letting them see it. Otherwise, you're done.

"Another thing about the money you're going to take out of the bank: most banks don't have that kind of money on hand, people never make withdrawals like that. You have to call ahead and arrange a pickup time. The banks get their cash deliveries once or twice a week and have to put in special orders for large amounts. So with the schedule you're on, you have to call them today, get it sorted out. Because it could take them three or four days to have it. Then they are going to want you to come in at a certain time to pick it up. You'll have to sign some documents, a waiver saying you know it's not safe to have such a large amount, that you don't hold the bank responsible if you get ripped off on the way home. And there's one last thing you need to know. If they are suspicious of you, if the teller or manager you deal with has any kind of hunch, they're supposed to file an SAR, a Suspicious Activity Report. That's definitely something you don't want. So you have to have your story straight and you have to be cool once you're in there. They're not looking for someone like you, they're looking for hoods and terrorists. But it only takes one cowboy minimum-wage motherfucker, and he'll file the SAR. Then who knows? They don't even tell you they're filing it.

"One more thing before you get out here and Billy will sit down with you and tell you more. A paper trail is more than just money. It's phone records, receipts, credit card activity, e-mails, even the sites you visit on your computer. Try to use stuff that's not connected to your name whenever you can. If you're using your own gear, wipe it every chance you get. Go to Wal-Mart and pay cash for a TracFone, they only cost thirty bucks. And when you use it, drive away from your house and get up on it through a cell tower that's not easily connected to you. It seems like a hassle, but it's not. Then you want to dump the phone after a while. Don't pass out the number over the phone, send it in the mail to the people who need it. Use the post office for everything—it's one of the safest things we have—because postal inspectors need a warrant to open first class mail. Use a fake return address, but make sure it's an actual address or they'll check it. Don't put anything in the letter to tie it to you. If the letter gets lost or takes too long to get there, ditch that phone and start over."

"Do I have to do all that this one time?"

"You're pristine for now, James. But the thing is, you don't know what they know about the people you're dealing with. If they figure out one person, it spreads through the system and contaminates everyone. Another thing is, you don't know where this might go. You want to establish a good business model, be disciplined, lay a foundation for a long and lucrative future."

"That's not my plan," I told him.

"That's what they all say."

The last thing I asked Darren was, "Do you think this is going to work?"

"Of course it's going to work," Darren said. "Because everybody needs it to. People like you, people like me. Even the bad guys. They wouldn't have jobs if it weren't for us. And if it weren't for them, our product would have no value."

I had the MetLife checks with me. That money had given me some peace of mind throughout my life. Now it was giving me the chance to do this. How was I going to explain that part to Kate?

I did the math again as I drove from the beach into town. We had $3,000 from Eric and a little more than $5,000 left from the first trip. So I had to get $17,000 more. I drove to the WaMu branch in the strip mall near my mother's, sat in the car outside. I couldn't get the cash directly from MetLife; they weren't a bank and didn't work like that. Instead I'd have to write a check to myself, deposit it into my WaMu account, and then withdraw the cash.

I called Mason from the car before I went in.

"How's Florida?" Mason said when he picked up.

"I'm outside my bank. I've got a trip put together. I would have called you sooner, but it all went down yesterday. Now I have to get everything together and jump on a plane. I'm calling to ask how much you want."

"Are you kidding me? I want one. No, two. Let me make a couple phone calls and call you right back."

Five minutes went by. Then five minutes more. It was the same as when I'd waited for him in Austin. I listened to the Killers, Damian Marley, drummed my fingers on the steering wheel. Then I had another idea, called Rita in Sacramento. When she picked up, she said in a whisper, "James? Are you here again?"

"I will be in a few days."

"I'm at work. Can I call you tonight?"

"I have to know right now."

"I'll take a break and call Henry," she said, still whispering.

There was a coffee shop a few doors down from the WaMu. I went in and ordered a drip. I bought a copy of the *Herald-Tribune,* scanned it with my phone out on the table as I waited. The front page above the fold was about the Sarasota real estate implosion: the massive condo project was indeed about to go bust. I couldn't care about any of that. In a minute, my phone rang.

Rita said, "How much if we get a pound this time?"

"Five grand."

"Then we'll have the money ready."

I hung up and did the math on my phone. Now I needed the rest of the baby's college money. A minute later, Mason was calling. I held the phone to my ear, glanced at the other people sitting at their tables. They had no idea what I was doing. Mason said, "I want two this time."

"Can you really handle that much?"

"I met new people because of what we did."

"You have to send me half the money."

"No problem, James."

"It has to be cash."

"How am I supposed to do that?"

I remembered what Darren had said. I said to Mason, "Money orders. I'll explain it later, but do it just like I say. Go to three different places and get an order at each place for one and a half. Then go to one more place and get a final one for five hundred, and mail them all to me. You have to get them in the mail today to give me enough time."

"I'll get on it right after work. I can't tell you how much I appreciate this."

I crunched the numbers on my phone, calculated the gross and net. Could I really make that much? I called Darren as I walked over to the WaMu. "Everything still on track?" Darren asked.

"Everything's great. But I don't need ten now, I need thirteen."

"Same guy?"

"Other people, other places."

"Billy will have everything waiting for you."

"Thirty-two five?"

"That sounds right."

"Holy shit, Darren."

Darren said, "It's just the beginning."

In the WaMu lobby I wrote a check to myself for $19,500, deposited it in the ATM. That was it, every last penny of the baby's money. I put the receipt in my pocket. Inside, a young guy was at the welcome counter in his blue uniform. I approached him.

"What can I do for you?" he asked me as he typed on his cell phone.

"I just put a check into my account. How long before I can get the cash?"

"Assuming sufficient funds?" he said without looking up. "Three business days at the latest. But it could clear overnight. You can get a hundred bucks of it right now if you want."

I took one of the business cards from the tray, slipped it in my pocket. I drove to the house, went to our room, took the baby from Kate, and put her on my shoulder.

"Everything okay?" she asked nervously.

"Everything's fine. Mason has to get some money here, but that's it."

"Are we still set to make the same amount of money?"

"We're going to make much more."

"How much more?" Kate whispered.

"If Mason comes through with what he's supposed to, we're going to make over thirty-two thousand."

Kate let out a long, slow breath. Then she said hurriedly, "What do you want me to do?"

"Can you take care of the baby?"

She took the baby from me. I pulled out the business card, called the WaMu. I held up my finger to tell Kate not to say anything. A woman answered and recited the branch location. I said, "I'm calling to arrange a large cash withdrawal."

"I can help you with that," she said in a serious tone. "Approximately how much will you be withdrawing?"

"Nineteen thousand five hundred dollars."

"May I ask why you need to withdraw such a large amount?"

"I'm going to buy a car and the seller wants cash."

"Oh, that's not a good idea," she told me. "You should write a check."

"He doesn't want a check, he wants cash."

"It's unsafe to deal with cash in that amount, sir."

"Nonetheless, I want the cash."

"You'll have no recourse if something happens. There's no valid reason why someone needs cash like that."

"He wants cash, and I'm not worried. This is what I want to do."

"Let me get my manager."

My heart was racing. Was she going to file a Suspicious Activity Report on me? A man came on and said, "You want to make a large cash withdrawal?"

"Nineteen thousand five hundred dollars."

"You want hundreds?"

"Yeah, hundreds."

"You have to come in and fill out a withdrawal slip. The money will be here on Friday."

"That's it?"

"That's it."

Then I said to him, "The woman I spoke to sounded worried."

He snorted. He said, "Susan's just like that."

Kate's eyes were wide when I hung up. She said, "You're using the baby's money?"

"If we want to make this happen, I have to, Kate."

"What if something happens to you out there?"

"Then we're going to have a lot more to worry about than that."

I went to the bathroom, shaved off my patches, combed my hair, pulled on a blue Lacoste polo from our Austin days. Would cleaning myself up be enough to keep the people at the bank from being suspicious of me?

The woman I'd talked to on the phone was standing inside the WaMu entrance when I drove up a half hour later. She was taller than I'd imagined, her hair pulled back in a tight bun. "It's your money, you can do what you want with it," she said, shaking her head as she walked me inside. "But I'd really advise against it, sir."

I filled in the boxes on the withdrawal slip, 1 9 5 0 0. Then I gave it to her and she ran it through her terminal. "All set," she said. "Come in on Friday afternoon and we'll take you in the office. I urge you to have some safe way of transporting the money. The bank bears no responsibility once it leaves the premises."

"We only live five blocks away."

"Cash can't be replaced, Mr. Lasseter."

Back at the house, my mother was setting up for mahjong, the baby was asleep in her crib, and Kate was sitting on the bed, her glasses on, circling courses in the community college catalogue. She lifted her eyebrows at me when I came in. "Every-thing go okay over there?" she asked.

"Everything went just fine."

"They're offering late-starting courses I can still enroll in."

"Do what you need to, Kate."

"It's going to cost us real money, James."

"We'll have it when I get back."

I lay on the floor with the laptop and found a flight to Red-ding for $670 one way. Flights to Sacramento were half that price. I called Darren.

"I can get to Redding, but Sacramento's easier. Can your guy come down and meet me?"

"Sac's no problem. Billy takes stuff there all the time."

I booked a US Airways flight through Charlotte and Phoenix, leaving Saturday at 6:55 A.M. and arriving in Sacramento at three in the afternoon — $365 on the credit card. I knew I shouldn't use it, but what other choice did I have? Besides, it would only be this one time. I'd land in Sacramento, meet Darren's guy, grab the stuff, hop over to Rita's, then get myself on the road.

I searched rental cars; I knew I wanted a hatchback. I'd learned in my reading that most smugglers used cars with trunks because the cops had to get a warrant to open them. The cops profiled vehicles with trunks for that very reason, so I didn't want one. A four-day, one-way economy hatchback from Sacramento to Sarasota $700. Why so much? I called Avis to talk to a person. The woman said, "The surcharges and recovery fees on the one-way are what make it so expensive, sir."

I reserved it anyway. I already had a thousand dollars in expenses. MapQuest said the drive across the country would cost me $360 in gas. Even adding another $200 for motels and food on top of that, we'd still be clearing $31,000.

I stayed on the computer through the afternoon. The route

would be I-5 south through Cali, then across to Barstow and the Mojave. Needles, Flagstaff, Albuquerque, Amarillo on the 40. Then Austin lay at the center of Texas with no direct interstate access. What would be the best way to go? I went to Kinko's, printed out routes that would take me through Roswell and Carlsbad, down to Pecos, and onto the I-10 in Texas. Or was that route too rural with not enough cars to hide in? How about cutting through Clovis, slipping back into traffic at Lubbock? Or should I just stick to the crowded inter-states, head all the way to Oklahoma City, drop down through Dallas–Fort Worth? With maps and travel documents scattered over the floor, our room felt like army headquarters. Of course we'd locked the door against my mother.

Mason's money orders came to the house via FedEx on Thursday afternoon, two each from the post office and Money-Gram. "What did you get?" my mother asked. "Plane tickets," I told her.

"Plane tickets to where?"

"Sacramento. Got an interview out there this weekend."

"They're paying for the trip?"

"Flight, hotel, per diem."

"Thank God. They must really be interested in you."

I texted Mason: "fedex came thanks."

Mason texted back: "c u mon/tues?"

"let u know."

"b safe. u got our life savings with u."

"ours too."

Kate and I put the baby in her car seat, drove up the Tamiami Trail to Bradenton, and cashed the money orders. I went into three places, Kate went into one. The one Kate went into paid out in twenties. I made her go back in and get hundreds. After seeing the sheer bulk of that drug money at Eric's, I began to understand the importance of hundreds, obviously for their

value, but also for their compactness. I already knew I was
going to carry the money onto the plane hidden somewhere
on my body.

We went to the Sarasota airport, parked in the short-term
lot, took the baby inside in her stroller. On the second level
was a bar and grill, and from its seats we had a view of the
security screening point. The travelers were winding their way
through the cordoned lines. Kate said in a whisper across the
table from me, "I don't feel good about doing this."

I'd been on enough flights to know I would have to pass
through security only once on the trip. We watched the TSA
officers wave their wands over people, send a few of them
into the bomb-sniffing booth. They called aside a middle-aged
woman in a business suit. A female TSA had the woman raise
her arms, ran her gloved hands closely over the woman's body.
She touched her upper body, her legs, her stomach, her waist;
the only places she didn't touch were her crotch and the soles
of her feet. However I ended up carrying the money, I would
have to beat that kind of pat-down.

Kate whispered, "We shouldn't have brought the baby here.
We can't do anything that'll get her taken away."

"We'll never do anything that would ever involve the two of
you."

"What if you get caught?"

"You'll say you didn't know."

"I'm your wife. They'll never believe I didn't know."

"You'll say I did it behind your back."

"And if they don't believe me?"

"They're going to believe you."

"But what if they don't?"

"Kate, they always leave the wives alone, okay? They're not
interested in breaking up families."

"How do you know that?"

"It was in everything I read."

"What if everything you read is full of shit?"

"I'm leaving the day after tomorrow. Do we really have to do this right now?"

I watched them pat down another guy: the arms, the legs, the front, the back. But not the crotch.

Kate said, "Are we done yet?"

I said, "Yeah, we're done. Most likely, I'm going to walk through the detector and nothing's going to happen. But there'll be a moment when I don't know."

"And then?"

"I'll call you when I've gotten through."

"What if they find the money?"

"I'll have the receipt on me."

"But what are you going to say about having that much money on you?"

"I'll say I was going to gamble it in Reno."

Kate shook her head. She got up, grabbed the stroller by the handles. She said as she walked away, "This is so fucking stupid. You know they're not going to believe any of that."

When I caught up to her, I grabbed her arm. "What's the matter with you?" I snapped at her so loudly the people around us turned their heads to look.

We were quiet the whole ride home. As I pulled into my mother's driveway, I told Kate, "Don't you know how fucking nervous I am?"

"Well, I'm fucking nervous, too. We can't do this if we can't handle the stress. We definitely can't do this if it's going to make you mean."

Thursday, the check cleared. Friday afternoon, I drove to the WaMu to pick up the cash. Should I dress up again? I didn't. I was leaving tomorrow no matter what, and if they were going to file a Suspicious Activity Report on me, so be it.

Susan and the manager took me into a spartan backroom. We sat at the desk and Susan walked me through a security document while the manager looked on like he was bored. She was required to tell me that it was unwise to take into my personal possession such a large amount of cash, that the bank offered more secure monetary instruments like checks and wire transfers, that my account was covered by FDIC, that the bank was solvent, that the money would be my responsibility now, that the bank could not be held liable in the event of a loss. She ticked off the boxes beside each point on the paper as we went through them, then we took turns signing at the bottom of the page. She told me they would have to file a Currency Transaction Report and would need a copy of my driver's license. I pulled out my wallet, gave her the license, then she left the room. What were they thinking about me?

The manager leaned back in his chair. "How about those Patriots?"

"The football team?"

He made a face at me like he couldn't believe it. "You're not following the undefeated season?"

Susan returned with my license and a stack of money an inch and a half thick. The hundreds were crisp and new, not a fold in any of them. I dealt them out onto the desk, once, twice, one hundred and ninety-five bills. It was all there both times. I gathered the pile, knocked it into a stack, and put it inside the empty laptop case I brought with me for that purpose. The manager stood up, offered his hand. "We'll be here if you want to put it back."

Eight months later, WaMu collapsed.

• • •

When I returned from the bank, I showed the money to Kate, everything we had in our lives boiled down to a stack the thickness of a paperback. I added the money we had left from the first trip, the money from Mason, the money from Eric Deveny, wrapped it with a rubber band: $32,500, enough to buy thirteen pounds of Siskiyou County weed. I unzipped my jeans, stuffed that brick between my legs, inside my boxer shorts. I walked back and forth in the room for Kate to see.

"That's not going to work at all, James," she said. "You look like you crapped your pants."

Could I tape it around my ankles? Stuff it under the insoles of my shoes? My flight to Sacramento was in less than fourteen hours. How was I going to hide the goddamn money?

I checked my e-mail to take a break, found a foreign number waiting for me, called it through Skype. Darren sounded groggy when he picked up. It was hot in Bangkok, he said, the flight had been brutal, and the ladies had been tiring him out even more. After a few more days of fun and adventure in the Big Mango, he'd be heading up to the tranquility of his farm at Chiang Rai.

"You all set?" Darren asked.

"Everything's fine."

"Tell me how you're feeling."

"Nervous and ready at the exact same time."

He gave me a number, a 530 NorCal area code. When I Skyped it, a man with a western drawl picked up.

"This James?"

"Billy?"

"Nice to meet you on the phone. Listen, all is well, all is well. I'm heading down to Sacramento, laying up in a hotel tonight."

"Where are we going to meet?"

"I'll sit at an exit south of the airport. Call me when you land and we'll hash it out. Remember to keep it simple on the phone. How you feeling? Feeling all right? Darren says you're a first-time dude."

"I'm feeling as good as I can, I guess."

"All is well, all is well. That's the way it's supposed to be."

There was nothing left to do but figure out how to hide the money. I set the stack on the edge of the bed. Kate and I looked at it. Then Kate handed me the baby. She said, "Spend some time with her already. Don't you know you've been an absolute madman for three straight days?"

I looked at my daughter and she looked at me. When I smiled, so did she.

Kate winked and said, "Tightie-whities? I'd be happy to run to the store and get you some."

I told her, "I'd rather quit the whole fucking thing."

We looked at the money, the money looked back at us. "Pantyhose," we said at the very same time.

She grabbed a pair from the suitcase she was living out of and took the baby from me. I stripped off my jeans, rolled on the hose. They were too tight, too short, but they were clearly going to work. I pulled them off, grabbed scissors from the kitchen, cut them off at the knees. Then I rolled them on again. I separated out the cash into four thin stacks, slid the stacks into the pantyhose at the tops of my thighs. The hose held the money against me like my very own skin.

That was it, everything was figured out. Tomorrow I would go to the airport and discover my fate. But right now it was time to be with my wife.

We lay in bed in the dark, our baby between us. Then I kissed the baby, put her down in her crib. Finally Kate and I were alone.

"Are you worried?" I asked her.

"I just want you to be okay."

"Everything's going to be okay. No matter what happens to me, everything's always going to be okay."

"I don't want to have to raise these babies alone."

"You're not going to have to."

"What if something happens to you?"

"I promise nothing will."

"Call me every chance you get, okay?"

"Be patient while I'm driving."

"If anything feels wrong out there, I want you to walk away."

"You know I will."

We made love once, twice. I lay awake the rest of the night, holding her as close to me as I could.

I showered, shaved off my beard patches, dressed in my lucky flannel jacket and jeans. Underneath my jeans were the pantyhose, the money tight against my skin. At the airport, Kate gave me JoJo Bear. I checked in at the counter and we went up the escalator to security.

"I have to leave now," Kate told me once we got there. "There's no way I can watch this, you know?"

We kissed, I kissed the baby, then I stared after them as they went down the escalator. Kate's back was to me, her long black hair. Would I ever see them again? I turned away, joined the security line. When it was my turn to show my driver's license, the agent, an older guy, looked at it and said, "Texas, huh? Don't mess with Texas."

I took off my shoes, belt, jacket, put everything in a bin. My backpack full of boxer shorts I tossed on the conveyor belt, too. All that was left to do was walk through the metal detector. A TSA agent was waiting at the other end. He was big and bald, looked like a bouncer. He beckoned me forward. I knew my face looked calm, nothing at all like the inside of me. Suddenly the money began to itch against my skin as much as my heart was pounding. I stepped into the metal detector like I was making a leap of faith.

"Come through, sir."

It didn't make a sound. I picked up my things from the conveyor belt like nothing had happened. I texted Kate—"made it"—as I put on my shoes at the bench afterward. She texted back: "love u."

The first flights went fine; I felt calm; I wasn't doing anything yet. In Phoenix, I went to a men's room in the terminal, took off the pantyhose, transferred the money to my backpack, and tossed the hose in the garbage.

When I landed in Sacramento at three, I called Billy. "Del Paso Road," he told me. "The lot at the In-N-Out Burger."

I took the courtesy bus to the rental car plaza, gave the Sikh at the counter my reservation and credit card. Soon enough he handed me a set of keys. It was cool and windy when I walked onto the lot, a Northern California winter day. I'd been traveling for eleven hours; I felt dizzy. My car was a Chevy Cobalt with California plates. Three cars down the line was a Mustang from Wyoming; two cars after that was an Aveo from Texas. Texas plates? What if I could get that car? I went back in and saw the Sikh.

"I don't really dig Cobalts. You think I could have that little Aveo?"

"I'll check the availability," he said. A minute later, he handed me the Aveo's keys.

I adjusted the mirrors and the seat, figured out the signals and wipers, got comfortable in that little cockpit. I drove off the lot, turned south on I-5. The Del Paso Road exit was on me in minutes.

The traffic was heavy here, the beginning of rush hour. After several stoplights and strip malls, I saw the In-N-Out Burger. A towheaded man in a Carhartt work jacket stood smoking beside a beautifully restored blue Ford pickup from the seventies with a camper shell on the back, looking at the evening sky. He was lanky, older, early forties maybe, seemed like a hick down from the mountains. He pulled a cell phone out of his jacket pocket when I called.

"James?"

"Looking right at you."

"Texas plates?"

"That's me."

"How'd you get those plates?"

"I saw them in the line and asked for them."

"Great fucking job on those plates," he said.

He hopped in his truck and I followed him out of the lot. We drove on Del Paso for a few more lights, ended up at the side of a Rite Aid away from the road, next to an empty field of weeds. There was no one around. Still, it felt way too exposed. We stepped out of our vehicles, shook hands. He was taller than me, crow's feet around his eyes, a scar across his chin like he'd been cut. His hands were rough and thick; they were a farmer's hands. Was he the one who grew it?

"You have to peel that car," Billy told me, pointing to the bar code stickers in the corners of the back windows. "Dead giveaway it's a rental. Don't do it here. Do it tonight when you stop. Stash the stickers somewhere safe. Put them back on at the end."

I had so many questions, didn't know where to start. Instead he said to me, "You want to try your stuff?"

"Are you kidding?"

"Some people smoke the whole way," he said. "Pop the hatch."

I hit the button on the clicker. Billy ducked into the cab of his truck, took out a huge black duffel bag, unzipped it for me to see: it was full of packaged weed. Then he zipped it shut, tossed it in the back of the Aveo, slammed the hatch down. It didn't take three seconds.

"Money," Billy said.

I handed him the backpack. He leaned into the cab of his truck with it, then came and returned it to me. "Don't want your underwear, dude. All is well, all is well. Everything is vacuum-sealed—I wouldn't open any of it. Don't get pulled over in that rental. You waived your right to refuse a search when you signed the agreement."

I hadn't thought of that.

Billy went around, hopped in his truck. "Drive fast and swerve a lot," he said and waved from the window. Wait! I wanted to shout. But he peeled out and was gone.

What about the sit-down? What about all the information he was supposed to explain to me? I got in the Aveo, drove away from that place. Had anyone seen the exchange? I looked into the rearview, scanned the traffic. Was that a cop? Was that a cop? My knuckles were white, my heart was pounding. I started coughing. I didn't want to do this anymore.

"Fucking breathe," I told myself. "Just drive the fucking car. You can't get pulled over. You can't get pulled over."

I turned into the parking lot of a Wendy's, went inside, washed my face. The bathroom was small and empty. I looked at myself in the mirror. My skin was blanched, my hands shaking. Should I call Darren, fucking yell at him? But I knew there was nothing more he could tell me that would make this any easier. If I wanted the money, this is what I had to do. I said to myself, "You're just another guy on the road, all right? Cut it out already."

Back in the car, I sat in the parking lot with the engine off, took some deep breaths. I was in a rental and couldn't refuse a search. Of course that was true. Why was I such an idiot? I'd have to have my story ready in case I got pulled over: I'd flown out for an interview, had time on my hands, wanted to drive home one way and see the country. I didn't have a family or anything like that, was stopping here and there to visit old friends. Then I shook my head at the thought of it. What a stupid story.

What if they called for a dog? What if they popped the hatch? JoJo Bear was in the passenger seat; I pressed his belly and he said, "I love you." I took another deep breath, turned on the engine, checked around for cops. There was nothing left to do but do it. I got on the road.

Rita was waiting for me when I knocked on her door with the duffel bag thirty minutes later. She yelled at her boys to go upstairs as she let me in. We stared at the thirteen big packages of weed as I unloaded them one by one onto her kitchen table. It was a mountain of marijuana, more than a hundred thousand dollars in street value.

"What's the name?" she asked as she sorted through the bags.

"I didn't ask."

"Some of it looks even better than the last stuff you had."

She picked out her bag. The buds in it were thick as pinecones, pale green, the color of money. She gave me a rumpled envelope. "It's only four grand," she said. "We're short a G for now."

"Rita, are you kidding? Why would you do this to me?"

She put up her hands. "We did the best we could! You know we'll get you the rest as soon as we can."

Had I ever felt so angry? I noticed her boys in their pajamas peeking around the corner from the staircase. I shook my head. What could I do? I had to get moving. Even if Rita stiffed us what she owed, I'd still made $1,500 on the pound she'd taken. I hurried out to the car, popped the hatch, tossed in the duffel, got back on the road.

Five hours later I was in a Motel 6 in Bakersfield; my heart hadn't settled down at all. In a dark area of the parking lot I peeled the bar code stickers off the car with my fingernail, stuck them far under the dashboard for safekeeping. When I went to the room, I spread the packages out on the bed like loaves of bread. So much weed! Mason would be happy, Deveny would be happy. I parted the drapes to look at the lot. What if anyone knew?

The next night I was in Tucumcari, New Mexico. A thousand miles in a day—I'd broken my rule and driven until midnight; I wanted the trip to be done. The night after that, at Mason's, I was shaken, burnt out. Of course I hadn't eaten. Of course I hadn't slept. Wherever I stopped, I hadn't been able to say anything more to Kate than "Everything's okay, everything's okay. Just fucking let me drive, all right?"

When I dumped out the weed on their living room floor, Mason's and Emma's mouths dropped open. Mason owed me $5,000. Of course he didn't have it. Three thousand dollars would have to do for now, everything he did have. "You're not upset, are you, James?" Mason asked. Goddamn stoners! What could I do but sigh it away? He had a six-pack of cold Lone Stars waiting for me in the fridge; I poured bottle after bottle into my face. Out on the porch as we smoked cigarettes, Mason said, "I want to do it, too, man."

I shook my head, told him, "Believe me, you don't."

"That bad?"

"Oh yeah."

"So you aren't going to want to do it again?"

"Hell fucking no, Mason!"

The car was looking ragged. In Houston, in the morning, I pulled into a self-service car wash and scrubbed off all the accumulated dust and bugs. In the evening, I crossed into the Florida panhandle, stopped at De Funiak Springs. Tallahassee was only an hour away, but driving through Louisiana had been terrifying. I knew too much about the state's draconian laws, the insane sentences that could put me away for as long as thirty years. And then there had been those minutes in Sulphur, the most terrible of the trip.

I had seen plenty of cops along the way: a couple CHPs in the Mojave, a half-dozen troopers in forested Arizona, three black-and-tans through New Mexico's Navajo territory, a dozen on patrol in Texas. They were mostly hidden in speed traps, seen only at the last heart-stopping instant, but a few zoomed up on me from out of nowhere, then hurried by to bust someone else. But nothing was like Sulphur. I knew going in that the town's interdiction point was one of the toughest in the country; it lived up to its reputation. There was a trooper hidden after the crest of every rise, troopers parked in the median in SUVs. Some of the SUVs had K-9 on them, and they all bristled with antennas. I knew they were profiling each car as it passed, calling in suspects to be pulled over down the road.

And people really were pulled over, blacks, Hispanics, beat-up cars, new. Every single vehicle had out-of-state plates: New York, Georgia, Oregon, New Jersey. And they were popping trunks. I held the steering wheel, maintained my even breathing, talked to JoJo Bear the whole way.

And then a cruiser came up on me. He rode me a mile or two, came so close that I could see him in the rearview. He was square-jawed, clean-shaven, in his crisp uniform and wide-brimmed hat. Behind him was the cage he wanted to put me in. I left the car on cruise control, let it drive itself. When the cop finally swung around and alongside me, we looked at each other a moment. Did he have a family? Children at home? Then he gunned it up the road like a jet.

From the dirty motel in De Funiak Springs that night, I called Kate. "We're in the same state," I told her. She yelled at me, "This is a fucking nightmare!"

Later, I called Eric Deveny. He said, "I'm ready and waiting for you, my man."

I didn't sleep, hadn't in days. Still, I took my time in the morning, as though I didn't really want to leave that room. This was it, the whole thing at hand. I thought of that gun Eric had. What if he wouldn't give me my money?

At one o'clock that afternoon, I pulled onto his street. There was his same big house, his same long, black car. Suddenly I felt like I was dreaming.

"I'm outside," I said when I called him.

"Side door's open," he told me.

I left the weed in the car, went in through the unlocked side door to the kitchen. The gun wasn't there this time. Eric was wearing a white tracksuit, like he was heading to the gym. "Welcome back, my man," he said and winked at me.

"Your brother here?"

"I sent him away."

"I'm freaking out."

"Believe me, I know that."

The coffee table in the den had been cleaned and cleared; the gun wasn't in that room either. The orange Nike box was open on the table with the money in it. "James, there's your money. Doesn't it look pretty? It's still short a couple Gs. I have to run out right now and finish it. If you want, you can drive around town and I'll call you when I'm done. Or you can just chill right here."

What should I do? If it was a sting, I was busted already. If he was going to rob me, there was nothing I could do. I said to him, "You want to see it?"

He said, "If you're ready to show it."

I went out to the car, looked around the neighborhood. No one else was there. I pushed the button on the clicker, the hatch popped open. I carried the duffel bag in on my shoulder, unzipped it, dumped the pounds out onto Eric's couch.

Eric picked one up, squeezed it, fingered a bud through the plastic. Then he tore it open. "Beautiful work," he said as he smelled it.

He left me alone in there. If the cops were going to rush in, now was the time. But a minute passed, then another, and the cops did not rush in. The house was silent around me. I sat on the couch beside the weed, took the rubber bands off the stacks, counted the money. Forty-five thousand in tens and twenties. It took me twenty minutes.

I was numb, cold, exhausted. I zipped up my jacket. What was taking him so long? Was I really alone in here?

I began to walk around the house. The rooms in the front were as dark and empty as they had been before, his loft upstairs the same as it had been with the flag. Behind the flag when I pushed it aside was only the bare wall. The unfinished basement was empty and silent. When I went back upstairs to the den, the weed and the money were still there.

A few minutes later, Eric came in through the kitchen and tossed two more bundles in the Nike box. Then he closed the lid and gave it to me. "You want to have lunch?" he asked.

"I want to go home," I said.

We went out on the deck, had a cigarette together to end it. I held the money in the box under my arm the whole time. Eric told me, "There was a day when I'd done all the work and my first big payoff was sitting right in front of me. I was exactly like you—I couldn't believe it. There's so much about this that isn't about the money. You know what I mean yet? You will. Enjoy the moment, James. Inhabit it. It only feels like this once."

As I left, he grinned and said, "Call me when you've settled down, my man. I know you'll want to do it again."

The money was in the shoebox on the passenger seat, JoJo Bear sitting on top of it. When I added the money I'd collected from Rita and Mason, the total came to $54,000; $29,000 of that was profit.

I counted down the mile markers to Sarasota, drove perfectly. The last five hours wouldn't end. I had to suck down these big, big breaths every inch of the way. What if I got busted now, with the money in my hands? The Texas plates were a long, long way from home. I could still easily get pulled over.

But I didn't get pulled over. I coasted up to my mother's house in the night, and Kate opened the front door as I did. She touched her finger to her lips when I walked in. "Everyone's sleeping," she whispered.

We tiptoed through the house to our room. Kate locked the door behind us. I looked at my baby asleep in her crib. I set the shoebox down on the bed.

I opened the lid.

There was the money.

I fell on my knees and pumped my fists. I let out a long and silent "Yeeeeeeeessssssss!" Kate and I leapt into each other's arms. Then we threw the money all around us in the room.

3

The Dark Mule

THREE AND A HALF months later, I had a new career. I was a full-time drug mule. I'd done the run six times, always dropping off weight in Tallahassee, Sacramento, and Austin. Kate and I had nearly $175,000 in dirty drug money sitting in two anonymous safe-deposit boxes the size of microwave ovens at the Florida Vault Depository. Gone were the days when we'd kept $25,000 in a shoebox hidden under a pile of clothes in the dryer in the little house across town from my mother's that we'd since rented, another $25,000 in a plastic grocery bag under the pots and pans in the dishwasher. Safe-deposit boxes at banks were out of the question because you had to give them personal information to get one. Then I found the Vault Depository online.

It was in downtown Sarasota, five blocks south of the city jail, in a solid concrete building with a luxury antiques shop on the ground level. The entrance to the Vault was under a discreet awning on the side, like the doorway to a private club. First you were locked in a small vestibule facing a bulletproof glass window. When you punched in your secret code on a keypad, the guard behind the window looked up your account in his file. He'd pass you the sign-in sheet through the slot; you'd mark an X, a squiggle, whatever you liked; and he'd buzz you in through a thick metal door.

The guard's name was Duke—it said so on the plate beneath his badge. He was burly and balding in a neat uniform, always polite, always kept the conversation on the weather. "Former law enforcement?" I'd asked him immediately. He'd shaken his head and said, "Nope." He never once asked me who I was or what I did for a living. He'd give a cookie to Romana that she'd grab tightly in her little fist, tell me how much she'd grown since the last time he had seen her. She was six months old now, a happy, baldheaded kid. Did he ever want to know my name, I sometimes asked Duke. He'd just shrug at me and say, "I'd only forget it."

The Vault wasn't a busy place; no one else was ever there. Inside, Duke would walk me down a carpeted hallway, lined with framed oil paintings of thoroughbred racehorses, and let me in through a last metal door. In the steel-lined vault itself, I'd put my keys in the slots of my boxes, Duke would put his in beside mine, the little metal doors would swing open, and he'd leave me alone with whatever it was I had.

What I had was cash, hundreds of bundles of tens and twenties folded in half and secured with a rubber band, each bundle a thousand dollars. I'd put one heavy box on the rolling cart they had there, then the other box, lift Romana in her car seat onto the cart, and wheel us into the counting room like we were going grocery shopping. I called it the counting room because I liked to count my money in it, but it was really just a small room with a locking door where the clients could have privacy with their things. It was always silent and peaceful inside the Vault, no more so than in that little room. Duke had told me when I'd first checked the place out that they'd put so much reinforced concrete into the building, it would survive a category 5 hurricane.

In the counting room, I'd lift Romana out of her car seat. She'd crawl around on the carpeted floor, sit up, clap her hands, and I'd toss her a few thousand-dollar bundles to play with. I brought her with me to the Vault almost every time I went because I always had a ton of cash on me. I had the idea that people might be watching who went in and out, that someone would jack me there. I figured with the baby in my arms, at least they wouldn't shoot me. I also started wearing sunglasses around town, as though that would somehow protect me. On the drive home from the Vault, I'd take a zigzag route on side streets until I was sure no one was following. Why had somebody built the Vault? The cocaine trade in the eighties? Retired tax evaders? It wasn't even expensive; my two boxes cost less than a thousand dollars a year.

The muling was never easy, but there were times on the road when I'd fall into a deep and meditative state. A hundred miles would pass in an instant, and I couldn't recall thinking about anything. Other times I had trouble keeping myself awake. JoJo Bear was always beside me to make me feel safe. "We're passing Window Rock," I'd tell him. He'd tell me, "I love you." "We're crossing the Big Muddy," I'd tell him. He'd tell me, "I love you." Billboards along the way were blank of advertising now. Every time I came home from another run, Kate and I were thirty thousand dollars further away from all of that.

Could I do this forever? I asked myself. Sometimes I felt like I could. I knew I'd never have another chance in my life to make this kind of money. I had all these crazy goals now that didn't seem that far out of reach: to put away a hundred thousand dollars in a deposit box just for Romana, and another hundred thousand for the new baby. A couple hundred grand in a box for Kate and me. Money for my mother, more money in case anything else bad should happen. Once I got all of that done, maybe I'd put a little away for Kate's parents, too. Out-of-work guys were spinning signs on corners everywhere now. I'd glance away whenever I'd see one. I'd never let what had happened to Kate and me ever happen again.

"Chance of a lifetime," I'd tell Kate. She'd shake her head at me and say, "Is that what you're going to say when you get caught?"

"You know I'm not going to get caught, baby."

"Isn't that what they all say, James?"

Just before Easter, we had our first problem. Mason had fronted two pounds to a kid named Russell, a guy he grew up with in Biloxi. It soon became clear that Russell had stolen our weed. It surprised me, wasn't something I would have done. But what kind of imaginary world had I been living in? The cost on Mason's end was eight thousand, the cost on mine, five. Not a lot of money to either one of us anymore. But it wasn't about the money. "This guy was my own blood, James," Mason said. "We went through the hurricane together. If he really did this to me, I'll fucking kill him." It brought all this anger out of him that I hadn't seen before; it was like the hurricane was still tearing around inside him.

Mason and I had become tight during those months. He and Emma were making over six grand a run, on track to make more than $130,000 for the year, all without doing any driving. One night on his porch, after I pulled into Austin with another load, he said, "Life is so amazing, James, you know what I mean? One day a hurricane takes away everything you have, the next day a guy comes running up the stairs with bags full of gold. Sacramento, Austin, Tallahassee. Man, we have to come up with a name for this shit."

"The Cross Country Couriers," I said and laughed.

"The Capital City Capitalists." He laughed back.

"The Capital Cities of Chronic."

"You know anyone in Santa Fe? You know anyone in Jackson? We should try to move weight in every capital of the states we run through, connect the dots, own the whole southern half of the country."

"The Capital Cities Connection," I said.

"That's it. That's who we are. Man, we've got to get some T-shirts made."

"Baseball caps."

"Fucking business cards, bro."

What could we do but laugh and laugh? I was running so much weed through Mason's apartment it felt like an assembly line, a repeating scene in a dream: get to Austin late at night, hurry up the stairs, dump twelve or thirteen pounds of weed on his living room floor. We didn't even get excited about it any longer, it might as well have been potato chips. Mason was working hard, had gotten to know a lot more people in Austin since we started. Still, Eric Deveny was the key to our whole operation. If he decided to bail on us at some point, the Capital Cities Connection was over, and we both knew it. Rita and her crew couldn't handle more than a pound or two a run. Mason couldn't move enough weight to make just a Sacramento-to-Austin delivery worth the risk. So we tried to come up with new ideas on how to move more weight in case Deveny quit.

That was how Russell had come into the picture. He lived in Biloxi, a few blocks inland from the beachfront casinos, two miles south of I-10, a perfect drop-off point halfway between the Texas-to-Florida leg of the trip. It was also a great place to melt bulky drug cash down to hundreds. I could hit three or four casinos, trade in a few thousand dollars for chips at each one, play the Pass Line at the craps table, win a little, lose a little, who fucking cared? Then I'd take my chips to the window and get the precious hundreds I needed to strap on my body and fly out to California.

Russell was a big Mississippi bubba, thick-lipped and fat. He had a piggy set of eyes and his dirty-blond hair spilled out of the edges of his threadbare Peterbilt cap. His cover story was that he installed carpeting for a living, but he mostly sponged off his girlfriend, LaJane. She was a bigmouthed redhead, sharp-nosed but nice-looking, a croupier at Treasure Bay, attractive in her black-and-white casino outfit. She and Russell had two big dogs and a filthy house; when I stopped by there the first time and opened their fridge for a beer, there was nothing in it. Mason and Emma had come along to visit and make the introduction. It had also been a chance for me to show Mason how to do the drive.

Emma had gone ahead in their Corolla with Bayleigh in the backseat and scanned the road for cops. Mason and I trailed ten miles behind in my latest rental car. "So we're coming up on this semi," I told him during that training run. "You want to leave at least five car lengths ahead of you so you don't get pulled over for 'following too close.' Now you want to start your signal, leave it on as you make the switch, otherwise they can get you for 'improper lane change.' You've got to make sure no one is coming up fast on you or they can get you for 'impeding traffic.' I like to keep my speed the same—don't accelerate to pass, the speed limit isn't any different in the fast lane. Signal again, and now we're in front of the truck. Being in front of a truck is a great place to be. It's like a wall at your back, and you only have to worry about what's waiting up ahead."

"Got it, brother, getting it all written down," Mason said, cribbing notes on the legal pad he brought with him.

"This isn't fucking college, Mason. Don't write it down.

Just try to make it part of who you are. You have to constantly check your rearview for cops. Pretty soon you'll be able to spot them by their shape. At night, you'll figure out what their headlights look like—they're different from other cars'. When you see one, don't change your driving. Your heart'll start racing, you'll want to throw up. Pull off at the next exit if they aren't up on you, and calm down. But never, never pull off when they are, or they might think something is up. You have to get ready for it, it happens on every trip. Have faith in your lucky charms and eventually they'll pass." At that, I patted the head of JoJo Bear, seated on my lap. By that point I had all kinds of lucky charms: fortunes in my wallet from Chinese restaurants I had eaten at along the way, pennies I'd found on the ground while gassing up, interesting rocks, a pair of my daughter's pink socks. The fortune I liked best read, "A long, even journey lies before you."

"So when am I doing the drive?" Mason was always asking me.

"We'll talk about that later," I'd tell him. The truth was I never wanted him to do the drive, because I didn't want to give up any of the money.

When we reached Russell's that night, it was all hugs and kisses between the redhead and Emma, a long hug between Mason and his friend, a rib barbecue out back, stories about their lives in Biloxi before Katrina had wrecked them. Russell's and the redhead's Mississippi accents were indecipherable, and the half dozen friends of theirs who came over talked like that, too. There was a lot of drinking, a lot of smoking blunts. It was hard for me to evaluate Russell in that environment. I liked that Mason vouched for him, but I didn't like it that Russell wasn't married, didn't have any kids. And then there were all those bright casinos beckoning five short blocks away.

Midway through the party, when we were alone, Mason

asked me, "What do you think about him?" I stared at fat-lipped Russell and told Mason, "You know I'll take your word for it."

When Russell's friends left to hit the casinos at the end of the night, I went out to the rental, a Mazda 6 with Alabama plates, brought in the duffel bag, and unzipped it in the bedroom for Russell to see. The redhead was passed out on the couch, the dogs were on the floor and snoring. Emma and Bayleigh were sleeping in the dark and quiet living room down the hall. Russell's face did what everyone's did the first time they saw that much weed: his eyelids snapped open like he'd been hit with a cattle prod.

How much did he think he could move? Mason asked him. Russell rubbed his stubble-covered chin, said he guessed he could move a pound pretty quick. The very next run, our greed made us front him two pounds, and then ten days went by with no word from him.

Something in me knew from the start what had happened. I said to Mason on the TracFone, "You think he could have ripped us off?"

Mason said, "Who ruins a lifetime friendship for a measly eight grand?"

When I passed Biloxi on my next run, I pulled off the highway and drove by Russell's house. The shotgun dump that it was looked dark and empty; his crappy truck out front was gone. Should I call Mason and let him know? I decided to leave it alone. I went to the casinos, got my hundreds. In the evening I was on the road.

A distance had sprung up between Kate and me; we didn't have time to lie on top of each other all day anymore. She was busy taking classes, I was gone every other week. And even the times I was home, I was caught up in my head, getting ready for my next run, turning things over about the business. In the beginning, we had arguments about it, about continuing to do it at all. But I wanted the money from the first, and there was nothing she could do. Besides, Kate liked the money, too. Once it really started pouring in, she thought we'd already made enough to go out and spend some. I shook my head. "Didn't what happened frighten you at all?" I asked her. She said, "It not like I never had to live that way. Besides, why are we even doing it if we can't spend the money?"

"Can't we just have it to have it, Kate?"

"What kind of life would that be, James?"

We were having a boy; we'd paid cash for a sonogram to find out. Kate had hired a holistic midwife. We were going to have a water birth this time.

This pregnancy was like the last one: Kate was sick all the time. On my second run from Cali, I'd brought her a pound of weed. It was supposed to be for her to sit on and smoke, to help her keep down food, but sometime between the day I gave it to her and the end of my next run two weeks later, she'd started selling it at the college. There'd be bags from Saks and Macy's on the kitchen table when I'd come in. I knew she wouldn't have dipped into our savings to go shopping like that.

"You selling that pound?"

"Maybe I sold a couple ounces to some stoners I met at school."

"A couple ounces let you go shopping like this?"

She blushed. "Maybe it was more than a couple ounces. You knew when you gave it to me I couldn't smoke it all."

"First of all," I said in a condescending tone that even I hated, "this is a terrible idea. Why would we take on an additional risk? For nickels and dimes? When I'm making what I'm making? Secondly, you're pregnant. What kind of people are we supposed to be if you're dealing when you're pregnant?"

Kate made a face at me. She said, "What's being pregnant got to do with it? Are you really that much of a jerk? Besides, I'm not showing yet, nobody knows but you and me. And it's not nickels and dimes, James. I'm pulling in double an ounce compared to what you get."

"Double?"

"More than that. I've already cleared three Gs and have over half the pound left."

I thought about that for a moment. Then I said, "What if somebody figures you out over there?"

"I say I have a hookup, a friend of a friend. Nobody knows that the friend is me."

"You'd better not let them know where we live."

"Do you think I'm stupid?"

Kate never had to do it. Even after we were set up at the Vault, we kept a few thousand dollars for groceries in a tea-pot on the stove. But it was how the thing worked. It paid in cash, was an instant reward, and more than anything else, it was easy. So Kate wanted to make some spending money? Fine with me. I knew if she was as into it as I was, she'd stop com-plaining and I'd be able to operate however I wanted.

Because Kate wasn't completely into it yet. I'd be sitting at the laptop booking flights for my next trip, and she'd be stand-ing beside me with Romana, whom she was stuck with all day. "Ever going to find any time to help me with this kid, Mr. Big-Time Drug Dealer?"

"I'm not a big-time drug dealer," I'd say and wave her away with my hand. "I'm a freelance courier — learn the difference."

"You're going to get caught."

"I'll get a slap on the wrist."

"A felony will ruin you for any other kind of work."

"If you'd let me work in peace, we won't have to work again."

The idea of getting rich was already growing in me, had started with something Billy had said. When I met him the first night of my third run in Sacramento, he had a room waiting for me at the Days Inn downtown. He came in through the adjoining door when I unlocked it, the duffel bag over his shoulder.

"What was it you did before this, James?" Billy asked me, his feet, in muddy work boots, up on the desk as we drank our way through a twelve-pack of Fat Tires. "Writing? This is better than writing. This is something that can actually make you rich. I've seen a dozen guys do it. Work hard, pay your dues, don't think too hard about the money. One day you'll wake up and realize you're loaded. Then you don't have to deal with the world again."

"So why aren't you rich, Billy?"

He rubbed the scar on his chin. "I make plenty of money, don't worry about me. But not everyone in the world gets the kind of opportunity you have. With the guy you have over there taking the weight he does? A connection to Darren on this end? You'd better not let them meet, James. They'd cut you out. Or pay you less than half. Then you'd just be a slave to them. Keep yourself in the middle and the only question is, how much are you going to make off it?"

"How rich have you seen people get?"

"I knew this big-balled Asian chick who socked away a million and a half over a couple of years doing SoCal runs twice a month. She was smart, got herself a HazMat license—they never check those trucks. Then she opened a couple of nail salons, cleaned up all her money. She's way into skydiving, the last I heard."

Kate, too, had made a friend, a woman her age, one of the academic counselors at the community college. They sat down together at the beginning of the semester, mapped out the courses Kate needed to take to get her degree. I was away on the road at the time. Kate took Romana with her, and the counselor fell in love with our baby. When I came home, Kate told me to shave off my beard patches, that we were dropping Romana off at my mother's, going out on a double date.

At dinner, we quickly understood that this couple was rich—at least the husband was. The wife, Sarah, had worked for a jeweler in Tampa, met the husband, Kyle, when he came in to shop for a birthday present for his mother. His family owned a chain of liquor stores up and down the state, Sarah explained to us, smiling at Kyle, but that hadn't stopped him from getting a law degree. From Duke. He hadn't made partner at his firm yet, but they both knew it was on the way. We had upscale Thai food at St. Armand's Circle on his expense account, then followed them over the bridge to their place on Longboat Key.

"What do you do for a living?" Kyle asked me at dinner.

"I did journalism before the publishing world tanked. Now I'm doing this import-export thing."

"Import-export?"

I glanced at Kate, then said, "Spices from the Orient. Supplying Chinese takeouts in half a dozen states."

"On the road a lot?"

"Every other week."

"Doing well?"

"Doing great."

"That's great to hear. Not a lot of stories of people landing on their feet out there right now."

In the car on the ride over to their house, Kate shook her head and said, "Spices from the Orient? That's what I'm always going to have to say?"

I smiled and said, "What's wrong with spices from the Orient, Kate?"

Their place was a gargantuan Spanish-style manse on the water. Kyle drove a Porsche, Sarah an Audi SUV. The house was decorated straight out of a lifestyle magazine. Sarah showed us their master bedroom, the electronic fireplace in it. In back of the house was an infinity pool that seemed to flow right into the bay. Kyle turned on the lights so the water glittered before us. He said, "I haven't jumped in it all year."

We sang eighties songs on their karaoke machine, drank red wine at their wet bar. Sarah was so happy to meet Kate, she said again and again, someone real, someone like herself. She was going to introduce Kate to the Young Professional Women's Club she was in. They could go to charity fundraising events together, laugh about the pretentiousness of it all.

When we left their house, Kate said to me in the car, "What did you think of them, James?"

"I think they're nice."

"Sarah only works because she wants to."

"He hasn't been in his pool all year."

We grabbed Romana from my mother's, drove across town to our rental house on 8th Street. Kate had found the place while I was away on the second run; it was a simple one-bedroom in a working-class Hispanic neighborhood, cars parked on the lawns, kids running in the streets. The rent was low because every third house was a vacant foreclosure now. We were still trying to be frugal back then; the day we moved in, Kate tied on a blue bandana, pulled on rubber gloves, and attacked the walls with bleach. "It's cute, right?" she kept telling me, as if trying to convince herself it was true.

As we pulled up on 8th Street, she muttered something under her breath.

"What did you just say?" I asked.

"I can't fucking believe we live here."

· · ·

Three weeks into our mess with him, Russell finally called
Mason, woke him up in the middle of the night. Mason wasn't
convinced yet that Russell had burned us, was more concerned
that something had happened to his friend. The story Russell
told him was this:

"I got pulled over by a trooper, Mason. He busted me with
an ounce. I had to spend a week in jail. They raided our house,
tossed around all our shit. They found both them pounds. It's
gone, man. Gone forever. I can't begin to tell you how sorry I
am. Both me and LaJane. Now I have to get a lawyer and go to
court. My life is fucked up. I'm worse off than before."

Mason told me about it on the phone as I was gassing up a
rental in a Flying J off the 40 in Albuquerque. I was already in
a crappy mood. It was a bright and cloudless day, a stressful
day for driving because when the weather was nice like that,
you knew the donut shops were empty. What could I say to a
story like that? Panic shot through me and I said, "Is he going
to talk?"

"Man, he'd never rat on us."

"How do you know for sure?"

"He's my own blood. Same as family."

"People can get crazy in times like this, Mason."

"We went through the hurricane together, James."

Darren Rudd had been giving me advice on Skype from
Thailand. As the Capital Cities Connection grew, he said I
should start setting aside a portion of my take for legal fees,
to protect "my people" in case anyone ran into trouble. Knowing the emergency cash was there would give my people confidence; they'd work better when they knew they'd be taken
care of. What he did was set aside five percent. On my last run,
I had told Mason we should do the same thing, set aside money
for a lawyer in case one of us went down. Now Mason brought
up our legal fund. "Maybe we should front him some cash," he

said. "I know it was the first time we did something with him, but he got busted out there while he was slinging for us."

Something about this smelled off to me. I told him, "Let me think about it and call you back." I hung up and scanned the traffic on the highway. Then I went inside the station, scarfed down a PowerBar by the postcard rack. I was always eating peanuts, trail mix, energy foods. I was always throwing the wrappers away before getting back in the car.

I turned it over as I ground out the miles toward Tucumcari across the flat and endless plains. What happened to Russell during his week in jail? What had they asked him and what had he said? Should I be worried enough to skip Mason's this time? Mason would be the first one they'd bust. Russell didn't know my last name. So maybe they already had Mason's place staked out, twenty-five jackbooted DEAs hidden in a moving van in their riot gear. Maybe they'd wait for me to pull up, then toss a percussion grenade, loose the dogs, hit me with a Taser. Maybe I should just dump the load somewhere, go home as fast as I could, throw away all the phones, be done with it forever. Take Kate and the baby somewhere safe for a while. Be grateful for the money I'd made, begin a tamer period of my life.

But I liked this period of my life, liked it a lot, the excitement of it, the thrills: pulling on the pantyhose, flying the money out to Cali, jumping in a rental car, making the switch with Billy. Stopping off at Rita's and dumping a pound or two on her, getting myself on the road. I felt challenged and busy like I never had. In fact, I probably wouldn't have taken my old career back even if I could have found any work in it. More than anything else, I liked making all the money.

Then I began to ask myself these other things. If they'd found the two pounds, would they have really let Russell out of jail? What would the bail have been on that? Why had the redhead left him in there so long? And why hadn't either of them called Mason sooner? I looked at JoJo Bear on the passenger seat. I already knew what he had to say about it.

I took the 285 south, pulled off at minuscule Vaughn, parked outside Penny's Diner, pulled out a TracFone, called Billy.

"James? Where you at?"

"Eastern New Mex. You?"

"Santa B. Just came in from the swell. I'm running the dogs on the beach. Beautiful day, free time to enjoy it. All is well, all is well. You?"

"Everything's fine. Listen, we fronted this guy two big ones last month, didn't hear anything from him. Now he called and said they got him, that we hadn't heard from him because he'd been down at county."

"Bad, bad, bad. Nightmare stuff. What do you think? Is he gonna tell a story?"

"I have no idea. He wasn't one of mine."

"Has he got your name?"

"I doubt it."

"Cauterize everything on that end."

"I'll lose my guy in Texas."

"So lose him. Close the wound, stop the bleeding. That's what our friend in Thailand would say. Hell, our friend in Thailand would pay your friend in Texas a nasty visit just for allowing a thing like this to happen. Why'd you let him get you caught up in this stupid shit anyway? Aren't you smarter than that, dude?"

I drove on to Roswell, parked downtown across from the UFO museum, the six-foot bug-eyed alien out front. Would I really have to cut out Mason? A black-and-white cruised down the street. But I was nobody doing nothing, right? Just another dude on the spaceship? I ducked into an alley off the strip, stood by a dumpster, called Billy again.

"Would they have let him out if they found two big ones on him?"

"What state?"

"Ole Miss."

"Were the big ones together or were they split apart?"

"He says they caught him with an ozone in the car. The real weight they found at his house."

"That's intent, bro. That's twenty to thirty. Unless your guy had a big pile of cash lying around, he definitely wouldn't be out on the street."

"Well, he definitely didn't have a big pile of cash lying around."

"Then it definitely sounds like he burned you."

I switched phones, called Mason, began to explain it to him. But he cut me short. "I already know," he said and sighed. "I checked it out online." Since we'd talked last, he'd Googled it and hadn't found an arrest listing or a mug shot for Russell anywhere. "Not in Biloxi, nowhere around there. I called people we know. They say they've seen him around. One dude said he saw him in a bar, putting money on the pool table, buying shots. I feel like my heart's been ripped out by this. Didn't the fucking hurricane mean anything to him?"

I pulled into a Motel 6 in Pecos that night, had a couple Lone Stars in a dumpy cowboy bar on the drag, then grabbed a Modelo six-pack from a gas station to ease me into sleep in the lonely room. When I called Kate, she said, "Everything going okay out there, James?"

"Everything's fine. Hunkered down for the night. I'm missing you guys is all."

"We miss you, too, you know."

Why did Kate sound in love with me only when I was away? At home she could feel like an adversary with how much she nagged at me about quitting. She'd be at her wits' end when

I'd get back, would say to me as soon as I walked in the door, "Welcome home. You're on baby duty starting right now."

Baby duty meant the nighttime feedings Romana still wouldn't give up, changing the diapers, never getting a good night's sleep. But it also meant my daughter's pretty eyes on me. Every day when I was home, I'd take her the two blocks over to Avion Park, push her in the baby swing, enjoy her happy laughter as the wind rushed against her face. Then I'd think about all these things. Darren Rudd ruled an empire. Eric Deveny did, too. As long as I could keep them apart, wasn't there plenty of room for me to build a happy little something of my own in the three thousand miles that lay between them? Couldn't I make myself rich for my daughter?

In that motel room in Pecos, the night we knew Russell hadn't been arrested, I thought about Eric Deveny. From things he'd told me, I'd pieced together that he moved his weight through a bunch of different guys, some at the school, most of them not. Almost none of them knew each other. No one had any real idea how big he was. His operation had taken him years to build; it wasn't something just anyone in the world could have done. But for how much I admired him, part of me disliked him, too. I didn't like how cocky he was. I hated the thought that he could end our business.

"So you think you got ripped off, my man?" he'd said to me at the end of the last run, when I'd told him my suspicions. We'd been at lunch together, my way of thanking him for everything, at a Japanese place called Sakura, two blocks from a busy Tallahassee police station. He'd led me there, speeding past the cops on our way, knowing my rental car was full of weed and money, had some kind of weird fetish for making me sweat. He'd been dressed in white, as dark and handsome as always. If he had any loose nerves in him, I hadn't seen one yet.

"Happens to the best of us, James. The thing is, how are you going to handle it if you want to stay alive in this business? Either you can let him get away with it and prove you're the pussy he thought you were in the first place. Or you can do what you're supposed to do."

"What's that?"

He laughed and shook his head. "You're supposed to fuck him up." Then he cocked his chin at two silky-haired coeds sitting at a table across the way; for sure he'd have their numbers before we left. That's how it was with him. Then he winked at me. "Want me to get someone to do it for you? Fucking whack him? It wouldn't even cost you that much.

"You want to know something, James? I feel like I witnessed your birth in my very own house. I really didn't expect all of this from you. In fact, I didn't expect anything from you at all. I thought you'd go home the first time, change your shitty shorts, retire with your one little war story, and I'd never see you again. Aside from all the money you've made me, do you have any idea how happy I am that you manned up?"

The last thing he said to me was "Interested in doing a little side work for me?"

"What kind?"

"I want you to run some stuff to New York."

But in that dirty motel room in Pecos, I knew Eric Deveny was Eric Deveny, and I wasn't like him at all. It was the weed trade, after all, right? Peace, love, and all that jazz? So why couldn't everybody just relax? I turned on *Cops*, smoked and drank in bed, the duffel bag under the covers beside me like a body. Russell had stolen our weed and I had no idea what to do. Couldn't we just be grateful he hadn't really been arrested? Couldn't we just let it go and keep on making money? In Austin the next night, Mason went on and on about it; what could I do but shake my head? I needed a shower, a shave, needed a few hours' sleep on his couch. There would be plenty of time to figure it out later. In the morning, I was on the road.

The story I told my mother about where we got our money, could afford to rent our own house, was that I'd landed a spot on a yacht-detailing crew up in Bradenton. They were picking up non-union guys like me in the bad economy, hiring us off the books. The rich still had money; there was plenty of work. The pay was decent enough for what was going on out there; if I stuck around a while, the bosses said, they were going to teach me how to work fiberglass. My mother said, "You should be careful with under-the-table kinds of things, James. One thing leads to another when you deal with people like that." Half the times I'd drop by and visit her, she'd shake her head as she watched the evening news. "I've been prudent throughout my life. But now? What in the world is a credit default swap?"

"If you ever need money, Ma, please just ask."

"I'm the one who's supposed to be helping you."

I didn't like lying to my mother, but what other choice did I have if I wanted to keep on doing what I was doing? I'd never been able to get away with anything with her when I was a kid, but I was certainly getting away with something now. Just before I'd left on my second run, I'd told her the crew had invited me along for a few days' job across the state in Vero Beach. The next run, we were working in Daytona; the run after that, all the way up in Pensacola. They were assigning me work phones, too, a nice perk. We had to check them in and out; my number would be changing a lot. I told my mother the story so often, I sometimes wondered if it was true.

But the story wasn't true. She'd call me after spending the afternoon with Kate and Romana, to tell me all the new things Romana had learned to do. I knew she was in her armchair in her living room, eating a TV dinner on her fixed income. Unbeknownst to her, as we talked I was gassing up the car in the snow in Williams, Arizona, or under the blue dome of the sky in dusky Amarillo, Texas.

"You're missing so much while you're gone," she'd tell me.

"I'm just glad to have work," I'd tell her.

My mother was also watching the baby over at her place the nights Kate had school; she and Kate were getting along much better now that they weren't under the same roof. "I couldn't do it without her," Kate would tell me when I'd come home. "It just makes me feel so dirty to have to hide all my stuff around her."

By "stuff" Kate meant all the things she'd begun buying with her drug money. "When'd you get this?" I'd ask, picking up some new little black dress that still had the tags on it hanging in our closet. She'd shrug and tell me, "I have to go to this thing with Sarah at Saks on Saturday night."

"What's the thing?"

"A fashion show fundraiser for the Humane Society."

Our plan was still the same: if I got caught, Kate would deny knowing anything. Whether that would work or not, neither of us seemed to care. We were making too much money. By the end of March, Kate was pulling in more than a thousand a week, had her own phones, was taking weight from me on every run. She was friendly, could tell a stoner a mile away; she identified a dozen of them in her film class alone. Even though we'd agreed she wouldn't let them know where we lived, a few of them were coming over now. They were kids, girls, eighteen, nineteen. They chewed through gas station candy, talked about problems with their boyfriends, their parents, their minimum-wage jobs, watched black-and-white Hitchcock movies with Kate on the couch. The rest of them needed the weed delivered, and of course I was the one who had to do that.

Then she started working with a couple of small-time dealers in Bradenton, who texted her day and night.

"So let's hire somebody," Kate said when I complained about having to drive to their trashy trailer park neighborhoods again.

"Who do you know that we can hire, Kate?"

The kid she wanted to hire was Nick, a pretty, blond-haired skater boy from her statistics class who didn't seem to own a shirt. For an instant when he first came over, I had the idea Kate might be in love with him. But then he pulled out a BB gun, challenged me to a sharpshooting contest in the backyard.

"You ever skate, Jimbo?" he asked as we plinked away at a Coke can.

"Way too old for that," I said, knocking the can off the stump with a shot.

"There'll never come a day when I don't skate," he announced.

There were crumpled lottery tickets and empty water bottles everywhere in Nick's Escort when he came over for his driving lesson. I told him to clean out his car, that the cops could use the mess for "reasonable suspicion" to search. I yanked down the evergreen tree air freshener from the rearview mirror, told him he could get pulled over because it "obstructed the driver's view." As far as the driving he had to do, it was all city traffic, nothing to it really, he simply couldn't speed, had to signal when he turned. And if he ever did get pulled over, I told him, he had to refuse a search.

"Tell them your stepdad told you to refuse, and don't say anything else. Nineteen grams and under is a misdemeanor, twenty-plus is a felony. So figure out when it's worth it to make two or three trips. Stay away from school zones, never drive around with more than one bag. If they nail you, say it's your stuff—they'll charge you with simple possession. Kate will bail you out and pay your fines. If you ask the judge for drug court, your record will be clean in a year. But the other thing that will happen is your driving days will be over."

"I'm not going to get caught, Jimbo."

"Don't call me Jimbo."

"Then Jim."

"Why can't you just say James?"

After the kids left one night and we were cleaning up the candy wrappers, I said to Kate, "Are you having fun with all of this?"

"Fun? I wouldn't exactly call it fun, James."

"Then what would you call it, Kate?"

"I'd call it a lot of hard work."

"Aren't you enjoying it at all?"

"I'm enjoying the money."

"You know, if we get raided and they find your weight, they'll take away the baby."

Kate made a face at me like she hadn't thought of that.

After another couple weeks of not answering his phone, Russell finally admitted to Mason that he hadn't been arrested. When Mason asked him why he lied about it, Russell told him he'd felt like he had to. When Mason asked him why he'd felt like he had to, Russell told him, "Because, man."

"Because why, man, Russell?" Mason had told me he yelled at him.

"Because I had to, Mason."

"Why did you have to, Russell?"

"Because I sold the weed."

"You sold the weed?"

"Yeah."

"What happened to the money?"

"I spent it."

"You sold the weed and spent the money?"

"Yeah."

"What'd you spend the money on?"

"I spent it on a ring for LaJane."

"Why would you spend our money on a ring for LaJane?"

"I was afraid she was going to leave me."

"You were afraid she was going to leave you?"

"Yeah."

At that, Mason was quiet for a long time. He tried not to let it affect him. He tried to hold in his anger. Then he exploded. "You have to give us our fucking money!"

"I'm going to give you your fucking money!"

"How are you going to give us our fucking money?"

"When I find a job."

"When you find a job?"

"I'm going to start looking just like everybody else."

"You're going to start looking?"

"Yep."

"You owe us eight thousand dollars, Russell."

"Once I find a job, I'll pay it all back little by little."

"Who decided that?"

"I did, I guess."

"Well, that's a bunch of shit."

"Well, that's the way it is, Mason."

"He never planned on paying us, James," Mason told me on the phone as I gassed up in Barstow. "He knew I trusted him, figured he could do whatever he wanted. He's still calling me 'brother' to this day. I want to kill him, James. I want us to drive out there and kill him."

I was looking at a beautiful SoCal day where I was, knew Mason didn't really mean that. I said to him, "What if I said I wanted to let this go?"

"You want to let this go?" Mason sounded like he was wincing.

"Listen to me, Mason. Why would we want to mess with this when everything else is going so well?"

"Because of the principle of it. He cheated us, James."

I sighed, got back on the road. I holed up for the night at the Red Lake Hostel off the 40, at high elevation in northern Arizona. The hostel was really an old motel attached to a gas station. Once the attendant turned off the station lights and went home for the night, I was alone up there. This was my third or fourth time staying there. I liked it because it was far off the highway, a lonesome outpost in the hills. I didn't get cell reception, so I didn't have to talk to anybody. It started to snow, and I stood outside my room and smoked a bunch of cigarettes in the dark. The falling snow made everything feel even quieter than it was.

Mason wanted the money back, but did I really care? I didn't need that money anymore. It pissed me off that I hadn't read Russell better; I knew I couldn't be any good at this if I ever let that happen again. But what was coming through to me now in Mason's voice was that this was always going to be a problem for him. What was Mason's deal anyway? Why did he always call me about everything?

I suddenly realized I was the leader. The thought of that kind of humbled me. The snow was falling on the darkened lot; the landscape had no lights in it. I had never been the leader of anything before. Did I even want this?

I called Mason from Winslow in the morning, told him, "We're going to give him one more chance. We're going to let him pay us back little by little. You guys were friends, let's see if he lives up to that. If he continues to fuck with us, then I promise we'll do something."

I heard Mason take a hard drag on his cigarette. He sighed and said, "You're right, James. You're always right. We'll give him a chance and he'll pay us back. I just got hurt by this is all."

Through the end of April and into May, Russell kept in touch, telling Mason he was beating the bushes high and low for work. Then spring came in full force on the highways with its wildflowers everywhere, and Russell stopped answering his phone again. The second week of May, Mason heard from a guy in Biloxi that Russell had bought into a Texas hold'em tournament at the Imperial Palace Casino.

"How much was the buy-in?" Mason asked the guy.

The guy said, "A thousand dollars."

Mason called me, so upset he was incoherent. When he calmed down enough to explain what had happened, I asked him, "What do you suggest we do?"

"You know what I want to do," he said.

I said, "Can't you ever take it easy? Text me his number and I'll talk to him."

I was at the Sarasota skate park that afternoon, Romana in her stroller with me, watching Nick and his buddies grind their skateboards down the rails. I'd wanted to stay home, but Nick had dragged me out. Why would I want to sit at home watching *Cops* all day, he said, when it was so beautiful outside?

Now I called Russell, figuring he wouldn't answer. But he did.

"Who's this?" he barked at me right away in his muddy accent.

"This is James. How you doing, Russell?"

Russell was quiet a second. Then he said in a cautious voice, "I'm fine, I'm fine. How you doing, man?"

"Listen, I know you and Mason are having a problem. And I

know you owe him money. I'm calling you to urge you to take care of it. Not trying to threaten you or anything like that. Just calling to say you should take care of your commitments."

"Oh yeah?" he said.

"Yeah."

He was quiet. Then he said softly, in this treacly voice, "Man, I've been trying to talk to Mason about all of this. But you just can't talk to the dude. I keep telling him I can't find any work. If I can't find any work, what am I supposed to do?"

"The thing is, Mason does want to work with you. He's willing to be patient. But you have to get the ball rolling on your end. Send him something. Send him anything. Send him a hundred bucks as a peace offering."

"Maybe I could get my hands on a twenty."

"Put it in the mail tomorrow. How can any of us do business if we don't live up to our commitments, right?"

"You're right," Russell said. "Uh, my girl's here. Gotta go."

I called Mason. "He's going to put something in the mail for you tomorrow," I said.

Mason said, "James, thanks for calling him for me. I know you were a lot more rational about it than I've been. Every time I talk to him, I start screaming. People who go through shit together, I think they should know how to treat each other, you know?"

Out in the skate park, Nick landed some kind of trick. Then he skated up to me. "You see that? You see that? That's what I'm talking about, Jimbo."

A week passed, then another. No money came from Russell. Mason unloaded himself on me about it the next time we talked: What the fuck were we going to do?

Now I was pissed off, too. I called Russell from my back-yard. Kate and the baby were sleeping inside. Outside, it was a thick and sweltering night, the beginning of the brutal Florida summer.

Russell answered. He said, "Who's this?"

I said, "This is James, who you owe money."

"I don't owe you any money, dude. I owe that money to Mason."

"Mason owes me. So now you do, too."

He was quiet for a long time. Then he said in this deliberate voice, "I'll tell you what. I'm getting sick of the two of you. So I'll tell you what I'd tell him—go fuck yourself."

"What'd you just say?"

"Go fuck yourself."

Then he hung up.

By that point everyone owed me money. Not Eric Deveny, of course, he was way too top-of-the-food-chain for that. But at any given time, Mason was in the hole to me for between five and seven thousand dollars, the Sac crew was always in arrears two or three grand. I kept the numbers written down in my wallet, didn't worry about it much, knew they'd pay me as soon as they moved their weight. And they did; money orders from them came in the mail almost every other day. I'd save up a stack, then put on my sunglasses and spend a few hours cashing them in all over town.

I was still using my credit card to pay for the flights and one-way rental cars, hadn't figured out a way around that yet. I didn't like it, but didn't know what else to do. I knew I'd have to come up with a story in case anything happened, figured I'd just keep my mouth shut, let whatever lawyer I'd hire tell me what to say. I was staying on my regular schedule for Deveny all of that time, had made so much money that even in an hour in the counting room at the Vault, I couldn't get through it all. It was two hundred thousand, then a quarter of a million.

Sometimes I'd feel so overwhelmed by the sight of it I'd start laughing.

Other things had been happening, too. Back in early March, I'd bought a new car for Kate, to tell her exactly how much I loved her. Or was it just to keep her quiet about us ever getting out of the business? We went to the dealership with the baby on a Wednesday afternoon. Kate had picked out a Suzuki Crossover because it was ten thousand dollars cheaper than what she'd really wanted, a fully loaded white Subaru Forester with a retractable moonroof, $27,000.

"You sure you don't want that pretty Forester, Kate?" I'd asked her on the lot after she'd made her final decision.

She'd shrugged and said, "You know I do. But aren't you the one who's always saying we need to be careful about our money?"

We went into the office with the salesman, haggled with him briefly, then he and I stood up to shake hands on the deal. But before we did, I asked, "Still have that pretty Subaru out there?"

"Yes, we do."

"Then I want you to give it to her."

I turned around and looked at Kate. I'd never seen her so happy.

I told the salesman we'd pick up the car the following week; I had a contract to finish before I'd have the money. "What kind of business are you in?" he asked me, concern written all over his face. He'd mentioned that 2008 had been horrible so far, nothing moving at all. I knew he was worried we wouldn't show up and he'd lose his commission.

"Import-export. We deal with a lot of cash. Any problem if I give you the down payment that way, too?"

"Not as long as it's American cash," he said and smiled.

Before taking me to the airport that Friday morning, Kate

had hurriedly stuffed money into my pantyhose, told me as she did, "You know I always want you to make it home safe, don't you? But please really make it home safe this time."

The following Tuesday afternoon, I did. We hustled to the dealership, and I put nine thousand-dollar bundles of tens and twenties from the fifty Eric Deveny had given me that morning on the salesman's desk, a small pyramid of rumpled drug currency, just under the amount that would trigger the filing of a Currency Transaction Report. Everything had been happening so quickly that I hadn't put any thought into how to clean up our money; it felt good to get rid of that big stack. At the same time, what could the salesman be thinking with so much filthy cash piled before him like that? But he slid it aside with his forearm, as though he hadn't noticed it at all, and passed me the pen. The good thing about selling Subarus, he'd told my wife as he gave her the keys, was that it was a repeat business; the bad thing was that the damn things were so reliable, he knew he wouldn't see us again for at least ten years.

As she sat behind the wheel and drove us up the Tamiami Trail with the moonroof open, her long hair whipping in the wind, Kate said, "They know we're drug dealers, don't they?"

"I don't think they care."

"Everybody just wants the money?"

"Everybody just wants to get by right now."

"I can't believe you really bought me this."

"I want you to know that your Mr. Big-Time Drug Dealer really does love you."

"I'm sorry I ever called you that."

"Just enjoy your car, Kate."

Then, in early April, we had ourselves a new house. Ever since I'd made the comment to Kate about the baby being taken away if we ever got raided, she'd been quietly looking for a safer place for us to live. She'd searched Lido Key, Long-boat Key, had found a dozen different condos and waterfront houses she'd loved. The rental agents had told her they'd have to run a credit report; she'd have to provide references, sign a lease. Finally she'd found something on the north end of Siesta Key, a spacious white three-bedroom Florida-style bungalow on a canal with the beach four blocks away. The old guy who owned it had recently remarried, was in a rush to get it rented and didn't need any of that. It was secluded under old-growth oaks, jacaranda, and frangipani. The crushed-shell driveway was lined with pampas grass, and there was a colonnaded patio with a screened-in swimming pool out back. Would he take the rent in cash? Kate had asked him as they stood on the patio. He'd said, "As long as you don't mind that I'll keep homestead-ing it."

Kate had taken me over to see it. What would we tell my mother? I'd asked her on the way. But as soon as I saw those high-ceilinged rooms, the Mexican tile, and the white car-peting, I knew we'd come up with something. The old guy chucked Romana's chin as he walked us around, then asked if we would be interested in taking the furniture, too, because his new husband didn't want it at his place. Yeah, we'll take the furniture, too, we told him. What about the utilities? he asked. I said, "Can't we pay you those for now?"

The next morning, I flew out to Sac, came back in a red Charger with Texas plates five days later. I'd lost a day because of a freak snowstorm in northern New Mexico, had crawled along for hours, semis jackknifed around me like great car-casses. "You're losing a G late fee on this," Eric Deveny told me on the phone when I called him and explained what was happening.

"Even for snow?"

"You're the mule. I'm the money. It's not my problem, my man."

Kate was waiting for me when I pulled in. She grabbed a chunk of the latest round of Deveny's cash, hurried through town and across the bridge to Siesta Key. Had the extra day lost her the place? she asked the old guy when she ran in. He accepted the money from her, first month, last month, security deposit, $10,000 total, and said, "Not in this awful market, my dear." We had chestnut leather couches now, a walnut sleigh bed. We brought over the baby's crib, and we never stayed at the 8th Street house again.

After Romana went to sleep in her own room that night, Kate and I spent the evening on the patio, enjoying our view of a flock of white ibis stalking with their curved beaks as they foraged in our yard. We sipped a Napa Sangiovese, the 2006 Altamura; Darren had sent me a case of it via Billy in Sac when we'd made the switch. "He's thinking of you over in Thailand," Billy had told me in the motel room when he'd dropped the case on the bed. "He wants you to know he appreciates everything you've rolled our way, hopes you won't be too put out that his numbers have to go up for a while."

Darren and I hadn't spoken in almost two months. I was finally established, and the mentoring part of our relationship had come to an end. I said to Billy, "His numbers have to go up?"

"It's almost summer, dude. The numbers always go up in the summer, until the harvest starts coming in. A lot of his stuff is in bunkers—he could keep his prices flat if he wanted to, but he's a businessman before anything else. You'd be wise never to forget that, James."

Anger had shot through me. Yeah, I'd known from the start that Darren was a businessman. But I also knew Deveny wouldn't pick up the costs on this and I'd be down a couple Gs a load for now. Then again, did I really care? A thousand dollars had become like a hundred to me; I knew I'd still be making huge money. So I'd let the anger go, uncorked one of the bottles with Billy's Swiss Army knife. We slugged the warm wine together in the motel room, celebrating how much money I was making for all of us. Were he and I friends? He'd said, "You going to remember us when something else comes your way?"

"When something else comes my way?"

"Moving the kind of weight you've been? Tons of people would love to meet you now, James."

I was on my way to rolling Darren Rudd half a million dollars from something that hadn't existed six months before. I was aware of it, thought about it all the time. What kind of windfall had it been for Darren? I knew exactly what kind of windfall it had been for me. A life changer. The chance to become the person I'd always known I was meant to be. Sitting on the patio sipping wine with my wife that late-spring night, I let the success of what I'd done settle into me for the first time. I'd never lived in a place as nice as this one. I knew my parents had never had as much. Kate and I were doing so much better than everyone else out there right now, and I knew there was something tragic about that. Were we going to miss out on some kind of collective pride everyone was going to feel for having survived this worsening economy at the end of the day? And how bad was it going to get? At the same time, we'd already gone through plenty of it ourselves, and I'd worked hard for what we had. A thought passed through my mind like a whisper: You're risking your life. But the night was lazy and wonderful, and I put that thought away.

"Don't you feel like we're moving too fast, James?" my wife asked from across the glass table.

"Don't think about it, Kate."

"But don't you ever get afraid?"

"I'm not afraid right now."

She was quiet a moment. Then she said, "What do you really think of this place?"

"I think I'm happier than I've ever been."

"You're not upset about the money?"

"I know we're going to make more."

Kate was quiet again. She set her hands on her belly like she was thinking about the baby growing inside her. She said, "Is it really always going to be like this? Couldn't we have had this some other way?"

"You know the answer to that."

The car, we told my mother, was bought with my income from the yacht-detailing crew. The house on Siesta Key we didn't even try to explain. We visited her at her place; when she'd ask us why no one was ever home on 8th Street the times she'd dropped by, Kate said, "We have busy lives now, Lynne. We're not the homebodies we were when we first got here."

"Then I'm so happy for the two of you."

No one from the business would ever know about the Siesta Key place; we didn't want any of them to figure out how much money we were making. We paid Nick to stay at the 8th Street house from time to time, to babysit our weight. Then we just enjoyed our lives. I liked swimming endless laps in my pool. I liked staring at *Cops* in my boxer shorts on my big-screen TV. I liked watching my daughter learn to stand up against the coffee table. I liked it when my wife crawled across our big bed with something really randy on her mind. Sometimes when I checked my beard patches, I imagined they were growing in. Whenever I pressed his belly where I kept him on my nightstand, JoJo Bear would always tell me, "I love you."

· · ·

The last thing Kate and I did with our new money before Mason and I dealt with Russell was plan a vacation in Europe. Sarah and Kyle went there often, and Kate had been nagging away at me. Why shouldn't we go, too? Besides working so hard at the business, she was getting straight A's in school. On top of that, she'd be having her birthday soon, number twenty-nine. Okay, okay, okay, I said at last. Of course I hadn't mentioned to her the shit with Russell I'd been dealing with. We applied for passports, circled the dates in June. Then I went to talk to Eric Deveny.

I'd been telling myself from the beginning that I didn't work for Deveny, but the truth was more complex. He was the one who had the money; I was the one who wanted it. It's not like he was hard to please: he wanted color in his weight, he wanted stickiness and stink, and he wanted his deliveries on time. I'd tell him the names of the stuff Billy gave me in Sac: Lamb's Breath, Silver Needle, Blueberry, Diesel, OG, Orange Crush, so many different names, which ones were indo, which ones were outdo. But Deveny didn't care about any of that; he made up his own names. "On time" is what he needed more than anything else. Except for that one ice storm in New Mexico, I'd had no trouble giving him that, and he always sent me home safe with the money.

"Europe, my man?" Eric said when I brought it up to him in May. "That sounds really great. But let me ask you this: How am I going to get my weight while you're gone?"

"What if someone else drives it?"

"No one comes to my door but you."

"What if we went to Europe anyway?"

"I wouldn't be here when you got back."

We were having Greek food, calamari, souvlaki, saganaki, at a quiet place near Governor's Square Mall when I talked to him about it. I was budgeting a couple hundred bucks into every trip to pay for those lunches with him. Kate had been supplying me with clothes to wear in upscale restaurants: Sevens, Diesel, Volcom; we both had piles of designer labels now. Before I'd meet Deveny at the end of the runs, I'd strip off my lucky driving clothes in the last motel room outside Tallahassee, pull all the new stuff on. I'd also long since been wearing my hair short, to look innocent on the road. At a French place, in late February, the hostess had glanced at the two of us and said, "You guys aren't brothers, are you?" I hadn't missed the shadow that had crossed Eric's face. And he never seemed to want to give me credit for anything. When I'd explained how I moved the money through the airports in pantyhose, he'd shrugged and said, "That's not new." When I'd told him about walking the rental car lines and going back in to get Texas plates, he'd said, "That's just common sense."

In the French restaurant he'd looked me up and down and said, "You've cleaned yourself up, my man."

"Taking after the Superstar," I'd said.

Now, at the Greek place, a few months later, when I asked him if I could have some time off to take my family to Europe, Eric shook his head. "Having you gone right now would cost me too much money."

"What do you do with all your money, Eric?"

"All the same things you do with it, James."

"Ever think about getting out?"

"I'll get out when I've made enough."

"How are you going to know when that's going to be?"

He looked at me a moment with this strange grin like he was trying to figure me out. Then he said, "Worried I'm not going to have enough work for you, my man?"

The waiter brought our lamb dishes and refilled our glasses with retsina. When he was out of earshot again, Eric looked at me and said, "How do I know you'll come back?"

"We need the money now."

"Are you going to give me your connection if you get out?"

"We'll talk about that then."

Deveny nodded. "How does your wife feel about all of this?"

"I think I have to take my wife to Europe."

"You like being married, my man?"

"I like it well enough."

We picked up our cutlery and began to eat. Eric said, "There are a lot of fucking hassles involved in marriage, aren't there?"

"Not when it's working right."

"Would you ever want a girl up here?"

I shook my head.

He looked at me a long time then, sipped from his glass. He said, "Good answer, my man. I like all the things I'm learning about you. Stay out of trouble, stay focused on the work. You've got Cali, you've got me. Nobody has a setup like you. People would love to take it from you if they knew you had it. But nobody knows you have it, do they? I'm glad you're working it right, James. Other guys would have gotten distracted by a whole lot of ego-stroking bullshit."

At the end of the meal, he wiped his mouth, tossed his napkin on his plate. "Thanks for the feed, my man. You are granted my permission to go to Europe. You're working as soon as you get back. Then you're going to New York for me."

I watched through the window as he peeled away in his car. Would I ever be as cool as that handsome man? Dressed all in white? Driving that long black Mercedes?

When I got back to Sarasota in the evening, I checked in at the 8th Street house. Nick was lying on the couch in his boxer shorts and staring at *Cops* on TV.

"Everything going okay?" I asked, tossing him Kate's new pound.

"Just fucking driving all the time now, Jimbo," he said and pitched me a roll of money.

"How's the shit moving?"

"The shit's moving great."

"Anything else going on?"

"I want a goddamn raise."

"You'll have to take that up with Kate, my man."

At home in Siesta Key, I put the shoebox full of money Deveny had given me in the dishwasher, then stuffed Kate's roll of money from Nick in the pocket of her jeans on the patio as she kissed me to welcome me back. She had dinner waiting on the table, pesto linguine with garlic shrimp. I held my daughter on my lap as we ate, and Romana stuck her fingers into everything.

"So can I book those tickets already?" Kate asked.

"Go ahead. Out on June sixteenth, back on the twenty-ninth. We'll have two full weeks over there. I have to work right up to the day we leave. I have to be on the road the day we get back."

"What do you think about driving up to see the Alps after we're done visiting Rome, James?"

"Driving, Kate? Are you fucking kidding me?"

The passports came, the tickets were booked, and we told my mother we were going to see Kate's parents in California. Then it was time for the last run before Italy, and to go to Biloxi with Mason and finally do something about Russell.

I flew out to Sacramento with the money, grabbed a rental car, picked up the weed from Billy, the same old things. Two days later, I pulled into Mason's lot late in the night. I'd been putting off this thing with Russell for so long because I really had no idea what to do. What I hoped more than anything was that when we rolled into Biloxi, Russell wouldn't be there.

At least then I would have satisfied my obligation to Mason. Because what if Russell was there? Were we really going to fuck him up? Just like that? How would that get us our money? I'd only agreed to go so I could put the goddamn thing to bed before our trip.

I sat in the car. I started thinking all these other things. What if we had enough now? What if Kate and I didn't come back from Europe? Could we hide enough money in the baby's diaper to stay over there a good long time? To do the things I was doing, I'd had to build lies into myself. The main one, I knew, was that I'd never get caught. But there were a lot of others, too. That we'd had to start doing this because of the economy. That we had to continue doing this because of the economy. Yes, we were scared when we lost our jobs. But that seemed like a lifetime ago. Because weren't we buying all this other shit now? Because weren't we doing all these other things? So what if I was good at the muling? Hadn't I been scared every single time? More scared than I'd ever been about anything else in my life? Wasn't I scared right now, just sitting in this car? What I felt in that car outside Mason's that night was that I should just stay in it, turn around and drive home without seeing him or anyone else, go to Europe with my family and never, ever look back.

Then I thought about the money. God, how I wanted the money. I stepped out of the car, carried the duffel bag up the stairs.

"It's time, James," Mason said when I went inside. "It's tomorrow. I'll follow you there. We'll wait outside his place. We'll stake him out until he gets home, then we'll fuck him up. Then you'll go to Europe and have a good time with Kate and Romana, and nobody will ever fuck with us again."

I dropped myself onto Mason's couch. Where was Emma? Asleep in the bedroom with Bayleigh. I'd told Billy again about our problem in Sacramento; Billy had said what he always said: "Don't think so much, James. Hit the motherfucker in the face with a lead pipe." I'd also long since known what Eric Deveny thought I should do about it. God, what was so wrong with everybody? Now I said to Mason in a voice as exhausted by it all as I felt, "So we're just going to go there, wait for him, and then fuck him up?"

"Yeah."

"Russell's a big dude, Mason."

"We're going to surprise him."

"Have you ever done something like this?"

Mason rubbed his chin, didn't say anything.

I shook my head. I said, "What if we go there and he calls the cops?"

Mason thought about it. He said, "What's he going to say to the cops? That he pissed us off because he stole our weed?"

"What if the redhead calls the cops?"

Mason thought about it. "Then we'll fuck her up, too."

In the morning, I woke up as irritated about it as ever. Mason said we had to do some shopping first, so I followed him over to Wal-Mart. He grabbed rope, duct tape, two black pillowcases, a Louisville Slugger. I shook my head at the stuff in the cart. I said, "What, you gonna kidnap them?"

"I don't know," Mason said. "It's better to be prepared."

He wanted to buy rat poison for the dogs. I said, "Get a life, Mason." He wanted a gallon of paint thinner to burn down Russell's house. I told him, "That's not even his house!" At the register, I couldn't meet the checkout girl's eyes. What an obscenely stupid collection of items.

We put those things in the back of my car, a big silver Chrysler 300, right beside the duffel bag of weed. I'd been getting upgrades from the rental agencies, my ego had finally decided to let me take one. I'd also just made Silver status on Star Alli-

ance because I'd flown so many one-ways to Sacramento with
them. Mason winked his headlights at me from where he sat
across the aisle in his Corolla. Then we pulled out of the Wal-
Mart lot, got ourselves on the road.

In the evening, we turned off the I-10 and entered the ugly
city of Biloxi, Mississippi. We drove past Russell's sad and
dumpy house in the fading light. No one seemed to be there.
We parked the cars, went up on the porch, peered in the front
picture window. The dogs inside began to bark at us.

"He's still living here if the dogs are here," Mason said.

"Why don't we just break in and steal something?" I said.

Mason said, "Why don't we just wait until he gets here, fuck
him up, and then steal every single thing he has?"

When we went back to the cars, Mason popped his trunk.
"Look at this," he whispered. When I looked in the trunk, I
saw the samurai sword from his wall. The scabbard wasn't
on it.

"What'd you bring that for?"

"I'm going to scare him with it."

"Goddamn it, Mason. Leave it in the fucking trunk."

As the evening settled down, we drove to the beach and
walked on the sand. There were cigarette butts and broken
bottles everywhere. Why were so many places on the Gulf of
Mexico such shitholes? Mason had all these plans he wanted to
talk about, how we should start buying vehicles, register them
in different states, set up drivers for every leg of the trip, one
guy coming in with the dope, another guy meeting him with
the cash for the next run. Then we could sit back, let other
people take the risks, make a shit ton of money.

What I wanted to say was, If it was that easy, Mason, don't
you think we'd have done it already? Instead I said, "We have
plenty of time to talk about all of that." I thought again that I
shouldn't come back from Europe.

When we went back to Russell's, it was night. We parked our cars far up the street; the cracked and broken neighborhood around us was dark and silent. I took the Louisville Slugger out of my car, Mason took the samurai sword out of his. "Give me that," I said and grabbed it from him, tossed it in my trunk. I took the tire iron out of the wheel well, since Mason had to have something.

"Come on," Mason said when I gave him the tire iron. "It'll scare the fuck out of him. What's scarier than a pissed-off Asian dude with a samurai sword?"

"Mason, give it a rest. You're a redneck from Biloxi."

"What are you talking about, James? I'm full-blooded Korean, been over there twice."

"One of those times you were a baby."

"One of those times I wasn't, all right?"

We went around back, crossed the darkened yard, hid in the brambles growing over a dried-out culvert. The lights went on in the rear windows of the shotgun house next door. A few minutes later, the lights went off. The darkened house on the other side of Russell's was vacant.

When I lit a cigarette, Mason hissed, "He'll see the glow of that." A half hour later, he was smoking one, too. We spent so much time in those brambles, smoking cigarettes, waiting. What would we have looked like to anyone who might have seen us?

It must have been past midnight. Still no Russell. "Can I go home now?" I said.

"You can't leave me here."

"Can't we both go home?"

"I'm not ready to go home yet."

After another twenty minutes of waiting, Mason gave in. He was frustrated, tossed down his cigarette and ground it out hard under his heel. When we went around to the front of the house, a pickup truck was coasting toward us in the middle of the street with its engine off. Its headlights were off, too. I knew right away it was Russell. I now understood that he really had been hiding from us. Everything felt real in a way it hadn't before. Mason and I raced around to the back, ducked in the brambles. We lay beside each other on our bellies in the dirt and watched as Russell and the redhead climbed into their own house through a rear window they'd slid open.

"Why are they doing that?" I whispered.

"Because they're fucking assholes," Mason said.

The lights went on in the other back window. Mason and I crept through the yard to the back of the house. First Mason climbed into the open window, then I did. It was their bed-room. It was a mess, clothes piled everywhere, the sheets twisted on the bed and the mattress showing. They were such dirty people. Poor people. Mason and I stood with our backs against the wall by the door. Mason ducked his head to look through the doorway. Then I did. I saw the backs of their heads over the back of the couch, the TV beyond with a NASCAR race on it, on mute. I smelled the scent of burning weed.

The redhead said in a normal voice that didn't know we were there, "How about your mother?"

"She don't fucking care," Russell said in a voice that also didn't know we were there.

"I'm not living in that campground, Russell."

Suddenly the dogs were barking in the doorway. Mason sidled toward them; when he was close enough, they sniffed his hand and remembered who he was. Then they were bump-ing against my legs, whining to be petted. When I looked in the living room again, Russell was brandishing a golf club.

"What the fuck you doing here! What the fuck you doing here!"

The redhead was standing, too, bug-eyed, frightened. Could

someone really be that scared of me? Mason stepped carefully
into the room. He had the tire iron raised in his hands, was
hissing under his breath, "Calm down! Calm down!"

"What the fuck you doing in my house?"

"We want our fucking money!"

"I'll fucking kill you!"

"I'll fucking kill you!"

The redhead yelled, "Give them some money! Give them
some money!" Russell glanced at her with a twisted face that
said, What the fuck? and Shut the fuck up! at the same time.

Mason and Russell squared off like swordsmen with those
weapons in their hands. But there was still a good distance
between them in the room. Mason barked out of the side of
his mouth at the girl, "Give me that motherfucking ring," and
she twisted it off her finger, tossed it to him. Mason stuffed it
in his pocket. He said, "I want more shit."

"Don't fucking give them anything," Russell shouted at her.

"I thought you were my friend," Mason said. "You ain't my
friend."

"Go fuck yourself," Russell said.

Mason barked at the girl, "Get all your fucking shit together.
We're gonna go sell it."

Russell said, "All we got left is the goddamn TV. You want
the goddamn TV?" He swung the golf club and smashed the
TV.

It was then that I saw that time had slowed. Because only
then did I notice that the dogs were going crazy, running
around Russell's and Mason's legs with their tails between their
legs and their shoulders hunched as though they expected to
be hit. They were making awful crying sounds, too.

Mason said, "Give us our weed."

"It's gone."

"Give us something."

"Go fuck yourself."

Mason ran howling across the room. He swung the tire iron. Russell stepped back from it. Mason glanced over his shoulder at me as if saying Help me! I sprinted across the room and hit Russell in the face with the bat as hard as I could.

He dropped like a sack. Then Mason and I were whaling on him. Somewhere the girl was saying, "No! No! No! No! No!" I managed to stop myself. I grabbed Mason and stopped him, and we were both panting, and I had no fucking idea who we were.

The girl went to Russell's side and crouched down. She said to us, "Let's help him up." We took his arms and pulled him up. His eye was swollen and his mouth was welling blood. He was stunned, swaying. He lifted his hand to explore the damage to his mouth. I could see the blood all over his teeth.

"Okay," Russell said in a normal voice.

"We want our fucking money," Mason said.

"Okay." Russell nodded. "I'll take you to an ATM."

The girl said, "I'm not going anywhere."

Mason grabbed her hard by her upper arm, shook her. He said, "Fuck yeah, you are! You spent our money, too."

"What the fuck, Russell? What the fuck, Russell?" the girl screamed at him, as if it was all his fault. But she was letting Mason hold her arm, wasn't fighting him at all.

"Gotta get my wallet," Russell said. We followed him into the bedroom, Mason yanking the girl along. Russell found his wallet on the dresser in the dark, and we all went out the window one by one. "Landlord changed the deadbolts," Russell said as he climbed down.

Mason said, "You stole our money and couldn't pay your rent? You're a fucking dumbass."

We went up the street, I pushed the clicker for the 300. We

all got in, Mason and Russell in back, the girl up front beside me. I had the baseball bat between my legs. I started driving. At the corner, I said, "Which way?"

Russell said, "Left."

At the ATM, we sat in the car with the girl and watched Russell stand under the security light and push the buttons on the machine. He looked off into the night while he waited, then took his money. When he was in the car again, he said, "It's two hundred. It's all I have."

"You think I believe that?" Mason said.

The girl said without turning around, "It's true. That's all that's left."

Mason said, "Then we're going to your fucking mother's."

Mason gave me directions in a calm voice and we drove onto the highway. Everyone was quiet. We crossed the water, got on the eastbound 10, drove awhile. Mason told me to take the next exit. There was a sign for a wildlife refuge, sandhill cranes. We crossed over the interstate and turned northbound on a dark country road. Russell said, "Can I smoke?"

Nobody said anything, and I realized he was asking me because it was my car. I said, "Yeah, you can smoke."

"Got a cigarette?"

"Jesus Christ," Mason said. I heard him rummaging around and then I heard the flick of a lighter.

I said, "What are we going to do at his mother's?"

We drove along and nobody said anything.

Russell said, "Gotta pee."

We drove along. It was dark.

Russell said, "Gotta pee like a fucking horse."

"Me, too," I said back to Mason.

We drove along. Mason said, "Fuck it, turn here," and I turned onto a dirt track into the woods, the headlights playing over the trunks of trees. The car banged up and down over stones in the dirt, and there was nowhere to stop. As we went deeper into the woods, the redhead said, "Where we going?"

Nobody said anything.

She said louder, "Where we going?"

Mason said, "Shut the fuck up, LaJane!"

The dirt track opened onto a field with the moon hanging over it. The plants at the field's edge, lit by the headlights, were young, knee-high. "Park," Mason said, and I did, turned off the car and the headlights. Once my eyes adjusted, I saw how big and flat the field was. The silver moonlight dappled the plants and made the field look like the sea; the backlit clouds drifting across the sky looked like ice floes. We all got out, except for the girl. I heard crickets. "What kind of crop is this?" I said as I walked off, unzipped.

Russell said, "Cotton."

"Pop the trunk," Mason said, and I pressed the button on the clicker in my pocket and started peeing. The car beeped behind me in response. Russell ambled off, smoking his cigarette. He wasn't peeing. I heard the tire iron thump against the bottom of the trunk. Then Mason walked by me with the samurai sword in his hands. The moonlight glinted on the blade; there was nothing I could do. Mason walked up to Russell and said, "You gonna apologize to me?"

Russell turned around. Before he could say anything, Mason drew back, plunged the sword all the way into Russell's belly. I'd never seen anything happen like that. Mason pulled out the sword and started slashing Russell's body as he went down. Then Mason was sticking the blade into Russell's back over and over.

I heard a car door open behind me, turned and saw the girl sprint from the car and into the cotton. Mason saw her, gave chase. She was running, he was right behind her, and they made it a good long way into the field together under the moon. Then Mason swung the sword and clipped her on the side of the head and she tumbled down. He started swinging that sword on her like he was chopping wood.

On the ground where he lay, Russell lowed like some kind of ancient species of cattle. It was the worst sound I'd ever heard. Then he was wheezing like a bellows. Then he wasn't making any sound at all.

Mason walked toward me through the field from that long way off, the sword dangling from his hand. He looked like a field hand returning home from work. He stopped out there, lit a cigarette, and then started walking toward me again. He was breathing heavily when he threw the sword at my feet.

"You kill that girl?"

He didn't say anything.

"Why'd you kill that girl?"

He turned and looked out at the field. Everything was quiet, sickening.

Mason held a cigarette out to me from his pack. I watched my shaking fingers take it. He lit it, said, "You gonna tell?"

I couldn't speak.

"James? James? You gonna tell?" He shouted, "What about my family? What about my kid?"

I'd been thinking, Don't panic, don't panic. Now I was thinking, Can I turn him in?

Mason said, "You did this, too."

"No I didn't!"

"You were standing right here. You didn't even try to stop me."

"Stop you?"

We were quiet. Then Mason said, "We have to get them out of here. Someone'll come and find them."

Then he said, "James!"

I shook my head. I said, "How the fuck are we going to get them out of here?"

"In the car."

"We can't put them in the car."

We smoked. I said, "I'm leaving. You're turning yourself in."

"No way."

"I'm not getting in trouble for this. I didn't have anything to do with it."

"Yes, you did!"

In a minute, I said, "Where could we even take them?"

"We'll dump them in a lake."

"What lake?"

We smoked some more. I looked at the moonlight on the plants, then at the moon. I was going to vomit. What could I do? I had to save my life. I opened the door of the car, grabbed one of my phones out of the glove compartment. I called Eric Deveny. What if he didn't answer? What if he did?

Eric Deveny was at a loud party. He said through the phone, "Why you calling so late? You busted?"

"No, no. Nothing like that."

"James?"

"I need your help. I've got a huge fucking mess on my hands."

"Calm down!"

I took a deep breath. "Something happened, Eric. I can't say it on the phone."

Eric was silent. I heard the noise of the party receding as he left it. If he didn't say anything, I had no idea what to do. Then he said, "What happened?"

"The guy who ripped me off? Something went down."

"He do something to you?"

"No, no. The other way around."

"The other way around?"

"It's over."

He was silent. Then he said, "It's over?"

"Yeah."

"What's over?"

"The guy."

"The guy's over?"

"Yeah."

"For real?"

"Yeah, for real. There's two of them."

"Two of them?" He was silent. I couldn't hear the party anymore. Then he said, "Anyone see you?"

"No, nobody saw."

He was quiet for second. He said, "Why didn't you just call me and let me do it?" Then, "Where are you? Can you get the mess here without anyone seeing?"

"I'm in Biloxi. I fucking have to."

"Get it here, I'll help you. It's going to cost you. You're going to have to give that weight to me. Don't come to my house. I'll text you an address. Wait there when you get there, then don't do anything. Don't call this phone again. You'd better not fuck this up."

I grabbed the duffel bag, tossed it in the backseat. My hands became bathed in blood as Mason and I wrestled Russell's heavy body into the trunk. Then we walked out into the cotton field. At first we couldn't find her, had to hunt all around. Could she have gotten away? Then we found her. She was lying face-down in the plants like she was sleeping. But she wasn't sleeping. She was almost weightless when we carried her out of the field. We put her in the trunk on top of Russell, shut the lid on them. Mason handed me the bloody sword. I opened the trunk, averted my eyes, threw it in.

"We have to pick up all these cigarette butts," I said.

We started doing that. Then I said, "Forget it. We have to get out of here."

I drove us back out to the road with the headlights off. I was trembling. "If we get pulled over, you did it. You tell them you were going to kill me, that you made me drive."

"Fine."

I turned on the headlights, drove us back to Biloxi. The baseball bat was beside me; I chucked it out the window on the way. Mason smoked, didn't say anything. When we arrived at his car, he started to climb out. "What are you doing?" I said.

"I can't go with you."

"I can't do this by myself!"

We sat there saying nothing. There was no one around. It was the middle of the night. We couldn't sit there forever. Mason opened the door again. He said, "Please let me go. Please let me go. You know you can do it."

What could I say? I said, "Get the fuck out of my car."

I put the 300 in gear. Then I stopped, powered down the passenger window. I said, "Throw that fucking sword away." I popped the trunk, Mason took out the sword, put it in his car. Then I pulled away. Then I stopped, reversed back. I powered down the window. I said, "You have to let those dogs out. You have to be careful."

"Okay."

"What the fuck is wrong with you? What if I get caught out there?"

I got on the road. Mason had killed two people. There were two dead bodies and weed in my car. I knew I couldn't think of that.

My phone lit up. It was a text, directions. I drove through the night. My mind was in this dead zone. The stripes of the roadway flashed in the headlights and I was the only car on the road. Every inch of the way I knew that my life was at stake.

I found the place at first light. There was a two-car garage on a cement slab in the woods with a big pond beside it. The garage was yellow. No one was there. Crows and starlings were flying around everywhere. There was blood on the steering wheel, dried blood all over my hands, bloody handprints on the dashboard where Mason had touched it. I lay in the backseat of the car with my jacket tight around me, looking at the tops of the pine trees waving in the wind.

Someone rapped on the window and startled me. It was Eric Deveny and his bearded brother. I got out of the car, crammed my hands deep in my jacket pockets. Nearby was Eric's Mercedes, a white utility truck parked beside it. The brother walked to the garage, unlocked the overhead door, and yanked it open. I could see work benches and tools inside. Eric was dressed in white. He said to me, "You all right?"

"No."

"Show me."

I popped open the trunk. Eric looked inside. He bit his knuckle and his eyes lit up. He said, "Holy shit! Hand-to-fucking-hand."

I gave him the duffel bag of weed, which was his payment, and took a walk along the pond. I stared at the trees reflected in the water and wondered if there were any fish in it. Time passed. I heard a generator come to life behind me. Then I heard a Skilsaw start up in the garage. I crouched and washed my hands at the water's edge, walked along, crouched, and washed my face. In the distance I saw Eric in his white clothing striding around the pond toward me, floating like a specter. He was smiling when he reached me, and he said, "You okay?" I shook my head. He asked me, "How much did they take from you?" I said, "Not much."

"Did you do that to them?"

"It wasn't me. It was a guy I work with."

"But were you there?"

"I was there."

"Did you plan it?"

"No."

"Where did it happen?"

"In a cotton field."

"And nobody saw?"

I shook my head.

"If your guy talks, you're fucked," he said. "So maybe you should bring him here, too. Somehow that girl was still breathing. Don't worry, she isn't anymore." He put his arm around me and led me back to the garage. "It's okay. It happens. Give it a couple days. Then don't think about it again."

When we reached the garage, I could see parts of Russell's and LaJane's bodies on the floor, red and meaty where they had been cut by the saw. The 300 was parked outside, dripping because Eric's brother had washed it out with a hose they had.

Eric smiled and said, "You okay to drive?" He laughed and shook his head. "I know what you're feeling, believe me. It's fucking heady, isn't it?"

I got in the car, started it, put it in reverse. Then Eric and his brother trotted up to the window. His brother's clothes were covered in blood like a butcher's. When I powered down the window, they were laughing. Eric's brother was holding something out to me on his bloody palm. It was a tiny curled finger with a red-painted fingernail on it. The brother said, "You want it, dude? You earned it." I was gagging as I reversed past the Mercedes and all the way through the trees to the road.

Kate, Romana, and I flew to Rome the next day. It was hot there. Everywhere we went, I saw statues and paintings, and all of the statues and paintings were dead bodies. Kate kept asking me, "What the hell's the matter with you?" and I kept saying, "Nothing" or "I don't feel good, Kate." "Well," she kept saying back, "you're ruining my fucking trip." Kate bought a lot of clothes with the money we'd brought with us in Romana's diaper, and in Milan Kate shopped all day for leather boots, trying on dozens of them in a dozen different stores before buying three pairs. "Why do you need three pairs?" I asked. She said, "It's my trip, isn't it? Mind your own business."

I expected men to come up to me with guns drawn, to knock on the door of our hotel room and arrest me. But nobody came up to me and nobody knocked on our door. After Milan, Kate made me drive us to the Alps, and then to Lake Como. The mountains were beautiful, the lake was beautiful, and for the three days and two nights we had there, I calmed down. As we walked along the lake, Kate asked again and again, "Do you love me?" I answered her every time, "Of course I love you."

I didn't want to go back, and I couldn't go back, and I knew I could not tell Kate. At passport control in D.C., I knew they'd surround me, take me into custody, but the bored immigration officer stamped my passport and said, "Welcome home." When the taxi dropped us off at Siesta Key, our house was waiting for us like we had never left.

I turned on the news. I'd been checking the news every day, many times a day. There was never any news. When I called Mason, he said, "Nothing's happened. Nobody knows. I'm fucking sorry. I'm so fucking sorry. It's all my fault. You didn't have anything to do with it. I shouldn't have made you come. I'm the one who's crazy. I'm the one who has to live with it. Did you tell Kate? Tell me you didn't tell Kate."

I did not want to do this anymore. I e-mailed all the editors I had ever worked with and asked them if they could use any travel articles about Italy. Most of the e-mails bounced back, because those editors had lost their jobs by now. The only one I received read, "Not in the budget. Good luck, sorry."

Five days later, I was parked in the lot outside Mason's apartment building with a duffel bag full of weed. I sat there for a long time. I did not want to go up there, and I did not want to go up there, and I did not want to go up there. And then I went up there. We had a cigarette together on his porch, and he said, "Everyone thinks they ran away together. We weren't the only people they owed money. Nobody is searching for them and nobody knows. I'll understand if you don't want to be my friend anymore."

We had another cigarette. I said, "Did you let those dogs out?"

He said, "Yeah, I carried them out that window and shooed them away."

"Did you take the tags off of them first?"

"Yeah, I took off the tags."

"What did you do with the tags?"

"I threw them away at a gas station."

"What did you do with the sword?"

"I threw it in Lake Pontchartrain."

Then I remembered the ring. I said to him, "What did you do with the ring?"

He dug in his pocket and took it out. He held it up and we looked at it together. He gave it to me and said, "I owe you a ton of money. I'm going to pay you all your money."

"Something is fucking wrong with you, Mason."

"I know, I know. I'm sorry."

"There's no way I can stay here!"

Mason grabbed my arm. "You have to! What would Emma think if you didn't?"

Kate saw me looking at the ring in our kitchen a few days

later. She said, "Where did you get that?" I said, "Somebody gave it to me who owed me money." She took it, looked at it, then handed it back to me and said, "It's small. It's ugly. I don't want it. I'll let you buy me a better one to make up for how crappy you were in Europe."

I carried the ring around with me for days because I didn't know what to do with it, didn't want to throw it away. Then Kate and I and the baby were shopping at St. Armand's Circle. All of the stores were having sales because of the economy. Some of the stores were going out of business. I said to Kate, "You sure you want a ring?" Kate said, "Yes." I tossed the dead girl's ring into a garbage can. I bought Kate a nicer one with $4,000 of our drug money.

PART **Two**

4

Skinning Mules

To anyone with any sense, it was obvious I'd been doing a lot of things wrong from the start. First, I wasn't taking any breaks. But I also wasn't sharing the workload, wasn't doubling up on weight to reduce my risk on the road. It was tricky: being busted with heavier weight would mean more prison time. And yet they couldn't catch you if you weren't behind the wheel. I continued to use the credit card for flights and cars, had from the beginning because I'd imagined I'd be doing it only once. But since I'd opened that Pandora's box, it had become impossible to shut. With the card, I could book the flights online, didn't have to answer any questions, deal with anyone. And the rental car companies wouldn't easily give me a vehicle any other way. To pay in cash, I'd have to register two weeks in advance, hand them all my information, put down a big deposit. I also knew that renting a car with cash could raise suspicions. So wasn't it just safer to keep using the card? It's not like I had any other options anyway: I was leaving behind a long paper trail documenting all my one-way flights to Sacramento, my quick drives home.

I did have a story to cover all of that: I'd been having an affair with Rita, couldn't stand my wife, liked driving back to prolong my time away from her. That I'd been telling my wife I was researching a book I was going to write about everything that was going on right now in the country, to be called *The End of the Golden Dream: Returning East on the American Highway.* I was a journalist in my past life, after all, I'd say to whatever investigators interrogated me in whatever small room they'd shackle me in. Still, I knew it was a ridiculous story.

I was telling myself all these other things, too: that it was good I was keeping my loads small, that if I got busted it would be only for that one time, we'd only lose the cost of the weight they'd nailed me with, the maximum federal sentence on the weights I'd been carrying was just five years. Just five years? For everything I'd already gotten away with? It didn't seem that long anymore. Not for the safety I was earning for my family. It would be a first-time offense; if they didn't find out about the rest of it, a good lawyer could get me a reduced sentence. We had plenty of money for a good lawyer now. Maybe my prison term would be so short, the kids wouldn't even notice I'd been gone. Besides, didn't a part of me feel that I deserved to go to prison?

And the money—what were we going to do with all the money? Open a nail salon, beauty shop, massage parlor, laundromat? I knew from Darren Rudd that anything that worked with cash would get the job done, we wouldn't even need customers, the only business we'd really be doing was washing dirty drug money clean in the books. But that felt too complicated to figure out right now, was something I'd sit down and tackle whenever my time on the road was done. Instead I'd been stuffing a grand here, a grand there, into my bank account to pay off the credit card, the new car; I knew they could get me for "structuring"—money laundering—if it all went down. My planned cover story on that was I ran a part-time lawn service, payments in cash. "So where are these clients of yours who paid you all that cash, Mr. Lasseter?" I could hear the investigators asking. I knew I'd just smoke my cigarette and tell them, "I'd like to talk to my lawyer now."

Even sloppier than all that, to avoid the stress of going through airport security with the money on my body, I'd begun mailing it to Billy instead. I'd split up $36,000 into four $9,000 batches to mitigate losses and avoid a CTR if any of the money was found. And it was all twenties—I didn't have to waste a second of my life in shitty casinos getting hundreds anymore. I'd hide the money in copies of magazines I loathed because they'd never published me, *National Geographic, Men's Vogue,* wrap all of it in foil, wrap it again with packing tape. Then I'd seal those packages in Express Mail envelopes at the post office. I knew I couldn't use FedEx or UPS because they were private companies and could open anything you gave them—you waived your right to privacy when you signed their bills of lading. But the post office needed a warrant. I'd write "Do Not Bend, Comic Books" on the envelopes, put a phony return address on the forms; I used the address of the downtown shop that really did sell comic books. Then I'd mail them out to the different addresses Billy would give me, in McKinleyville, Mount Shasta, Etna, Montague, Crescent City, Happy Camp, small towns in far northern California.

I'd feel sick as soon as the packages left my hands. Why was I risking my money like this? Just for an extra minute of peace of mind at the airport? Just to not have to get hundreds? Billy had let me know that while people occasionally mailed him their money, packages could be x-rayed in a random check, and drug dogs at the sorting stations were trained to smell cash. He and Darren couldn't take responsibility if I used the mail. But he'd also told me that if any was found, it would only be "civil forfeiture," wouldn't lead to an arrest. Nobody he knew had lost money in the mail, he'd said.

I'd track the packages on the computer throughout the night. They'd arrive in Tampa by truck, fly out from there, make pit stops at various sorting stations in the middle of the country—Dallas, Denver—reach Sacramento in the early morning. By noon the next day, they'd be in vans for delivery. I'd swim, watch *Cops*, worry about losing my money the whole time; Kate had no idea. In the late afternoon my phone would ring and Billy would tell me, "All is well. All is well. Everything got here fine, dude."

And then there was Eric Deveny. I was having trouble putting him off on his New York run. "Way too busy," I'd tell him when we'd have lunch. He'd narrow his eyes and say, "Too busy, my man? I wasn't too busy to clean up those bodies for you."

One evening in mid-July, Kate and I dropped off the baby with my mother. We'd told her about the Siesta Key house at last, said we were watching it for one of Kate's professors who was away on sabbatical. My mother had swallowed the story whole, looked around the place and loved it for us—mothers will believe anything their kids tell them. That night, Kate and I went to a black-and-white party at a beach house off Midnight Pass, down the road from where we lived. The place was beautiful, belonged to someone wealthy Kate knew. The party was around the pool; young waiters came by every few minutes bearing silver trays of themed hors d'oeuvres and Oreo cookies, chocolate martinis and sweating flutes of sparkling wine.

I liked being included in that high society, felt I belonged to it now. Kate was really showing, people told her how pretty she was. Everyone was a doctor, lawyer, or in finance, all in their early thirties. They talked about the presidential election, the car companies, Bear Stearns, the price of oil, the housing market; they asked each other if they thought the stock market would crash. They seemed so surprised, as though what had happened to Kate and me a year and a half ago was happening to them only now. Because of our money in the Vault, I wasn't as consumed with economic fear as they were; for that reason I enjoyed the party all the more. When an attractive woman in a black-and-white Audrey Hepburn hat and form-fitting dress asked me what I did for a living, I told her, "Import-export."

"Import-export of what?"

"Spices from the Orient. Supplying Chinese takeouts everywhere."

"How's business?"

"Business is great."

"Even in this economy? I thought the restaurant business was tanking."

"We're insulated from it. Everyone still wants their takeout."

"So where are you keeping your money?" she leaned in and whispered.

I whispered back, "We're keeping our money in cash."

Kate said to me in bed that night, "Who was that woman you were talking to?"

"She was somebody's wife, Kate."

"What were you two talking about?"

"We were talking about the economy."

Kate said, "Were you attracted to her? Did you want to sleep with her? Don't act like you didn't notice how good-looking she was. Don't pretend like you didn't think about it."

Then she said, "I feel so ugly right now."

"That's what you felt like the last time, too."

"Where are you these days, James? Because you're never here."

"I'm working. I'm busy."

Kate turned from me. "Don't you know how fucking lonely I feel all the time?"

A house, a car, a vacation, college—hadn't I given her everything? I wasn't in any mood to console her. I said, "Want me to buy you something, Kate?"

In the morning, I caught a flight. In the evening, I was on the road.

Nick had been working hard. He'd had his hair cut, always wore a shirt now. By the middle of summer he was making deliveries all the way up to Tarpon Springs and as far south as Fort Myers. Was he skating anymore? I asked him when we were hanging out over Pabsts at the 8th Street house. Skating? Who had time for that? The only thing he had time for anymore was driving for Kate and making money. He had payments to make on the Impala he'd bought, the twenty-inch rims he'd put on it. He needed cash for fun and women. Would I ever let him drive for me, he wanted to know, cruise out to Cali with forty Gs, come back with the weight?

"No fucking way."

"Don't you want someone to give you a break from it?"

"Not if that someone would stress me out more."

"But don't you know I could do it?"

"Even if you could, trust me, you wouldn't want to."

Nick shook his head. "Of course I want to. I want to make the money, Jimbo."

Then Nick had this other idea. If he could move a pound at six and a half Gs for me, what would I be willing to toss him on that?

"Five hundred bucks," I said.

"What if it was two pounds?"

I thought about it. I told him, "I'd give you twelve hundred dollars."

He nodded, was happy.

"Where's the deal?" I said.

"Up in Orlando."

"Who's it through?"

"My boy at school has boys up there."

"Fronted?"

"Cash."

"A one-time thing?"

"Regular, if it moves right for them."

"The money has to come down here."

Nick shook his head. "My boy says his boys can't travel."

"Why can't they travel?"

"They'd get pulled over."

"Why would they get pulled over?"

Nick said, "They're, you know, hoods. I know that makes it sound sketchy. But relax, when you meet my boy, you aren't going to think that. Besides, it's thirteen thousand dollars, Jim."

Before I left that evening, Nick wanted me to see the house next door. The place had been foreclosed on, the family had just been evicted. It was a little yellow block house under a shady live oak. When we went through the plank gate to the yard, the side door was open. Inside, clothes and toys were strewn everywhere. It was hot in there because the power had been cut.

"We should stash our shit in here," Nick said.

I shook my head. "And give it away to vagrants?"

Nick was right, I did want help with the driving, felt almost desperate about it. But I also still wanted all the money. On the transatlantic flight back from Europe, I'd sketched out the details of the loop Darren Rudd had told me to build way back in the beginning. If anybody in Sacramento would be willing to pony up, for example, that person could carry the weight from there to Albuquerque, two days out, two days back. I'd pay that person a pound of weed, $2,800 cost on my end, and he could sell it for between $5,000 and $6,000, whatever he could get. Mason would be waiting in an Albuquerque motel, take the handoff, and drive the weight to Dallas the next day. Emma could pick up his pounds from him there that night; the round trip from Austin to Dallas was only six hours. The following day, Mason could make it all the way to Tallahassee, if he got an early start and could keep himself awake. Then I'd grab the weight from him, take it to Deveny. I'd pay Mason two pounds, the same as ten to twelve Gs to him. The whole thing would cost me only $8,600; I'd make almost twenty grand a run without doing much of anything. If it worked once or twice, I'd send the money back that way, too. I'd done so much for everyone, wouldn't they do this for me?

When I brought up the idea to Rita and Henry in Sacramento, asked them to drive, they said, "Hell no! Hell no!" as if the cops were already on their way over to bust them just by me saying it out loud. They had kids, they said, jobs. There was no way they needed the money that bad. All right, all right, I said, what about their old buddy Jerome? They said, Jerome? Yeah, Jerome might do it. He'd quit working at the bank, was slinging full time now. He was even carrying weight once in a while to various people he knew down in Riverside and L.A. counties. "Interstate?" he said when I asked him on the phone. "No way. Not everyone's got your death wish, dude."

Then there was Mason; he'd always wanted to do it. Plus, in theory he owed me fifty Gs, which I knew he'd never be able to repay. "Drive for you?" he said on the phone when I broke my plan to him. "Sorry, James. Not me or Emma. What if we got caught out there, you know?"

I said, "What do you think I've been doing out there all these months?"

"I never asked you to do all that."

"What about the Capital Cities Connection?"

"You know that was just a name."

"After everything I've done for you."

"I know, I know. And I'm sorry."

"What if I said I'd knock twelve Gs off what you owe?"

"It's tempting, brother. But not right now."

"I fucking hate you, Mason!"

There had been moments when I could be as paranoid about the business as anyone who's ever done it. I'd part the drapes to see if anyone was watching the house, would have the idea that even the grocery store checkout girls were narcs. Now I was making Kate run through our worst-case-scenario plan all the time. The worst case, of course, was if I got pulled over.

The main part of our plan had to do with the Vault. Our code for the punch pad at the door was 4-2-0, easy to remember, no problem there. Our one-page contract in case we lost our keys was folded and buried in the sawdust insulation in my mother's attic. But the keys to our safe-deposit boxes were the most important thing; they were the only way we could get our money and passports if anything ever went down. For that reason, Kate always carried them with her in her purse. If I was ever to text her the word "Emergency," no matter when, the first thing she had to do was hide those keys. For all we'd know, the cops would already be on their way to get her. And if they got her with the keys, they'd trace them, take all our money.

"Hide them where?" she'd asked me when I'd explained it to

her, the day we'd returned from my first trip to the Vault, back in late February.

"It has to be someplace no one but us will find them."

"How about over at your mom's?"

"They'll toss her place for sure. It has to be someplace not connected to us."

After a little thinking, Kate had said, "How about Sarah and Kyle's?"

I thought about that: her rich friends' place. "That might work."

"I'll drop them in their downstairs toilet tank."

"That's perfect, Kate."

The other things Kate would have to do if I texted her "Emergency" were to leave the Siesta Key house and her expensive shit behind in it, throw all the phones and the laptop into Sarasota Bay, call Nick and tell him to dump the weight, his scales, phones, whatever he had, and to disappear. Then she should go to my mother's with the baby, wait there for the cops with her hands in her lap like she didn't know a thing. Whatever money she'd have on her they'd take, so she should never roll with a lot of cash. It wasn't a lot to do, but she had to have it all done in fifteen minutes.

"Got the plan down?" I was constantly checking with her these days. She'd shrug and say, "Hide the keys, dump the phones, call Nick, wait." Or she'd sigh and say, "Do you always have to remind me we're doing what we're doing?"

"You've got to get behind the wheel for me," I would say to Mason every time I called.

"Sorry, James. Even if I wanted to, my smog sticker is expired."

"Your smog sticker?"

"And Bayleigh's been down with an earache. I can't leave Emma alone with her right now."

"An earache? Mason, can I ask you something? Do you even remember what happened in that cotton field?"

"Easy, brother. Let it go. I'm the one who has to live with that."

"Let it go? I have fucking nightmares!"

"Well, I do, too. Besides, I'd have to ask Emma if I could even use the car."

At the 8th Street house, there were a few pictures of Kate and me on the walls that we hadn't bothered taking down: the two of us in Austin when she'd been pregnant, and in the Dunsmuir cabin with Romana just after she'd been born. Whenever I'd hang out with Nick over there and notice them, I'd wonder, How could we have looked so happy when we'd been so worried?

"Listen to this, Jimbo," Nick said to me one day, telling me his usual drug-dealing stories as we played *The Godfather* on the Xbox he'd brought over. "The landlord sends over this contractor to fix a gutter at my parents' place. It's outside work, the landlord doesn't tell anybody. The guy comes around the corner while I'm in the middle of a blunt out back. What can I do? I smile, offer him a hit. He's like fifty, older. Right away he rips it. At first he's like 'no big deal,' says, 'Nice stuff, son.' Then he starts laughing, goes, 'This ain't the haze we get around here.' He's been scoring weight off me ever since. Fifteen-five on the Q.P., says the money's saving his family's ass right now.

"Then the cable's out at this chick's place I've been banging. I slip the Comcast guy fifty dollars when he gets there, he hooks her up with premium. Then I just had this feeling. So I pull out a bowl, ask if he wants to spark. He's over there with us the rest of the day, trying to get straight because he'd never smoked dank like ours. Now he picks up eighths a couple times a week.

"Now, my boy Micah at school, he's always on me about this deal in Orlando. Six and a half on the pound, two pounds, thirteen Gs. Roll up there, roll back, then you're going to toss that G-point-two to me. I have it all worked out. They leave the money in a motel room, pass us one of the keys, we go in there, make the switch. We won't even have to see them."

"The hoods, right?"

"Yeah."

"I don't know, Nick. I don't want to go up there and get shot by hoods."

"It wouldn't be you, Jim. It'd be me. Besides, Micah isn't like that. Micah is like a baby version of that weatherman on TV. Funny, right? Dude makes the dean's list. He's a scholarship kid."

"It doesn't sound like his Orlando boys are like that."

"We'd only have to work with him. Besides, haven't I been busting my ass for you guys? Don't I deserve to make some real money?"

He had to drop an ounce at Micah's right then, Nick said, so why didn't I come along and meet him? I had to get home and take the baby off Kate's hands, I told him. Come on, Jim, it'd only take thirty minutes.

We hopped in Nick's Escort—he wasn't dumb enough to use his Impala for work—cruised up there on the Trail. I hadn't been in a car with him since the day I taught him how to drive. The Escort was vacuumed and clean; Nick drove it like he was sixty-five years old. When I told him how happy I was with his driving, he shrugged and said, "Keep it tight. Live it like a baller."

The place in Bradenton was a rundown apartment complex

in a black neighborhood off 63rd. An empty Bradenton PD cruiser sat chilling in the lot.

Nick said, "I know what you're thinking. I thought it, too. Just give him a chance, okay?"

We went up the metal steps, stood in this open-air hallway, graffiti on the walls around us. Three little girls in braids raced by on roller skates, yelling at the top of their lungs. We knocked, waited, then the door cracked open. The kid who peered out at us was slim and dark, his Yankees cap cocked to the side.

"This the dude?" he said and looked me up and down.

"Relax, Micah," Nick said.

The inside was dark because the drapes were pulled. Still, I could make out two guys in high-tops passed out on couches. Fast-food bags, clothes, and empty pizza boxes littered the floor; the air smelled musty because they kept the place warm. We went down the hallway and into the kid's room. There was cash on the carpet, cash on the desk, all fives and ones. A spliff burned in an overflowing ashtray, blunt wrapper foils scattered everywhere. The closet door was off its hinges, the ceiling had water stains, there was nowhere to sit but the mattress on the floor. The only thing neat about that room was a row of sneakers on the windowsill, half a dozen pairs, the shoes on display on top of their boxes like they weren't meant to be worn.

Micah sat in the one chair he had, an office high-back missing two wheels. He rolled a blunt at his desk out of the ounce Nick had brought him, told us as he did that the guys in his living room were his cousins, that the PD car in the lot belonged to the cop who lived downstairs.

"You got a cop downstairs?" I said.

Micah shrugged. He said, "Dude has to live somewhere, right? He stays on his side, we stay on ours. We all got to live here together. We all know how to play that shit." To pay for the ounce, Micah peeled fives off a bankroll he had in a drawer, made up the remainder with a tall stack of singles. He was gramming out his dope if he was working in singles, hustling dozens and dozens of people, his name in the air all over town. I knew it was only a matter of time before the cop downstairs came with a crew and kicked in his door. He sparked the blunt, sat back, started jabbering. He said, "My boy says you were a writer. That's the same shit I want to do."

Nick listened when I talked about my other life? I said, "I hustled that until the economy killed it. Now I hustle this."

"The economy?" Micah said and made a face. "Don't cry that shit in here. From my point of view? Shit's exactly the same as shit's always been. Y'all feeling it for a change is all." He smiled at his hands. "I have to admit it. To tell you the truth, I kind of like seeing it."

I looked at Nick, Nick nodded at me. Then Micah said, "You're not writing no more?"

"Can't afford it."

Micah laughed and said, "Man, don't you got no struggle in you?"

He said, "Now, I mailed some of this up to my boys in O-Town. They're hoods, but they got the money. They usually cop haze, so they know they can move this shit easy. They want to do it right away. Twice a month is how it'll all go down once it gets rolling. I want four bills off the top every time."

"We can do that," I said.

"Want me to see if they can do three pounds?"

"Let's just start with two."

"Yeah, that's what I told those greedy mothers. So when are we taking it up there?"

"How do we know we won't get jacked up there?"

He made a face. "I'm the go-between."

"How do we know you won't jack us?"

He shook his head. He laughed and said to Nick, "Man, who is this dude, Detective McNulty? I thought you said he was cool." He said to me, "Look around. Can't you see I'm just a school kid? You see any gats lying around in here?"

I looked around the room. I said, "You don't look like a school kid."

"What do school kids look like over where you're at? I'm even on a scholarship."

"Then why do this?"

"Like you don't know? I'm sitting here wondering the same thing about you. They gave me that money at the end of foster care, like, 'Good luck, see your ass later.' You know it doesn't cover shit."

I looked around the room again. What was I supposed to do, take him on as a charity case? Help him get through school? He must have sensed I didn't want to do it, and he said, "What? You scared? Man, if I was white, I'd be moving weight, too. Making Al Capone money. But I can't, can I? Look who they put in their fucking prisons."

I hesitated a moment, then said, "I'll call the order in today. The shit'll be here in a couple weeks. Your boys have to have the money ready."

Micah said, "They'll have it ready. Thing is, these boys are the nervous type. They're my boys in the sense that I met them in the system."

"Don't get us into trouble, Micah."

"Trouble? I just want to make money like you do. We'll do this motel thing Nick's got planned. Everything will go down tight."

Then I said, "How're you getting up there?"

"Can't I roll with you?"

How could I say it? I shook my head. "We're going to have weight in the car."

Micah looked at me a long time. Then he smiled, sat back in his chair. He nodded and said, "It ain't you, right? Just the world we live in?"

In the car, Nick was happy. He said, "You liked him, didn't you?"

"Yeah."

"Told you. Dude made dean's list last semester."

I put the order in with Billy on my way home. Where was Billy right now? I asked him. He was pruning, checking pH, all week up in Siskiyou, he told me. I mentioned the new weight was for hoods. Billy said, "Hoods? What kind of hoods?"

"Bros."

He paused and said, "You think you're ready for that? Whatever, dude, money's money. Too much heat for me, but what the fuck do I know?"

I'd been feeling magnanimous since leaving Micah's, better than I had in a while; I knew Nick and his family didn't have shit either. I said to Billy, "I've got this kid, he's good. If I ever get out, could I pack him up, ship him to you?"

"How old?"

"Almost twenty."

"We could start him trimming. See how it goes."

"Change his life, right?"

"Oh yeah. But you know that already."

Back at the house, Kate had a friend from high school staying with us. The friend had been sitting in a holding pattern between jobs like everybody else. Kate had had this new loneliness thing going on; the solution had been to send the friend a frequent-flier ticket.

"What are you going to tell her when she gets here?" I asked Kate on the way to the airport to pick the friend up.

"Spices from the Orient," Kate said.

Cristina Freeman was tall and blond, a former cocktail waitress from Vegas. She and Kate had been on the cheerleading squad together at their little mountain high school. On our way home, Kate mentioned to Cristina that my beard had been falling out. Cristina laughed and said to me, "Don't worry about it, Captain Patchy. After all the shit I've been through? If I had a beard, it would have fallen out, too. My major problem now is just trying not to be angry. I just feel so screwed over, you know?"

All the shit she'd been through included losing her job, losing her house, having to sell her car, and living on a friend's couch for months like an economic refugee. Then she had to give away her dog. "You think things are bad out here?" she said as we passed the vacancies in the strip malls. "You should see Vegas. I tried everything, was so far underwater on my house I couldn't even lie to myself anymore. The only thing I miss now is my dog. I left him at this ranch. I'll get him back as soon as I'm on my feet. But when's that going to be, you know?"

Being with us perked Cristina up. She helped out with Romana, went shopping and had her nails done at the mall with Kate.

What was going on with me? Kate always wanted to know now when we were alone in bed. Nothing she needed to worry about, I'd tell her. Everything okay out there? she'd ask. Everything was just fine, I'd say.

And how was she feeling? I'd ask. She'd put her hands on her belly, tell me, "I just want you to be here when he's born."

"Don't you know I will be?"

Cristina loved swimming in our pool, was always telling us, "I'm so freaking jealous of how good you guys are doing."

I'd say, "The catch is, I'm always away."

She'd say, "When they can even find work, people have to slave. At least Kate gets to stay home with the baby."

But that didn't seem good enough for Kate. One afternoon, when Cristina was at the beach with Romana, Kate patted the place beside her on the couch. How long would I be home this time? she wanted to know when I sat down. Four or five days, I told her. Was I going to be busy while I was here? No, I had nothing at all to do. Was I going to have an affair with Cristina? Why would she ask me something like that? Because she was so pregnant and Cristina was so pretty. I told her, "I know someone prettier than her."

Kate said, "Something's been going on with you."

I thought about denying it. But what I said was "Do you really want to know?"

She looked away through the window at our well-tended yard, at the white and yellow frangipani trees in bloom, and she smoothed her gauze maternity dress on her belly, thought about it. Then she said, "No, I guess I don't. Sometimes I don't feel like we know each other anymore."

Did we really have to do this again? I sighed, said, "Look at me, Kate." When she looked at me, I took her chin in my hand. "We're exactly the same as we've always been, okay?"

"You're never home. I don't know what you do out there."

"I work out there."

"You don't have some girlfriend out there?"

"When would I have the time?"

"You don't need anyone but me?"

"I've never needed anyone but you."

"I feel so ugly right now."

"You're prettier than you've ever been."

"Promise me you'll be here when our son is born."

"I'll drop everything the second you call."

"Sometimes I wish we weren't doing what we're doing."

"Sometimes I wish that, too."

"We're not going to do it forever, are we?"

"Of course we're not."

"James?" Kate batted her lashes and smiled at me at last. "I've been having this other idea. What do you think about us getting a nanny?"

Trouble happened on the very next run, the first week of August. It went down like this: Five days before I was supposed to leave, I woke up in bed with a bad feeling and called Eric Deveny. I was tired, I told him, my new baby was almost here. Could I please take a week off? He thought about it a second, then said, "And have you owe me New York, too? No way. Not with school about to start. What's going on with you, James? Do I really have to bring up again that mess I cleaned up for you?"

"Didn't I pay you for that?"

"Yeah, you did. But don't you think it also took our relationship to a higher level? I've been feeling like it did. Relax, my man. I just want my weight on time. Let me ask you this: What's really going on with you? The James I know wouldn't want to take a break. The James I know would want to make his money."

Next I called Mason, told him I had this bad feeling. For how much he owed me, couldn't he do the drive for me this once?

Mason said, "If you have a bad feeling, how the fuck am I supposed to feel?"

"I'll take your debt down fifteen Gs."

"Sorry, James."

"I'll forgive you a straight twenty thousand dollars."

"Brother, it isn't in the plan. My uncle in Korea is sick. I'm stressed out about that right now."

"What fucking uncle?"

"My mother's older brother. Well, her cousin. It's the same thing over there. I'm really, really sorry. Drive fast and swerve a lot, okay?"

I swam, watched TV, paced the house the rest of the day. The girls were out and I was alone. Why did I feel like this? Just like I felt before my very first run. Shouldn't I be over this shit by now?

By evening I still hadn't shaken it. After everyone went to bed, I smoked cigarettes on the patio, looked out at my darkened yard. What if I just didn't go? I knew I'd never hear from Eric Deveny again. And without him, I'd lose my only way to make any real money. Was I really ready to give it all up? Strangle my golden goose and come back to reality?

I wasn't. In the morning, I packaged up the cash, drove to the post office, began to overnight it out to Billy. But even doing that, I didn't feel good, decided to hold half the envelopes back. Friday morning, I strapped on the pantyhose, stuffed in the rest of the money, took a taxi to the airport, was nervous the whole way. The TSA ran me through the bomb sniffer; I figured this would finally be it. "Why are you traveling with so much cash hidden on you, sir?" "High-rolling in Reno. Didn't want my wife to know." "Please step aside with us. We have a few more questions for you."

In the end, the machine puffed its air and the agent waved me through. Apparently, $26,000 in your underwear couldn't blow up a plane. In Charlotte, my connecting flight was delayed because of rain in Phoenix. Rain in Phoenix? Really? Was there any other way I could go? I asked. Since I was now a valued Star Alliance Gold flier, they told me, they would do what they could to reroute me. They sent me on to Memphis. The leg from there was canceled. How about Chicago, sir? I tried that, too.

From Chicago, I called Billy. "I'm going to be late. Weather."

"All is not well. I got a big handoff to make downstate. What if I miss it? You think Darren'll give a fuck about the weather?"

They flew me across to SEA, down to PDX, finally to SMF. At the Days Inn, Billy tossed two duffel bags on the bed. He said as he walked out, "I should bill your ass by the fucking hour."

I hopped in the rental, got on the road, drove all night across the Mojave. I felt hunted the whole way. In Williams, Arizona, the motels were full with summer travelers, and I felt hunted. Up the road, the Red Lake Hostel was full of Grand Canyon hikers, and I felt hunted. I spent the afternoon trying to sleep in the car in a Denny's parking lot in Holbrook. Couldn't.

The next day, I reached stark and empty west Texas. The only other cars on the road were cops, and I was terrorized by fear. I thought I was on the 180 South, hours went by in a straight line to nowhere, then I didn't know where the hell I was. Of course I didn't have a map in the car. Of course I hadn't taken the rental agency's GPS. By nightfall I was almost out of gas. Where was a fucking gas station already? Was I really going to have to sit in the breakdown lane in the middle of nowhere with all this fucking weed in the car? The needle dipped below E, then it started bouncing. I panicked, pressed JoJo Bear's belly; nothing happened. I pressed his belly over and over. JoJo Bear was dead.

All this insane shit began to happen. In the dark I saw lights, red flashing lights. Not cop car lights or anything like that, all these red lights flashing way up in the sky. Hundreds of them. Hundreds and hundreds of them. I gripped the steering wheel, craned my face close to the windshield to see. An alien invasion? Or something even worse? A host of wrathful angels coming down to punish me? The next thing I knew, they were gone. What the fuck had that been?

I reached a place called San Angelo. There were no rooms

at the Motel 6, no rooms at the Super 8. But at least I got some gas. Finally I found a room at this beat-up Bates motel; the East Indian behind the desk wanted $150. $150? What kind of room was it? A standard smoking king, sir. They were having a rodeo this weekend. If I wanted to try to find something else, it would be his pleasure to let me look.

I shook my head, gave him two C-notes; he gave me the key and change. I took the duffel bags out of the Mazda, shouldered into the room. At the light, roaches skittered across the walls. There were stains in the carpeting, like people had been stabbed to death in there. I lay in my driving clothes on the bed to calm down. What had those fucking lights been? Could it even have been me? Then I thought, How could I have let Mason kill those people? On the inside of the lampshade on the nightstand beside me, people had written, *Miguelito Sexy* and a phone number, and *8" Hung and Cut* and a phone number.

I stuffed the duffel bags in the closet, went back out to the Mazda, drove around town; I needed a drink right now like goddamn fucking hell. The convenience stores were already closed. I sucked it up, went in and bought a six-pack of Corona at a Mexican polka bar, where the prettied-up big girls were dancing for dollars. From the second I walked in, mustachioed ranch hands in their beautiful clothes and Stetson hats stared my gringo ass down.

"*Quieres limón?*" the lady bartender shouted at me over the brassy music.

"*Quiero partir,*" I told her.

"That's probably the wisest idea," she said, flashing her gold tooth at me.

San Angelo, Texas, in the middle of the night. JoJo Bear dead. Crazy red lights in the sky and a bad, bad feeling. I would bounce from this shithole at the butt crack of dawn. I'd get myself to Austin and force Mason to finish the drive.

But when morning came, JoJo Bear was still dead and I didn't get out of that bed. I turned on the TV; it was all in Spanish. Those duffel bags were in the room with me, the plates on the car, California. Nice fucking work on those plates this time, James. I couldn't do this anymore. How had I ever done it? How had I ever fucking done it?

Then it was afternoon, and I was still in that bed. The phone started ringing and ringing. Then there was a pounding on the door. It was the East Indian. Was I staying or was I going? he asked. I told him, "I don't know."

"You don't know?" he said, raised his eyebrow. "You are feeling all right?"

"I think so." I coughed and nodded.

Maybe I needed to see a doctor, he said. No, it was nothing like that, I said. Maybe I was driving too many hours from California? Yeah, maybe that was it. If I was going to stay another night, it would be $150. I gave him another bill and the change from before. He tried to look past me into the room as I closed the door on him.

Here are all the things I knew I was doing wrong from the motel guy's point of view: I showed up late at night in a car with California plates. Strike one. I hadn't bothered to peel the stickers from the car's windows, so he knew at a glance it was a rental. Strike two. I paid in cash. Strike three. I was acting weird. Strikes four, five, six, seven, eight, nine, ten. I fit the profile of a drug smuggler to a tee. If he was in cahoots with the cops for a percentage of the takedown, all he'd have to do was call. They could kick down the door anytime they wanted. If they did, everything in my life would come to an end in that filthy room.

I hopped on a TracFone to Mason. He didn't pick up. I called his regular cell. He didn't pick that up either. Who else could I call? My wife? Scare the fuck out of her? Eric Deveny? If he caught one whiff of the fear in my voice, who knew what his crazy Iraq-combat ass would do? Billy was in California, there was nothing he could do. Even Nick was three long days away. Couldn't I just get in the goddamn rental car and gut the fucker out? I could not. There was nothing left in me that could take another second of that kind of fear. This kind of fear in here? I could do this kind of fear. That kind of fear out there? No fucking way. Even my bones felt dead. I was going to lie in this bed until they kicked down the door. Then I was going to let them end it and haul me away.

How bad would prison be? Didn't I quietly chew it over all the time? Wonder if it would be peaceful, the stress over at last? Push around the mail cart. Get cozy in the prison library. Lots of time to read. Maybe even write again.

Or would it be something else? Something hellish? Would they try to punk me in there? Would I spend every moment fighting for my fucking life?

I had one last number to call: Emma.

Emma answered. She said right away in a whisper, "James? Is it happening? Did Mason get picked up?"

"Mason didn't get picked up. It's me, Emma. Something's wrong with me. I'm in a motel room in San Angelo."

"What are you doing way out there?"

"I don't know."

"Aren't you supposed to be coming here?"

"I can't get in the car."

"Why can't you get in the car?"

"I'm scared."

Emma was quiet for a minute. I could hear restaurant sounds in the background behind her. Then she said, "I'm leaving work right now. Don't go anywhere and don't do anything. I'll be there in three hours."

I lay in the bed like an invalid. It was warm, felt like a womb. If Emma didn't come and get me, I'd never leave this place. There were so many things I didn't allow myself to think about anymore. Instead I thought about our trip to Europe. In Milan, we'd gone into the cathedral, seen the high columns and the stained glass. Then we pushed the baby in her stroller all through the square. An old woman stopped and talked to us, told us that the city had been heavily damaged by Allied bombs during the war. Over time many of the buildings were rebuilt the way they'd been. As we looked at those old buildings, I asked Kate, Where had the money come from? Immense and ornate structures, it must have taken thousands of people to create them. Laborers, artisans, carvers, masons. All that stone. All that glass. Who paid for all of that? Verona was like that, Venice was even greater. What did it mean to have that kind of money? In the face of that, who could we ever pretend to be?

America was like that, too. Yeah, the country was hurting now, but there was still money everywhere. Working the business had certainly brought us our share. More than other people had. But where were we going with it? Where would it take us? What about all the lies we were telling? What about all the horrible things we did?

As I lay in that room, I understood you couldn't stop to think. If you wanted the money, you had to put your head down and plow ahead. The moment you stopped to think, you'd know you were wretched. Evil. More than cops and robbers and prison and getting away with it as long as you could, the real crime you were committing was against yourself. It had been decided that you shouldn't have money, that was your path, so you should find your happiness on that path. But you'd decided that was wrong, you deserved more. That you were a god upon the land, better than everyone else.

That was my problem: I thought too much. Prosaic things like how the work we did spread the weed through the country, how a bud grown in a hidden field in the Siskiyou Mountains could end up being smoked by a college kid in Tallahassee. But I thought of other things, too. Like whether my wife really loved me. If my wife really loved me, why would she ever let me take the risks I did? To run the chance I'd get caught, go to prison? For Gucci? For decaf soy lattes? Pedicures? A house she could show off to her friends? So what if we hadn't really known each other when we plunged into life together? We knew each other now. If she really loved me, shouldn't she have put her foot down, told me no from the start? The fact that she let me do it, did that mean she must actually hate me? And so maybe I hated her, too. For not making me stop. For letting me do the things I did. And what about our kids, our precious, precious kids? The one we had with us, the one soon to be born. How could either of us really love them if we risked leaving them parentless just so we could buy them shit? Fancy toys, fancy clothes, maybe even fancy schools later? So they could think they were better than other kids who had less money than they did? And what about myself? Didn't I hate myself, too? To risk my freedom? To think I was so worthless only money could make me better?

In that room in San Angelo, I knew suddenly and finally I was not the kind of guy to be doing this. For all my bluster about being on the road, I'd simply been scared from beginning to end. Frightened by what could happen out there. Frightened by the things the business could make me do. Frightened by how special it made me feel. Honestly, anyone could do it. You only had to have the invitation to try. Most people would have turned their backs on it. I hadn't.

Why was I doing this? And how was I supposed to get out of it now? What would I say to Darren Rudd? I knew he didn't care about me, just the money I made him. And what would I say to Eric Dead Bodies Deveny?

A knock on the door brought me back to that vile room, my reality in it. What the hell was I doing dicking around in here? James, wake the fuck up, asshole! I had sixteen pounds of weed with me.

When I opened the door, Emma was framed in it, a sturdy angel, a voluptuous goddess, a highway Joan of Arc who'd come charging across the battlefield to save me. I pulled her into the room, embraced her. I didn't really know her, but that didn't matter anymore.

"Not quite the five-star suite I imagined you staying in, James," Emma said as she looked around, tossed her car keys on the table. She gave me a Big Mac; I began to devour it. She pulled a Mickey's forty-ounce out of a brown paper bag; I twisted off the cap and chugged it like a prescription. "I think of you in some swank hotel, getting a massage, sitting in the Jacuzzi. Is this what it really is? Shitty rooms like this?"

"This is what it is."

"It's dirty," she said and made a face.

What about those lights, those red lights in the sky? I asked her. Emma laughed. It was a wind farm, she told me. They were everywhere out here. Hadn't I seen any on my way in? The lights were to keep planes from hitting them at night. So it hadn't been something wrong with my head? I asked. No, she said.

"Are you going to carry the weight for me, Emma?"

"If you're going to pay me."

"But I haven't taught you how to drive it yet."

"It's a car, James. You drive it. I've been doing it my whole life."

I looked her up and down. Could she do it? Of course she could. "Let's go," I said. "Enough of this screwing around. And enough of this motherfucking San Angelo." I parted the curtains to peek out at the lot. Sitting behind my Mazda was a black San Angelo PD cruiser. I let the curtains fall.

"There's a cop out there."

"There wasn't when I came in."

Fuck fuck fuck! When I peeked out again, he was still there.

"Where's your car?"

"At the McDonald's across the street."

"You didn't bring it here?"

"I'm not stupid."

I took the duffel bags into the bathroom, threw them in the tub, shut the shower curtain over them. Like that would do anything if they came in. But it was better than doing nothing.

"I'm going to go out and drive away. Don't do anything until he leaves. If you have to leave the shit behind, leave it."

"Okay."

"And whatever you do, don't talk."

I left the room, pulled the door shut behind me so it latched like I was leaving it forever. I could hear the sounds on the cop's radio, the pops and beeps and voices and static. He looked at me and I looked at him. This one wasn't wearing mirrored sunglasses. But he was wearing everything else. When I took the key into the motel office, the East Indian was standing at the counter with his hands flat on it as if holding it for support. I took one look at him and we both knew. This slow-motion feeling began and I tossed the key on the counter. "That room was a filthy hellhole," I said. He didn't even twitch his mustache.

"Gonna let me out or what?" I mouthed to the cop from the door to my car; I was trying to be a dick. He looked at me a long moment with that flat face they wear, then nodded almost imperceptibly. I thought, I am a bait fish and you are a shark. I am going to flee from here and you are going to chase me.

I sat in the Mazda, started it. The cop backed up to give me room. Evening was settling down on the town. When I pulled onto the road, he followed me. I drove perfectly all through San Angelo. The cop was right behind me. I stopped at all the lights, kept to the limit. What would his reason be when he pulled me over? Scrupulously obeying the traffic laws? We left town on some highway, I had no idea which one. I had no idea which direction I was heading. I knew none of that mattered now. The cop was in my rearview every inch of the way. Was he weaving, or was that just me? What would the accommodations be like at the San Angelo jail?

Six miles out of town, his lights went on, his siren went *whoop whoop* twice. I pulled over to the side of the road. It was flat and dull in that part of the world—who in the hell would want to live out here? But he did. I was on his territory now. He was white and tall, a big bad boy. He rapped his knuckles on my window and I powered it down. "License and rental agreement, sir," he said. I said, "What are you pulling me over for?"

"Headlights."

"What about them?"

"You haven't turned them on."

"You could see around to the front of my car?"

"License and rental agreement, sir."

Headlights. I closed the window, sat in the car and waited. Why did they make you wait so long? Mind games. To make you sweat. I hurriedly grabbed my phones out of the glove compartment, wiped all the calls off them, all the numbers, all the texts to Kate, then I shut them off. Just like that, I was completely disconnected from my world. I checked around the car for anything else. There was nothing else.

He was back. I powered down the window. He shined his flashlight around me in the car. It was already nighttime out there.

"California to Florida?"

"One way across the country."

"But now you're heading back to New Mexico?"

"Yes I am."

"Why are you heading back to New Mexico?"

"I don't believe I have to say."

"Okay." An immediate change of tone in his voice, a long ratchet down in unfriendliness. "Anything in here you need to tell me about?"

"Nothing that I know of."

"Any large amount of money?"

"No, sir."

"Would you mind leaving the keys in the ignition and stepping out of the car?"

Just this once, I didn't mind. Still, I was fucking nervous. "Happy to," I said.

He patted me down.

"Any sharp objects in your pockets?"

"No, sir."

"Anything else I should know about?"

"No, sir."

He put his hands deep into every pocket I had, pulled out my wallet, my phones.

"Why do you need three phones?"

I didn't say anything.

"Would you mind if I took a look in your vehicle?"

"No, sir."

"Stand over there and wait for me." Then he spoke into his shoulder radio, called for a K-9 as he lined up my stuff on the hood of his car like evidence.

I stood at the side of the road where he told me to, watched him look through all the windows in the car with his flashlight. He didn't talk to me, I didn't say anything to him. No other cars passed us on that road.

When the K-9 came, a second big bad boy came out, and the two of them met and talked. They were robots, no monkey business about them, no "Hey, how are you, Chuck?" The first one said to the second one, "California to Florida, one way. No luggage. Disposable phones. The rental agreement checks out, but now he's heading back to New Mexico."

"Sounds hot."

The first one came back to me and said, "I'm going to put you in the back of my car."

"Am I under arrest?"

"No, you are not, sir."

"Then why are you putting me in your car?"

"A safety precaution for us, sir."

From the cage he put me in, I watched them trot out the dog in the spotlights of their vehicles. I'd already given them permission to search, so why were they running the dog? Looking for secret compartments? Hoping to score some cash? The dog was a calm and obedient German shepherd; it kept glancing up like it was eager to please. I knew there wasn't anything in that car. But what if the dog found something anyway? The handler jogged it around the Mazda once, twice, then the dog jumped up against the rear bumper. The handler patted it, said something to it. When he popped open the hatchback, the dog

immediately leapt in. It scratched the carpeting where the duf-
fels had been sitting for the last fifteen hundred miles, barked.
I settled into my seat while they called in a bunch more cars.

This went on for a long time. Hours? My heart was in my
throat: they would tell me they'd found something, or they'd
plant something, and I had no sense of time out there at all.
What could I do if they did? They brought out tools, stripped
the Mazda down. The paneling. The sideboards. They pulled
out the air filter. They set the pieces down on the side of the
road. After they'd finished putting everything back, the extra
cops drove away.

The first cop let me out, gave me my wallet, phones, a ticket
for the headlights. "Our K-9 alerted on the back of the vehicle,
sir," the cop said. "At that point we had reasonable enough suspicion to conduct a thorough search."

I raced through the night to Austin. When I ran up the
stairs, Mason let me in. Emma had already gone to bed, he told
me. My weed was in the living room.

Now this thing with Micah, I'd included the weight to do it
in the load I'd just brought across. After Deveny's in Tallahassee, I cruised down to Sarasota, dropped the pounds off
at the 8th Street house, hid them in a closet there. I'd called
Kate from Austin on Mason's phone after what had happened
in San Angelo, told her that one of my Tracs had fried; she'd
given me all my numbers back. Now I called Nick, told him to
get the Orlando deal set up. I threw the duffel bags away in a
supermarket dumpster, then went home to Siesta Key. There
was a strange beat-up car parked at our place. Kate and Cristina were watching TV when I came in; Romana was in her
highchair being spoon-fed by an older Hispanic woman.

Kate sat up on the couch. "This is Mrs. Jimenez," she said.

I said to Kate, "You can't fucking feed her? You're sitting right there."

"What do you know about it, James? Nice thing to say when you've just walked in."

I gave the Hispanic woman a hundred-dollar bill; she took her keys and left. I picked up the rubber-coated spoon, finished feeding my daughter her pureed sweet potatoes. I gave her a bath, put her in PJs, carried her into her room. She laid her head on my shoulder as I held her against me.

"Did you miss me, little girl?"

Romana nuzzled me, sucked on her binky.

"I love you more than you'll ever know."

When I went back out to the living room, Kate told me she'd had contractions while I was away. Cristina had taken her to the emergency room. That was why the nanny had been here, if I'd even bothered to ask.

"Why didn't you call me?"

"I didn't want to worry you."

"But that's the time when I'm supposed to worry."

"I just know how you get when you're working."

Fine, Kate. Fine. I grabbed a Stella from the fridge, cracked it, changed my mood. Was Cristina having a good time in Sarasota? I asked her. Cristina smiled and said she was. "We saw the shark feeding at the Mote Aquarium today," she told me, "then we had brunch on the patio at the Ritz." She was feeling rested and relaxed for a change, grateful to be here. If there was ever anything she could do to repay us, all we had to do was ask.

In bed that night, Kate said, "I don't know why I didn't call you. I wanted to. But I knew it was only Braxton Hicks. You want to feel him kick?" She took my hand and put it on her belly. There it was, kick kick kick.

Was I going to be home for a while? she asked. Maybe I

wouldn't leave for three weeks, I said. Why not, was anything going wrong out there? Everything was going fine, I finally found a driver I could trust who was going to do some work for me.

Then I said, "You remember when we were in the cabin, Kate?"

"Yeah, I remember."

"What would you say if I said I really did want to get out of the business now?"

She paused. Then she said, "Do you think we have enough money put away?"

"We have a lot more money than we had at the cabin."

"We have a lot more to pay for now, James."

I didn't say anything. Then I said, "What are we going to say to the kids? What are we going to tell them about the things we did?"

Kate said, "We're not going to tell them anything. Or we're going to tell them that we did what we had to do to survive a frightening and difficult time."

"It was frightening, wasn't it?"

"Fucking frightening."

"And everyone else out there is still going through it."

Kate touched my face in the dark. "Are you ever going to write again? What about going back to a regular life? Are you even going to want that anymore after this?"

"Are you?"

"I haven't done all the things that you have."

"You've gotten used to the spending."

"What else have I had? It's not like you've been around."

"You think you could live without all the stuff?"

"What have I bought that I couldn't live without?"

"How about Europe?"

We were quiet then, thinking about it. I thought about the drive in the beautiful snow-covered Alps.

"Do you remember the little hotel on Lake Como, James? The bath we took with the baby? How big that tub was? How we all fit in it together?"

"I remember the mountains."

"It lived up to every dream I'd ever had."

"I'd go back to see those mountains."

Kate turned to me. She said eagerly, "I've been looking into flats in central London. We could get one next summer, right off of one of the parks. If you could get your work to where other people were doing it for you, you could commute back and forth, bring over the money, spend most of your time with us there. Think about all the frequent-flier miles you'd get. The kids could go to an English school. Then maybe they'd grow up talking like that. 'Morning, Mum. Morning, Dad.' How funny would that be?" She laughed. "What were we talking about again?"

"Going back to a regular life."

"It seems dull now, doesn't it?"

We thought about that a while; I thought about cutting the grass behind some little house somewhere. Did I want that? The stable life my father had had? Yes, I wanted that, at the very least I wanted that. I said, "We'd never have money like this again. No matter how hard we worked at something else."

"I know that."

"So how much do we put away before we're done?"

"I have no idea."

"Does it feel like enough to you yet?"

"I don't know. I guess not yet."

"A million? Two million? Or do we go on until the end?"

"Of course we don't go on until the end."

We were quiet. Then Kate said, "What do you think they're going to say when we really do want to get out of it?"

"I don't know what they're going to say."

"Do you worry about it?"

"We're making them a ton of money."

"That Eric guy, right?"

"Eric, yeah. But Darren, too."

"What would Eric say?"

"Eric wouldn't want it to end."

"Couldn't you let him and Darren meet? Maybe even get paid for it?"

I thought of the dead bodies. I didn't want to be one of those dead bodies. I said, "It may be too late for that."

"Too late?"

"I don't know that he'd want to let me go anymore."

"Not let you go? Why not?"

"I know some ugly things about him, Kate."

Kate was quiet a moment. "Would he try to do something to us if we wanted to get out?"

I didn't know what to say. Then I said, "Yeah, I think he probably would."

"Do you think he knows where we live?"

"I don't know what he knows."

"Do you think he checked up on us the way we checked up on him?"

"I'm sure he did."

"Could we ask Darren for help?"

"Darren's in it for the money, Kate. I don't know that he would care."

"Then we'll leave without telling either of them. We'll disappear to London."

"How will we live over there?"

"We'll go on working until we've made enough. Then we'll take enough with us for a long, long time."

I nodded. "What about my mother?"

"Your mother?" Kate thought about it. Then she said like a realization, "What really goes on out there?"

The baby began to cry in her room; I went in and picked her up. How warm she was, how small her limbs. Even after she fell asleep on my shoulder, I held her to me in the dark. I was thinking all these things with her body against mine, about how she was in the world now not having asked for this, about how we were doing all of this to her, too. Then I thought of my father, how sad his death had made me feel, sad even now. He'd had hard times, too. What a piece of shit he would have thought I was. What if something happened to us out there? Prison, something worse? I'd have to watch my daughter grow up through visitation room glass. Maybe wind up in pieces at the bottom of a quiet pond.

Enough. Way too much for now. I put those thoughts away, set down my sleeping child. Back in our bedroom, my wife seemed to be asleep. I stood awhile and looked out the window at the moon. What was the true meaning of everything I'd done?

Over the next few days, Kate pitched her camp on the couch with Cristina, was laid low with mild contractions. I paid the nanny to stay away so I could spend time with my daughter. As I pushed Romana in the stroller beside the pond at Payne Park, I called Mason on a TracFone, asked to talk to Emma.

"What do you want to talk to Emma for?" Mason said.

"I want to thank her again for picking me up when that car broke down on me."

Emma came on the line. Was she ready to do the long haul?

I asked her. She said quietly, so I knew Mason wouldn't hear, "How much are you going to pay me?"

"It depends. Can you do Albuquerque to Tallahassee?"

"How many days is that?"

"One day out, two days across, one day home. They will be real days, Emma, not like those three hours out of San Angelo. It will be dawn-to-dusk driving, twelve to fifteen hours."

"How much will I be carrying?"

"Sixteen or seventeen pounds."

She was silent. Then, "I don't want to know about all that. I'm going to tell myself I'm carrying clothes. Or nothing at all. I'm going to have to quit my job to do it. So it has to be worth my while."

"How about two pounds? You'll clear at least ten grand when you put it out."

"That sounds good."

"If you make everything go right, you can run that twice a month."

"Then you know I'll make everything go right."

I called Jerome, crossed my fingers. I knew he'd quit his day job. So he needed the money now, didn't he? "How much to get you behind the wheel for me, Jerome?"

He thought for a moment. "How much you got, James?"

We haggled. How far would he have to take it? Sacramento to Albuquerque, one long day. How much weight? Almost twenty pounds. Ten thousand dollars, he said. I said, Three thousand. At last we settled on a pound of weed. Then he said, "If I get caught, I'm giving you up."

"Fine. But you have to let me know where your family lives."

"What do you need to know that for?"

"So I'll know you won't steal from me."

Jerome hesitated. Then he told me, "I'll text it to you."

When I hung up with him, I looked at my daughter. Was this how it really was? Being a child in a stroller one day, growing up the next and offering your family as collateral so you could make some money? Yes, this was how it was, at least for some people. The address came in on my cell even before we left the park.

At the 8th Street house that evening, I asked Nick if he'd set up the Orlando thing yet. He'd been working on it, he said as he played Skate on the TV, but there had been a snag.

"What kind of snag?"

"They don't want to do the switch in a motel room anymore," he said, his eyes on the game. "They have some kind of address they want us to come to in motherfucking Pine Hills."

"What's the matter with Pine Hills?"

"Everybody up there calls it Crime Hills."

I parted the drapes to look out at the street. Nobody was out there. I said, "Who's doing the talking?"

"Everything's going through Micah."

"Tell Micah it's a motel or they can forget it."

"If we tell them to forget it, how will I get my money?"

One of my phones started vibrating. The baby? But it was an Austin number, Mason calling from his job.

"You've got my fucking wife working for you?"

"I don't like it either."

"Why the fuck does it have to be her?"

"I asked you. You wouldn't do it."

Mason started freaking out on me over the phone. He wasn't down with this—what would he do if something happened to Emma out there? He couldn't raise their daughter alone. He could barely handle it with Emma there anyway.

"So tell her no," I told him.

"I already tried that."

"What did she say?"

"You know what she said."

"She said she wants the money?"

"Yeah."

"Then that's it, isn't it?"

"Not if you don't let her do it!"

"Well, I've done enough, and I need a break."

"Well, what if I told you no?"

I sighed, said, "Emma's good. Emma's cool. Nothing's going to happen to Emma. And if something does, you know we'll take care of her. That's what the legal fund is for."

"The legal fund is bullshit, James! We both know it won't do shit against the kind of trouble she'd be in." He added in a pleading tone, "Come on, man. What if it was Kate?"

Could we talk about this later, please? I said. Mason said no we could not. He was pissed I'd gone behind his back. And he was pissed right fucking now. How could I break it to him? I said, "Remember that cotton field?"

"You know what, James? This has turned into complete horseshit."

"You're telling someone who knows that."

Mason hung up on me. My heart was beating fast, he'd gotten me so worked up. Of course I didn't like the idea of putting Emma out there. At the same time, what other choice did I have? Now Nick started in on me about Orlando again.

"What do we do if they refuse the motel? Can't you just let me cruise up there and make the drop myself?"

"Even Micah says these guys are sketchy, Nick."

"I can handle it, Jim. I've got it all covered."

"What do you mean, you've got it all covered?"

"You've seen how tight I hustle. You know I'm not afraid."

"You really want the money that bad?"

"Hell-to-the-fucking-yeah. Of course I do."

Looking at Nick was like seeing myself. The money. The money. The lust for the money. "If you go up there alone, you're done working for me. Even if everything goes perfectly, you'll never hear from me again."

"You that worried about it?"

"It just has to be done right."

"So how are we going to do it?"

I'd been thinking about it, how to do this deal, or any deal with people you didn't know. "There'll be two ends. They leave the money in the motel room, Micah gets a key from them. I get the key from Micah, I go in, get the money. I leave the key in the door, drive away. You wait until you see I'm on the road, then you go in and make the drop. Then you get out of there, too. They can pick it up whenever they want. But we're only there a minute."

"Two cars?"

"Yeah, two cars. I'll grab a rental and go up with the weight. You go up with Micah."

Another of my phones vibrated. Austin again. This time it was Emma. "Did Mason talk to you? He didn't change your mind, did he?"

"Don't worry, Emma. Mason didn't change a thing."

Emma said, "I didn't know he was so chickenshit. Just because he's scared, I'm supposed to be? It's just drive fast and swerve a lot. Isn't that all it is?"

There were a million things I could have said to her, the same things people could have said to me. What I told her was "Drive fast and swerve a lot. That's it."

Could she run something else by me? she asked. Of course she could, I said.

Her cousin was a sophomore at UT, she told me, and there was a guy in his dorm who was looking for weight. A college kid? Yeah, a preppie undergrad. Was he moving weight around or was he just getting established? Her cousin said the guy was moving weight around already. How much weight was he looking for? He was looking for a pound; he'd pay five and a half if he liked it—what did I think about that? Five and a half sounded good to me. Right, she said, because that's what she'd been thinking, too. But the thing was, how should she get it to him? That depended on her, I said. She could walk it right in if she wanted to. Well, she wasn't ready to do that yet. Would I come out there and do it for her the first time?

"If you pay for my flight, I'd be happy to, Emma."

"How much is the cost on that?"

"Probably four hundred bucks."

"So I'd still be making a crapload of money?"

"Getting it all figured out, aren't you?"

When I hung up with her, Nick said, "Why did you just tell whoever that was to 'walk it right in' when you're giving me so much shit?"

"Different story. That's a college dealer in a dorm room."

"So what?"

"He'll have way too much to lose to fuck around."

"Micah's a college kid."

"We're not really dealing with Micah on this, are we, Nick?"

A few days later, Kate and I went for a long walk in our bare feet on the white sand of Lido Beach. Though her due date was still two weeks away, she was miserable, wanted this kid out immediately. "Doesn't nature have to run its course?" I'd winked and asked her at the house before we'd left. She'd snapped back, "Nature can fuck itself, James. I've been pregnant for two years."

Of course the long walk didn't get the baby out. Then she asked if I would make the spicy penne pasta we had at the cabin the night she went into labor with Romana. I knew that wouldn't work either, but I picked up the stuff from Whole Foods, made it for her anyway. "Anything happening?" Cristina and I asked her all night after dinner as we sat in front of the TV. Kate just made pained faces on the couch; the only thing happening was heartburn. The next night, she tried jumping up and down. The pissed-off baby kicked her until dawn.

Then she wanted to drink castor oil. She'd read about it online, a hundred women on a discussion board said it had worked for them. What the heck was castor oil? we asked her. It was the extracted oil of some kind of bean, she explained. What the heck did they use it for? we asked. They used it to loosen people's stools, she said.

Cristina made a face. "How is that supposed to put you into labor, Kate?"

"It's supposed to make your bowels start cramping. Then the cramps spread to your uterus and then you have your baby."

"Sounds like an old wives' tale to me," I said.

Kate said, "Sounds like you've never been pregnant."

Could she at least wait a couple days before she tried it? I asked. I had to fly to California tomorrow. California? How long would I be away? she asked. Only overnight this time, I told her.

"What if the baby comes while you're gone?"

"Tell them to make it stay in."

"You really think I'm going to stop it if it starts?"

"Can't you just take it easy until I get back?"

I'd mailed out the cash to Billy in advance. Now I hopped a flight to Sacramento to grab the weight from him, drive it across town, hand deliver it to Jerome. Wouldn't it have been nice if Billy and Jerome could have met and taken care of it themselves? But I already knew how that conversation would go:

Jerome: "How much does James pay you for a pound?"

Billy: "He's paying us twenty-nine hundred dollars right now."

Jerome: "Well, I'll give you three and a half."

Billy: "Done."

I met Billy for burgers on Del Paso Road at the old In-N-Out after I landed. How was everything up Siskiyou way? I asked him. Everything was fine in the mountains, he said. Man, did I miss those beautiful mountains, I told him. It was a whole lot of beauty to miss, he said. Had he heard from Darren over in Thailand recently? Because I certainly hadn't heard from Darren in months. Yeah, Darren was doing fine, he'd been complaining about not being able to unload some big piece of land he had down in Santa Cruz, properties in SoCal—he was getting hit by the real estate market like everybody else. But business was rolling along, busy as usual. Darren was getting married to a Thai girl, a high school girl, something like that. Anyway, nobody knew their real birth dates over there, Darren had told him; the girl was definitely legal age, it just sounded complex.

Darren was getting hitched, huh? Yeah, Darren was getting married—so that definitely was a new thing for Darren, but probably Darren didn't plan on taking it too seriously. Because I knew what Darren was like, didn't I? Actually, I didn't know what Darren was like at all. Well, why did I think Darren was always over in Thailand? Wasn't he organic farming or some-thing? Yeah, maybe he was doing a little bit of that, but mostly he was over there lying low, chasing around the ladies. Lying low? Oh yeah, keeping his head down. He'd had a scrape up in Humboldt this last time just before he'd left. Hadn't he men-

tioned something about that to me? Yeah, maybe I vaguely
remembered something about that. Yeah, he'd caught a couple
inbreds skimming one of his grows, it happened there all the
time. But he'd taken care of it; those two definitely weren't
going to be doing that to him again.

Anyway, Thailand, yeah, Darren liked going over there to
chase tail. To chase tail, huh? Oh yeah, that's what they all did
over there in Thailand. You'd think that would help him work
out his aggressions. But no, not Darren, never Darren. What
a hard motherfucker he could sometimes be. Anyway, yeah,
Darren was getting married was the word on the street. Well,
good for Darren then. Yeah, we'll see how it goes.

What else? Nothing else. You going to vote this year? Oh
yeah, crazy old McCain. Pro–law enforcement, keep the prices
up. What about you? Obama. Fellow Chicago boy. Well, maybe
one of them can fix it. Yeah, we'll see; it seems like a lot to fix.
How's your kid doing, Billy? Corinne? Corinne's picking out
colleges this year. How about yours? Romana? Romana's got a
bunch of new teeth.

"I stuck an extra G in the stack for you, to make up for being
late last time."

Billy grinned and shook his head. He told me, "It'll barely
cover her application fees."

After we finished eating, we made the switch in the lot, two
duffel bags from his truck to my rental, right out there in the
busy afternoon.

"Drive fast and swerve a lot."

"You know I will."

"All is well, all is well. See you in a couple weeks."

When I arrived at Jerome's apartment downtown, his mother
was there, she'd made dinner for us. The signs of his new
money were everywhere: a big-screen TV, a new Mac setup,

electric guitars, piles and piles of designer clothes. His mother was like any other mother; she didn't seem to notice about her son what was obvious to anyone else.

Jerome adjusted his glasses, raked his fingers through his hair, explained to her that we were old friends from Sacramento State. "Are you in banking, too?" she asked me as we sat down to her lasagna.

"I'm in import-export."

She said, "How wonderful for you."

When we went out to the cars to make the switch, Jerome showed me a current Social Security Administration statement that had his mother's name and address on it, which I demanded to see to be sure the one he'd texted me was legit. He said, "If anything happens to her, I'll kill you."

"Don't disappear with my weed."

With the duffel bags stowed in the trunk of his freshly washed Honda Civic, we stood in the night shaking hands to seal the deal.

"Be safe out there, all right?"

"Thanks for saying that, James."

"Drive fast and swerve a lot."

"Same to you."

As a last thing, I handed him JoJo Bear. I'd opened up JoJo at home, changed the battery, stitched him shut myself.

"What's this for?"

"This is JoJo Bear. He's done every trip with me. Give him a squeeze." When Jerome did that, JoJo Bear said, "I love you." I told Jerome, "Set him on the passenger seat. He'll help keep you calm when you need it, an extra set of eyes on the road."

"A tracking device?"

I shook my head. "My daughter's teddy bear. Give him to the girl you'll meet in Albuquerque. He wants to get home safe as much as you do."

I caught the ten P.M. down to LAX, the redeye across to IAD. By eleven A.M. I was on the tarmac in Sarasota, and at noon I was home on Siesta Key. Cristina and the nanny were walking Kate around the living room between them, Kate looking like an injured football player.

"Baby on the way?" I asked as I picked up Romana. Kate just glared at me.

I drove to the Vault, had Romana with me. When we got there, Duke buzzed us in. How had he been? I asked. A little under the weather, he said, otherwise he couldn't complain. Could he give a lollipop to my little girl?

In the counting room, Romana sucked the lollipop, made a mess on the floor with the money I tossed her. The weight was moving across the country at this instant; at the end, the money would still be mine—$18,000. Not quite what I was used to making. All the same, how cool was this? Taking no risk, still making tons of money. Is this how Darren Rudd felt? What about Eric Deveny? I wasn't even stressed that Jerome or Emma might not make it. I was just glad not to be out there on the road. I counted money for a while, reached a hundred and fifty grand, wasn't through half of it, got bored. The world was going to run out of money the way I was socking it away in here. Afterward, I ate falafel at the Middle Eastern place on the Trail; my daughter liked the hummus. In the evening, I took her to see the ducks at Red Bug Slough. What a sublime way to make money!

The girls were waiting with dinner on the patio when we came home. Tonight it was Taco Bell. Taco Bell? Kate looked up from the chalupa she was devouring, smiled, and said, "Pregnant."

After dinner, I stayed outside with Cristina. We drank Stellas and smoked cigarettes, pleasantly poisoning ourselves away from the pregnant lady inside. Cristina said, "I've never seen Kate so beautiful."

"She was like this at the end of the last pregnancy, too." Then I cocked my chin at her, said, "What about you, Cristina?"

She looked out at the darkened yard, grinned to herself. "Me? I don't know, James. I guess I've kind of wasted half my life on completely unavailable men."

The TracFone on the table between us vibrated. I snatched it. I'd been waiting for this call all night. It was Emma.

"I'm in Albuquerque. Your California guy gave me this teddy bear." In the background, I heard the familiar "I love you."

"Great news, Emma."

"I'm staying in the Old Town. I've got a suite, rented a Cadillac, decided to do the whole thing in style."

"Do whatever you need to do. Drive fast and swerve a lot."

When I hung up with Emma, I turned back to Cristina. I said, "Tell me again what you were doing in Vegas."

"Before my whole life crashed and burned? I was a cocktail waitress."

"Short skirt?"

"Oh yeah."

"Good money?"

"Only until you spent it." Cristina cocked her head. "Tell me again what it is you do?"

"Import-export."

"Spices from the Orient, right?" she said and arched her eyebrow, because she knew.

"Kate tell you?"

"Of course she did."

I said, "You grew up with Darren Rudd, right?"

"He used to stalk my little sister."

"What else do you know about him?"

"Obviously not as much as you do."

I nodded, sat back in my chair. The evening was quiet around us. Finally I asked her, "So, what do you think?"

"What do I think? I think you're making a lot of money, Mr. Lasseter. After everything that's happened? How badly we've all been fucked? What else is there to think right now?"

The following evening, as Kate choked down six ounces of castor oil straight from the bottle, Emma pulled into Dallas with the weight. While Kate spent the night on the toilet shitting out her guts, Emma and Bayleigh were eating room service on a California king-size bed at the Fairmont Hotel as Mason looked on from an armchair, fuming. "What were you ever doing in that shithole in San Angelo?" Emma asked me when she called.

I laughed, asked her, "How was the heat out there today?"

"The heat? It was fine. Except for one crappy stretch on the 285 in north Texas."

"What happened on the 285?"

"Hang on a minute," she said, then came back on the line. "I'm in the bathroom. I don't want Mason to hear this. Have you ever done the 285?"

"I've always gone through Austin," I said, shaking my head.

"The 285 is two lanes for long parts of it, passes through all these towns. So I'm going along the Oklahoma border and I start to see these cops. They're cruising along by themselves, going ten miles under the limit. I saw the first one and my heart stopped. I didn't know he was going that slow until I almost rear-ended him."

"Jesus."

"I didn't know what to do. Pass him? Pass a cop? But at the same time, I was doing the speed limit. It was just me out there. No other cars, nobody to follow and figure out how to play it. So I took a deep breath, signaled, passed. And guess what? Nothing happened. He kept on driving slow, then disappeared in my rearview. I had to do that two more times. Imagine? So I think it's something they do over there, checking out people's nerves. If you were up to something, you'd be too afraid to pass, right?"

"You've got big balls, Emma."

"Drive fast and swerve a lot. One more day and I'm done."

"Mason taking your pounds home for you?"

"He's leaving with Bayleigh in the morning."

"Wait until you finish the run. You won't believe how good it feels to drive a car that doesn't have any weight in it."

"I believe you right now, James."

In our bathroom, Kate was dry-heaving into the sink from the castor oil, pale and sweating in her nightgown.

"How's it going in here, baby?"

"The castor oil isn't working."

Dare I laugh? I didn't.

"Why isn't it working for me? Why isn't anything working for me when it works for everyone else?"

"Kate, I have to overnight tomorrow up in Tallahassee."

She looked at me over her shoulder. "Gone? How long?"

"Leave in the evening, come back the next afternoon."

"What if the baby comes?"

"There's nothing I can do."

"Let me explain this to you," Kate said. "If you aren't here in time, I will hate you."

I drove up to Tallahassee the next day, in my own car for a change, the old Forester I'd started it all in, pulled into the Super 8 at last light. Emma was waiting in the lot in her Cadillac. She'd peeled off the stickers, everything she'd done had been exactly right. She tossed the duffel bags in my room when we went inside, then handed me JoJo Bear. I gave her the four padded envelopes with the $43,000 I'd decided to send back on the route. Did she want to go out and have a couple drinks, I asked, talk about the road? Sure she did, she said. She'd made it, after all. Popped her cherry on her virgin drive, made the big money for the very first time.

I left JoJo Bear to guard the weed in the motel room, and Emma followed me as I drove us over to the smoky Leon Pub. There, we muscled our way into the bar, and I ordered us framboises on tap. It was time to celebrate, wasn't it? The adventure a success yet again. Even sweeter for me now that someone else was doing it for me.

I texted Kate: "in labor?" She texted back: "not yet come home."

"emma made it safe."

"congrats to her come home."

"miss u."

"miss u 2 come home."

"love u."

"love u 2 come home."

I turned off my phone. I said to Emma, "How did it feel out there?"

"It felt like I was on any other drive."

"Think you could do it again?"

"As long as you'll let me."

"You know what, Emma? None of these people in here have any idea what you just did."

"I like how that feels."

"And you weren't scared?"

"I surprised myself out there. I even liked it. But what I like most about it is the money."

We drank our framboises and shot some pool. Emma could

hit bank shots with the best of them. I never noticed before how pretty she was. How had Mason ended up with a girl like her? At one point, Emma looked around the bar, leaned against the table. How many of these kids would smoke our weed? she asked. More than I would have ever guessed when I began this, I told her. Did any of them have any idea about the work we did to get it here for them? That was the thing, I said. As long as they never had to ask, we were doing it right.

Afterward, in the lot outside the bar, we hugged goodbye. Emma wanted to get on the road, hole up in a Mobile hotel a few hours from now, be home in Austin the following afternoon. Then she was going to rest. Because pretty soon she'd be doing it again, driving back across the country from Albuquerque with another heavy load.

"You're the only other person who knows what it's like," I said.

"A secret society," she said.

Then I thought of something. "Want me to mail JoJo Bear back out to Jerome?"

"Please do. I couldn't have done it without him."

"Drive fast and swerve a lot."

"You take care of yourself out there, too."

In my room, before sleep, I called to check on Kate. Was she feeling all right? I asked. She was fine, she said, she just missed me was all. I'd be home soon, I told her. Why couldn't I be home right now? she said.

In the morning, I drove across town to meet Eric Deveny. I pulled up to that dark and foreboding house of his, felt the same twinge of dread I had from the first. I went in through the unlocked side door to the kitchen with the duffel bags on my shoulders. Eric was waiting there for me, dressed in white, sipping espresso from a tiny cup.

"Anyone in here?"

"Just us mice, my man."

"Your brother?"

He grinned. "You're really afraid of him, aren't you?"

I said what I always said: "Got the money?"

He said what he always said: "Let's look in your mule sack."

We went to the den and I dumped out the pounds on his couch. He sorted through the bags, broke some of them open, so the stink filled the room. He said, "Names on this?"

"'Pineapple' on the yellow. 'OG' on the rest."

"How about 'Superstar Kush' for this really dark shit? I fucking love it when it comes back to me."

He was talking about how people would brag to him in bars about the killer dank they'd scored, hear them say the names he'd made up. Now he jogged up the stairs, came back with a shoebox.

"Want to count it?"

"Do I ever?"

"It's always nice doing business with you, my man. Every time I see you, I think, Look how far my boy has come. Because you were born in my very own house. Think I'll ever forget it? You look fresh today, like you didn't even drive it. Got someone out there muling for you?"

Could he already know? "What if I did?"

"Come on, my man, I'm not fucking dumb. I know the rules: get established, protect yourself and your source. I know you're putting Cali as far away from me as you can. Good for you, you're smart to do it. How much money have you made? A quarter million? Three hundred grand? More? Sell me your goddamn source already, James."

I shook my head.

"What if I just told you to give it to me?"

What could I say? I said, "I guess we'd have to figure that out then."

Deveny looked at me a long time, like he was considering it. Then he smiled and said, "Look at how far you've come."

"I learned it all from you."

Where was I going to feed him today, he wanted to know, and sit down and finalize this New York run? Because I was fucking doing that now, didn't I know that? Especially since I had someone else out there driving. Not to mention again that big mess he cleaned up for me. Like we could ever forget that. Like we wouldn't always have that between us. "Still doing okay with it?" he asked.

I shrugged.

"Ever going to tell your wife?"

I made a face, shook my head.

"Yeah," he said, "that's the way. Dump it. Or else keep it locked inside. There will come a day when you can let it all out. And then everything will feel fine, trust me. But let me ask you this: Why do you keep telling me no about New York?"

"What's up in New York you want so bad?"

"What do you think is up in New York, James? Money. Why don't you feel like you made a commitment to me when you brought that mess here to clean up?"

"You have that hanging over you as much as I do."

He thought about it, smiled, and said, "Maybe I do. But maybe I don't care about things like that at all. I'll come up with something else to keep you honest. Because I've been having this idea I have to keep you honest. All the money you're making me? Don't you know how important to me you are? Don't you know how proud of you I am? Born in my very own house. So where are we going to eat? Shula's for steak? How about that French place for duck?"

Could I just cruise home this one time? I asked. My wife was due.

He said, "A boy, right? Number two? They say that when you have a child, you learn the meaning of love for the first time. Is that true? Then I can't imagine how much you love those kids. Me? I'd never bring a life into this world. Not with the things I've seen. Not with the kind of people I know are in it. I'll get a present for your son when he's born. But what are you supposed to get for a kid who already has everything? Money? Parents who love it? I didn't have that. And I'm never going back to what I did have."

Deveny went behind his brass-topped bar, returned with a short green bong. He sat on his couch with those pounds of weed piled around him like pillows. He packed the bowl of the bong with bud from one of the pounds he'd popped open, sparked a lighter, started hitting it. "Did I tell you I was down in South Beach this weekend, my man?" he said, letting out a long plume of smoke. "Good times, James. You should be jealous. But you're not jealous, are you? You've got it all already. Kids. A wife who loves you. Because your wife loves you, doesn't she? Or does she just love the money? Europe? What else? She's spending it, isn't she?"

He hit the bong so it bubbled, his eyes closed like he was concentrating. It was so quiet in the house, it felt like there was some kind of sadness about it all. He tilted up his chin, let out the smoke. He tapped the bowl of the bong with the lighter to loosen up the weed. "Anyway, everybody down there is freaking out about the economy. I hate those fucking people—did you know that about me? Silver spoons, trust funds. That's who you get the pleasure of hanging out with when you're where I'm at. I love seeing those people scared. Know what I mean? To see them feel what we feel? To see them realize they live in the same world we do? My question is, if you're scared, shouldn't you do something about it? I did. You did, too."

He hit the bong, exhaled the smoke into the room. "We got

ourselves out of it, didn't we, my man? And I know I'm going
to keep myself out of it. And even if I could do something else,
and even if I could be something else, I wouldn't. Not anymore. Not until I have enough. Not until I know nothing can
ever fucking touch me. Is that how you feel? Tell me the truth,
James. Because I need you. Are you still in this with me?"

He'd never said so much to me. What I said to him was
"Yeah, I'm still in it."

"Superstar," he said and grinned. "I knew you had it in you
from the start. Remember how bad you wanted that money?
Hard to control, isn't it? No more excuses, my man. As soon
as that kid is born, you're going to New York. Dump your
phones, by the way. Heat's been off since that dead CI, but
that's no reason for us to get lazy. Get the fuck out of here. You
owe me a steak."

Deveny was talking about Rachel Hoffman, the girl who
was killed back in the spring. The Tallahassee PD had busted
her for a few ounces, scared her into working a sting with
them, sent her in alone on a drug and gun buy with $13,000 in
cash. Somehow they'd lost their surveillance; the hoods drove
away with her in their car, executed her. She was twenty-three,
not any kind of real drug dealer. The papers had been hammering away at the police ever since. At the time Eric had said,
"A civilian like her? That's the best they could do?"

When I pulled away from Eric's, I called Kate. Was she still
pregnant? I asked. Yes, she was still pregnant. Any contractions? No, she sighed, nothing at all. Then I threw away my
phones in a garbage can in a McDonald's parking lot, like Eric
had told me to. During the long, quiet drive down to Sarasota,
I thought about the things Deveny had said. Did my wife love
me? Of course my wife fucking loved me. Why was he trying
to get in my head?

Nick was pacing in a fury when I got to the 8th Street house, yelled at me when I walked in: "Why haven't you answered your phone? The deal is right now. We have to grab Micah and get up there."

"I can't go up there. Kate could have the baby."

Nick put up his hands to end the discussion. He said, "You're coming or you're not. The money's already in the motel room."

Money, money, money.

We didn't take two cars, we took one: no matter how much I did or didn't like Micah, I didn't want him to know the plates on my car, have something on me. Now we were too rushed to get a rental. We tossed the two pounds in the trunk of Nick's Escort, hurried up to Bradenton. As we watched Micah jog down the steps of his complex in a satin Yankees jacket with his cap cocked to the side, Nick turned to me from the driver's seat and said, "Check it out." When he lifted his shirt, I saw the handle of a gun tucked in his waistband. Nick whispered, "Told you I had it all covered."

"Is it real?"

"Hell yeah."

Panic tore through me. Right away, I said, "No no no no no!"

"What?"

"'Ten–twenty–life.' Ever fucking heard of it?" Micah was almost to the car. I said, "Ten years mandatory on top of anything else."

He said, "What do I do with it now?"

"Throw it out the window."

"Dude, it's my stepdad's."

Micah was in the backseat. "You Capones ready?"

I said, "Keep your head down."

"Because I'm black?"

"Come on, Micah. Like you don't know?"

Nick took us up on the 75, then across on the 4. There was a lot of high-speed weekend traffic, and we were past Disney and in Orlando in just over two hours. Micah bitched the whole way about having to keep his head down. When we got to Pine Hills, he said that if we really wanted to keep a low profile, he should be the one behind the wheel. "How many lightbulbs you see driving around up here? Pull over and get in back."

Nick turned into a Burger King parking lot. "Toss it in the garbage can," I hissed to Nick when we switched seats. But Nick looked at me like he was helpless. He said, "I gotta get it back before he sees."

Then Nick and I were hunched on the floorboards in back while Micah drove us along West Colonial. Every time I looked up, I saw liquor stores and PD cars. Nick pulled out his lit-up cell phone, showed it to me. The message on it read, "where the f is james??? why wont he anser his fon???" Of course it was from Kate. An instant later, another message came in from her: "everything ok??" Then we were idling somewhere. Micah powered down the window. "Got that key?" he whispered to someone. Someone with a deep voice out there in the night whispered, "Where your boys at?"

"They coming."

"They better be straight."

"Money in there?"

"Money's in there."

Micah powered up the window, pulled us away. He passed me back a keycard. When we were in traffic again, Micah said, "Who's going in?"

I said, "I'm going in."

"Room 151."

He wheeled us in somewhere, parked, turned off the car. When I looked up, we were at the Top Hat Motel; across the lot was the room. The lot was poorly lit, the few cars around us dark and empty. Why was I so fucking nervous? Micah slouched in the driver's seat, pulled down his hat. "It's your move," he said.

I opened the door, stepped out of the car, and walked across the lot to the room. No one was around. I slid the card in the slot, the lock clicked, I turned the handle, the door creaked open. I turned on the lights. The room looked like all those rooms did: shitty. There was no one in it but me. Where was the money? Nothing on the table, nothing on the bed. Should I leave? The bathroom. Why would they put it in the bathroom? God, would I have to check the fucking bathroom now?

Halfway through the room, on my way to check the bathroom, I saw that the adjoining door beside me had begun to open as I passed it. It was opening so slowly it looked like the nightmare was coming out of the closet. What should I do? I ran to it, even put my hands on it. It smacked the wall as they burst through. Four or five of them. All in hoods, two with guns. Their eyes were red. Were they high? Why would they be high? I put up my hands, let it all go.

"Face the wall, motherfucker!"

I faced the wall. "I'm cool. I'm cool," I heard myself saying.

"Shut the fuck up! You ain't cool," the one with the gun to my head shouted in my ear.

Another one was shouting in my other ear, "Want to get wasted? Want to get wasted? My boy will do that. My boy will do that."

The gun was pressed hard to the back of my head. They put a cell phone in my hand. "Tell your boy to bring the shit in here!"

The phone was ringing. Someone picked up. "Yo," Micah said.

"Get me Nick."

"Hang on."

Then it was Nick. Nick said, "What the fuck's going on?"

"Bring it in here."

"What the fuck?"

"Don't think. Just bring it in here as fast as you can."

"Open the door," I said to the room.

"Shut the fuck up!" Then they got quiet. Come on, Nick. Come on, Nick. Come on, Nick. I heard the door creaking, then the scuffle. Light splashed across the room when the lamp went over. Then I got hit in the back of the head, and I fell to the floor and stayed there.

"What you gonna do with this?" one of them shouted.

"No, no!" Nick said.

Then there were shots.

They banged out of the room, car doors slammed, cars peeled away.

Nick was lying face-down when I got to him. "Nick! Nick!" I turned him over. He wasn't shot.

I pulled at his shirt. "Get up! We have to get out of here!"

We ran outside. The Escort was sitting there. When I jumped in it, the keys were in the ignition. I drove us out onto the road, kept driving, realized my headlights were off, turned them on. Then we were up on a highway, then off of it. Then we sat in a 7-Eleven parking lot.

"Fuck! Fuck!"

"Jesus! Jesus!"

"Fuck! Fuck!"

"Jesus! Jesus!"

Then: "You all right, man?"

"Yeah, I guess so. What about you?"

I rubbed the back of my head where the gun had been. I said softly, "He left the keys."

Nick opened the door, started to get out. I said, "Where you going?"

"I'm done!"

"Get back in. Where you gonna go?"

Halfway home, near Tampa, Nick said, "I can't believe it!" A few seconds later he said, "He knew the whole time. He knows I'm going to have to see him again."

I told him, "Text Kate. Tell her I'm on my way. Text Micah. Text him, 'Fuck you.' Then tell him you want that gun back."

Nick did that. The text that came back from Micah said, "y u bring it? cost u a g."

Nick said, "What are we gonna do?"

I shook my head. I shouted at him, "You think we can do something?"

Nick looked out the window beside him in silence the rest of the way home.

When we got to the 8th Street house, he said, "I fucking quit!"

I said, "You can't quit. You owe me money."

I drove home. No one was at the house when I walked in. A handwritten note on the counter read, "If you can work it into your busy schedule, we are at the birthing center having your son."

I arrived at the birthing center, beside a Japanese pond. Kate's and my mother's cars were there. I ran through the doors. My mother was sitting in the lobby reading a magazine; I ran past her. When I entered the candlelit birthing room, Cristina and my wife were in the tub in the corner. I stripped down to my boxers. Cristina stepped out of the tub and I stepped in. Kate took my hands. She said between contractions, "I was worried. I was worried." Three hours later, our son Evan was born underwater, and I lifted him to the darkness to take his first breath.

My mother was always over. Kate's parents flew in from California wearing Hawaiian shirts and Bermuda shorts, began drinking Coors right away. They were so glad we'd sent them the tickets, so happy to be with us and the babies. Cristina, too, what a nice surprise to see her. She'd always been like a daughter to them. Florida was so warm and sunny, our house was so nice, they were thinking of staying forever. What did we think about it if they did?

I ran away with Romana to the park every day. Then Emma wanted me to go to Austin and help her with her college-kid deal, which I'd forgotten I'd said I would do. Fly out in the morning, fly home late at night—did Kate mind if I went? As long as it'd only be a day, she said; if she could get away from everything right now, she would, too.

I shaved off my beard patches, put on my work clothes, flew out early, and landed in Austin in the middle of the afternoon. Emma picked me up; Bayleigh was in her car seat in back. "Say hi to your Uncle James," Emma said to Bayleigh. Bayleigh said, "Hi, Unca James."

As she drove us into town, Emma asked, "How is everybody?"

"Everybody's fine."

"The baby?"

"Yeah, the baby, too."

"A lot more work for you guys now."

What could I say? I said, "What's two when you got one, right?"

We went to Trudy's on the north side, ate fish tacos. I drank a margarita to pass the time. Should I tell Emma about the gun to my head in Orlando? The margarita made me want to, but I knew I never should.

Emma explained the deal while Bayleigh colored on her placemat. She said, "I've got the pound in the trunk in a backpack. We pick up my cousin Sam. You go with him, tell him what to do. If everything works out, I'll run my stuff for this guy through him, let Sam make some money. They were all relocated here after the hurricane, just like we were. They haven't had shit since."

"Sounds good."

"Sam doesn't know I'm doing any driving. I told him you're the guy who brought it."

"That's fine."

"He's going to be nervous. He hasn't done anything like this before."

"It'll all work out."

We got stuck in traffic, the usual Austin snarl, and the cousin started calling: What were we doing, what were we doing? The dealer was expecting the shit at six. What if we pissed off the dealer? Emma said, "We'll be there in fifteen minutes, Sam. Just tell the guy to chill out."

The cousin was standing on the corner of 24th and Guadalupe, rooted in place like a telephone pole, a skinny, clean-faced kid in a Longhorns cap, his hands crammed deep in the pockets of his jeans. His face was white as he eyeballed the street. I could tell he was terrified. He jumped in the back of the car beside Bayleigh. He said, "You guys are late. You guys are late. He says he doesn't want to do it anymore."

I looked at Emma; Emma rolled her eyes at me. She glanced at Sam in the rearview, made a face. She said, "Fifteen minutes? What's wrong with this guy? Like he's never had to wait? Give me a fucking break." She wheeled us into the alley behind the Urban Outfitters. When she popped the trunk, the cousin looked around. He said, "Right here? Right here? What if somebody sees?" Emma rolled her eyes at me again.

Out in the alley, I grabbed the backpack, shut the trunk. Emma drove away. Then the cousin and I went around the corner and crossed Guadalupe over onto the UT campus. The weather was breezy, an early September day, laughing students were wearing backpacks around us everywhere. The cousin said to me under his breath, "Everyone's watching us, aren't they?"

"Nobody's watching us. Just get your chin off your chest, okay?"

Up in his dorm room, Sam called the dealer. The dealer didn't want to do it anymore. We were late. He'd scored a pound off somebody else in the meantime.

Scored a pound just like that? I shook my head. "Call this guy," I said. "Tell him he ordered it. It came across the country for him."

"You call him," Sam said, offering me the phone.

I put up my hand. "Emma's paying you, right?"

"Two hundred dollars."

"This is how you earn it."

He called the dealer while I looked around his room. It was so plain, textbooks and pencils, not much else, no posters on the walls, nothing colorful. Why was this frightened kid messing around with this? For two hundred dollars?

Sam hung up. Okay, okay, he said, the dealer said he'd look at a sample. Where did the dealer live? I asked him. He said, Upstairs, on a different floor.

I opened the backpack, pulled out the pound, popped it with my finger, fished out a pinecone bud. Sam stared at all the weed in the bag, got scared, went and put his ear against the door. Was he expecting anybody? I asked. No, his roommate had a night class, he said. So what was the deal with all this nervous shit? I said. He said, How could we be sure nobody knew?

I sighed. "Run this up there. Tell him I'm down here getting pissed off."

Sam put the bud in his pocket and left. Ten minutes went by. Then he was back, locking the door behind him. "He doesn't want it. He says it isn't good enough."

"Not good enough?"

"He says he isn't paying five and a half grand for something he can get for three."

I let that sink in, turned it over. Then I said, "He's lying. He can't get this for three."

"Well, he says he can."

"Call him. Tell him if he can get it for three, I'll buy it from him. This is what I do, Sam. And I know he can't get it for that."

Sam took out his phone, called him. He said quietly into the phone, "The guy says you can't get it for that price." He was listening. Then he said, "The guy says he'll buy it from you."

Sam hung up. "He doesn't want to do it."

I shoved the pound in the backpack, zipped the backpack shut, slung it over my shoulder. Take me up there, I said. Why, what were we going to do? Sam asked. We'd done a lot of work to get this here, I told him, we were going to go up there and talk to this guy.

We went up in the elevator. Sam shook his head. "I knew I wouldn't make that two hundred dollars."

"What are you talking about, Sam?"

"He's always bragging to everybody about what a big drug dealer he is. I'm not even sure he really is one."

On the floor the elevator opened at, there were guys in towels coming out of the showers, guys in soccer jerseys and cleats heading for the stairs. When Sam knocked, the drug dealer who could score kush for three opened the door of his dorm room. He had glasses, acne, slicked-back blond hair. He was wearing a puka-shell necklace with a wooden marijuana leaf hanging off of it. When he saw me, he turned pale.

"Where do you score kush for three?" I asked.

His eyes widened at how loud I'd said it. "Dude," he said to hush me, and looked up and down the hall, "not out here." He let us in. He had Bob Marley posters on the wall, a digital scale out in the open on his desk, bongs, pipes, baggies, all the paraphernalia. But I'd already figured everything out. He went and sat in his leather recliner, recovered himself, put on what I guessed he thought was a business face. Should I give him credit for being able to do that, at least? I said to him, "You just copped a pound from someone else?"

He cocked his chin at me. He said, "Sorry, man. You were late. The shit's already on its way over."

"Why'd you order it if you never really wanted it?"

"How was I supposed to know it would get here? From Sam? A guy like Sam? Man, I had to have my backup plan. I got a business to run, you know?"

I picked up a heavy textbook off his desk, looked at it. It was *Fundamentals of Cost Accounting*.

I said, "This your book?"

He said, "Yeah."

I stepped across the room, swung the book as hard as I could and hit him in the face with it. I dropped the book, punched him over and over. Then he was on the floor, and I was stomping on his head. I knocked all the shit off his shelves, yanked out his drawers, tore down his posters. Was he crying? Good. Could I even piss on him? There was a roll of money on the floor; I grabbed it. The nickel bags of seedy Mexican yard weed of course I left behind. When I shut the door behind me,

I saw Sam bolting away, already far down the hall. When he glanced back over his shoulder, I understood he was running away from me.

I took the elevator down, walked out. In the car, I noticed my knuckles were scuffed and bleeding. Emma didn't want the guy's money. She yelled at me, "What's the matter with you? That's my cousin! Don't you care about anything? Are you fucking crazy?"

At the airport, she threw the money after me onto the curb, pulled away. People were watching as I gathered up the money. I went through security, walked to my gate. Then I got on my plane. When I counted the money, it was $167. I stared out the window at nothing all the way home.

5

Mule in the Traces

IN MID-SEPTEMBER, I MANAGED to put off Eric Deveny on his New York run one last time. Two days later, my mother called and said a letter had come to her house for me. She let me in when I arrived, went back to watching the news. "Are you following what's happening, James? The Lehman Brothers bank last week, and today this AIG."

"Sounds like more of the same to me, Ma."

"What a bunch of assholes."

The letter was in a plain white envelope, no return address, no postmark, no stamp. When I tore it open, there was a single sheet of paper folded inside; on it was a photocopied picture of a turn-of-the-century western pack mule. The mule was loaded with baggage and ready for travel. There was nothing else in the picture but the mule. Under the mule was printed: "Operators of working animals generally find mules preferable to horses. Mules show less impatience under the pressure of heavy weight. The stereotype of a mule as being stubborn is unfair and inaccurate."

Under that was a line of handwriting: "Stop being so fuck-ing stubborn!!!"

"What'd you get?" my mother asked.

I rubbed my beard patches. "An invitation to this thing at work."

"Is your job safe? Are you and Kate worried about all of this?"

"We've been through it already. Besides, rich people still want their boats cleaned. I'm even managing my own crew over there now." I folded the letter into my pocket. Then I said to her, "You have a valid passport, by any chance?"

She nodded. "I had to get one for my cruise to Nassau."

"Maybe we'll all go on a trip together someday."

When the Cali load came in two Mondays later, I drove up to Tallahassee in the morning, met Emma at her hotel, grabbed the weight from her in the lot. I apologized again for what I'd done at UT, asked if her cousin Sam had taken the $500 I'd asked her to give him from me to say sorry to him, too. Emma shrugged. "He wouldn't touch it. He said he doesn't want our filthy drug money."

I nodded. "What about that stupid liar kid?"

"Stop worrying about it. He knows he can't say anything. Just keep an eye on your mental state, would you? You're get-ting to be as high-strung as Mason."

I gave her the cash for the next run, then drove the weight to Deveny's. His house was as dark and foreboding as always when I pulled up to it. I took my usual deep breaths, hopped out, and ran the duffel bags inside. Eric was standing in his wood-paneled den, dressed in white, his remote in his hand, watching the news on his projection TV. "Can you believe this shit?" he said, smiling when I walked in. "It gets crazier every day. It's down eight hundred points right now. What did they think would happen, wasting their money blowing up shithole countries? Who's laughing now, my man?"

I dropped the duffel bags on his couch, pulled the letter out of my jacket pocket, tossed it on his coffee table. The picture of the mule looked up at us in the dark room. When he noticed it, he picked it up and made a face like he was seeing it for the first time. Then he grinned at me and said, "An amazing animal, don't you think? Much better than a pig, for example."

"How'd it get down there?"

"My brother was passing through."

"You sent your brother to my mother's house?"

He turned back to his TV. He said, "Relax, my man. It's not like he knocked on her door. Sometimes people just need a kick in the pants. You're not the same guy who first came up here anymore, are you? That guy would've begged me for the chance to do some work. In fact, I think you did beg me, remember? Where is that guy now, that guy who was born in my house? Have you made enough money, James? Even with all this new shit that's going on? Fine with me. Give me your connection and go the fuck away. You'd make me very happy."

"You're not getting that."

"Then you're going to New York."

What could I say, No? Or better yet, Make me? I shrugged, said the only thing I knew I could: "How much are you going to pay me?"

He nodded as he watched the Dow Jones plunge. "Good news, my man. Great news, in fact. We've had such a productive working relationship, haven't we? Making money for each other. Getting our hands dirty for one another. Besides, I have this strong feeling you're going to enjoy yourself up there. All right, water under the bridge, back to business. Where are you taking me for lunch today? The restaurants are going to be fucking deserted I bet."

When I crawled into bed that night, Kate rolled over and whispered what she always did: "Everything going okay out there?"

I whispered back what I always did: "Everything's going just fine."

"Did you stop and see Nick?"

"Yeah, I picked up your money, Kate."

"How's Nick?"

"Nick's good."

"He doesn't want to stop working for us anymore?"

"No, he managed to get himself over that."

"What do you think was the matter with him?"

"People get frightened out there sometimes."

Kate said, "Did you look in at the babies?"

"You know I did."

"Aren't they getting big?"

"Yeah, so big."

"You're not going to see them grow up if you go on working like this, you know."

Then Kate asked, "Are you going to be home for a few days?"

"Why are you asking?"

"There's a function—"

"Take Cristina."

One part of my life really was going just fine: Jerome and Emma were conducting the cross-country runs from California like symphonies, bringing in the weight, taking out the money, passing JoJo Bear back and forth between them like a baton. I'd finally let Jerome and Billy meet in Sacramento, to save myself the hassle of having to fly out there. If they'd cut any side deals between them, which I assumed they had, I hadn't noticed yet. The dream of the Capital Cities Connection was up and running, tossing me eighteen to twenty Gs every two weeks for doing nothing more than putting up the cash. I should have been able to kick back, grow out my hair, get to know my kids, maybe even start writing again. But of course I couldn't do that. Now I was working for Eric Deveny.

The New York run was a three-day roundtrip up the eastern seaboard that took me through High Intensity Drug Trafficking Areas in Jacksonville, Washington, D.C., and Trenton, and overnighted me in Richmond on the way up and Savannah on the way back. Eight more states to add to my muling résumé, 2,200 more miles, and lots of congested traffic to hide in—so much easier than anything I'd done before that I didn't mind that JoJo Bear wasn't riding along with me.

I was carrying twenty-five-pound loads, made up of a little of my Cali kush and a lot of Eric's Miami haze, in two big suitcases in the back of our old Forester. At Dulles, I'd switch out the car for a rental with New York, New Jersey, or Pennsylvania plates. When I reached Newark, I'd park in the short-term lot, catch a prearranged town car to the city, finish the run at a Manhattan address on the north side of Gramercy Park. The building was old and beautiful, the ceiling in the lobby paneled and high, the brass banisters polished and gleaming. The liveried doorman would hand me a heavy gym bag, I'd unzip it and see that it was packed with cash, then he'd whisk the suitcases away into the elevator. Should I hang out for a while in the city? Have a little fun like Deveny seemed to want me to? I'd just earned another eight Gs, after all. But I'd take the same town car back to Newark, hop in the rental, get myself back on the road. Down in Tallahassee, I'd give Eric his money and go home with mine: $58,000. I was having to wait to get my fifty

Gs from him for the Cali pounds out of those New York gym bags now, too.

I did the inaugural run the first Friday in October, the second two weeks later. Kate didn't have any idea where I was going or what I was doing; when she'd even bother to ask, which was almost never, I'd tell her I'd been out in Sacramento, dropping off money with Billy. Why should Kate know anything? To feel as threatened as I'd felt when I'd opened that letter? To know that part of me had given up the idea of ever getting out at all? She was busy with the kids, her friends, school; we lived completely separate lives. Which sometimes felt right and good. At least one of us was enjoying the fruits of everything I was risking out there.

"Everything going okay?" she'd ask in her rote and uninterested way whenever I'd come home. I'd just grab the remote from her, plunk myself down on the couch, switch the channel to *Cops*, and tell her, "Yeah, everything's fine."

"So what do you think of the dealer up there, my man?" Deveny grinned and asked me in Tallahassee when we sat down to unfiltered Muscadet and escargot at Chez Pierre at the end of my first New York run.

"Didn't meet him. Made the switch with the doorman."

"The doorman?"

A shadow crossed Eric's face; he didn't like something about that. He beckoned the waiter for another bottle of wine, said, "Guess I'm going to have to make a fucking phone call."

"What's with the dealer?"

"Just wait, my man. You'll see," he said. "What about the skyline?"

"It was raining."

"Then you haven't felt it yet. A guy like you? A guy like you is going to love that city."

"What's a guy like me, Eric?"

"Don't you know yet, James? A guy like you is a guy like me."

"What if I said I didn't want to go up there again?"

"Hook me up with Cali."

What could I do but shake my head?

Someone else who wanted something from me now was Darren Rudd. Because Darren was back from Thailand and dealing with major problems. The stock market crash had flushed a ton of his cleaned-up money down the drain, along with everyone else's. And those big properties he owned up and down the state of California? Greedy Darren had been flipping them. Now he was caught holding the bag on a dozen jumbo ARMs.

Billy told me on the phone, "You don't want to talk to Darren right now. First he got taken for a big, big ride over in Thailand. Now he's hemorrhaging cash to stay out of foreclosure. I've never seen a dude so stressed out. He's running stuff all over the place to try and make up for it. He's laid off half a dozen guys out here, is doing time behind the wheel himself."

"What happened to him over in Thailand?" I asked, working my way through a six-pack of Yuengling in a dingy smoking room at the Relax Inn, Savannah, returning home from my second New York run.

"What do you think happened to him? Arrogant rich white guy. Underage bride. I told you she was underage, didn't I? He gets the idea he can do whatever he wants over there. He buys her whole village stuff, a fridge for her old man, clothes for the women. He slaughters an ox, marries her, takes her home to his humble abode. He doesn't even get to stick it in her before the Thai police are kicking down his door. Shooting his dog, beating the fuck out of him. Of course they'd seen his money.

They'd set him up to get their hands on it. Darren had to pay through the nose to get out of that cell. They confiscated his farm. They confiscated his vehicles. Then he's in a cab with the scumbag Thai lawyer who got him his passport back, sees the girl tooling around in his truck. He pays the cabbie to chase her down, she lifts up her sunglasses, laughs at him. Darren still insists he loves her. Anyway, that's how it ended for him in Thailand.

"He's pissed, James. He's had the shit scared out of him as much as anyone with money right now. But you know what I say? The power's still on. There's still food in the stores, gas at the stations. And even if we get down to a barter economy, what we have to trade will still have value. Anyway, Darren's getting sloppy, Darren's getting mean. He's chewing people out over nothing. Sometimes I ask myself if I want to keep working for the guy. It's not like I need the money, but it's not like they just let you walk away. After everything I've seen? Everything I know? I've watched dudes take that long walk in the woods. The Marble Mountains, the Trinity Wilderness. When the snow melts up there, the Forest Service finds the car, all shot to hell. But they never find the dude. Drive fast and swerve a lot, you know what I mean? I'm not breaking any kind of news flash to you."

I lit another cigarette, glanced at *Cops* on the muted TV, worried my beard patches. I told Billy, "You know what scares me? I'm not afraid of getting caught anymore. I'm frightened by not knowing what people are planning on doing. The guy who takes my weight, he's been playing mind games with me to get me to do more work for him. So I'm asking myself, What happens when I want to be done? How am I supposed to know he's going to let me go?"

"You can always get yourself out of the country."

"Sounds easy enough. But out of the country to where?

With what? Thirty or forty Gs? Maybe a hundred grand? What do we do over there when that runs out? All our money is stuck right here. Bricks of it. Bricks and bricks of it. And then there's my mother. What do I do about her?"

"You have to take her with you."

"My mother's in a mahjong league. She's not ready for this."

"You know what I'm doing when it's my turn to run?" Billy said. "First I'm telling Corinne to treat it like I'm dead, that she should go to the donut boys right away if anyone tries to fuck with her. She knows where everything is buried, it's always all been for her anyway. Then I'm grabbing the dogs, heading for the border. I'll go as far as the road will let me. You'll never hear from me again."

"No shit?"

"Oh yeah. I've had it all mapped out for years. Anyway, Darren's going to be calling you soon. My guess is he'll ask you to hook him up with your guy. You already know what my advice is. Don't fucking give it to him. You give him your guy, you got nothing. You always have to have something if you want to have any safety in this."

There was one more thing going on that none of us knew about yet—not me, not Billy, and especially not Darren Rudd. It was gathering like a thunderhead over the Siskiyou Mountains day by day, getting ready to release its mighty clap and drown us all in pain. Up in Siskiyou County, at Yreka High School in August and September, and then at Mount Shasta High School through the rest of the fall, a baby-faced twenty-three-year-old virgin cop fresh out of Narc Academy was posing undercover as a troubled, transferred high school student. Unlike most bacon in the world, this pig had no odor and possessed an actual gift for acting. He'd been setting up weight buys on school property to carry back to his "buddies" in L.A.

Unfortunately for the dealers selling to him, his buddies ate donuts.

The bad guys had been quietly taking down all these people through him, leaning on them with the school-zone laws, making them flip, clawing their way up the chain. Just a few months into it, they already had a surprising target in their sights: a Mount Shasta city councilman working the business on the side to pay for his model girlfriend's condo on Russian Hill, her monthly trips to Cabo. By the time Billy and I had that conversation in the middle of October, the cops were choking on their bear claws and Boston creams in their listening vans, knowing they were getting close to something real for once in their frustrating law enforcement lives. Eventually they would amass enough video and wiretap recordings to warrant a hundred-man joint task force operation involving Siskiyou County Narcotics, the California Department of Justice's Bureau of Narcotics Enforcement, the Siskiyou County Sheriff's Department, and the Yreka and Mount Shasta PDs. In the end, it would all go Fed.

As that interagency narcotics task force in Siskiyou County began to assemble their case in their secret war rooms in California through late October and early November, the country went nuts with election fever, Obama won, made his Grant Park speech, and I did a third and fourth run to New York. Had I met the dealer? Eric Deveny wanted to know each time I came back with the money. I had not met the dealer, I told him each time. Then Kate was planning a big Thanksgiving spread at our house, and I did the run once more before the holiday. The drive up was calm and easy; I had a beautiful view of the long and naked city from the back of the town car. When I ran the suitcases up the steps of the building at Gramercy Park, the doorman shook his head at me. He pressed the elevator button and said, "They want you to take it up this time."

I was wearing my lucky driving clothes that day, the same flannel jacket and beat-up jeans from our time in the cabin that had seen me safely through all these months and tens of thousands of miles. Did I care that I was dressed like that, in that beautiful building, in the great city of New York? I didn't. This was just work to me, and this was how I dressed when I worked. The doors of the elevator opened at the third floor. I lifted the two suitcases by their handles and began walking down the long red-carpeted hallway. There was a gilded mirror on the wall, two French armchairs on either side of a demilune table, and on the table a yellow bouquet in a porcelain vase—real flowers, amaryllises. At the door, I pressed the bell, heard the chimes inside. Soon there were soft footsteps approaching behind it. Then the door opened. Standing before me was a beautiful girl.

She looked me up and down. "So you're the famous courier I've been waiting so long to meet." She took the suitcases inside, came back with a heavy gym bag I knew was full of cash. She didn't look at me as she shut the door. I thought about her the whole drive home.

"Did you meet the dealer?" Eric Deveny asked me over porterhouse steaks at Shula's back in Tallahassee.

"I met the dealer."

"Her name's Danielle."

Two weeks later, Danielle invited me in.

The apartment had high ceilings, dark hardwood floors, faux columns around the arched doorways, ornate crown molding. The style seemed more suited to someone older than she was, but when she lit a cigarette in her living room, it all clearly belonged to her. Looking out the tall windows, I saw a pretty, gated park below; the next room beyond, I could see, was a library. I'd glanced around when I'd followed her in, trying to find her last name written down somewhere. But there was no mail lying about. No diplomas on the wall. The copies of *Vanity Fair* on the coffee table had been purchased off the rack. She was tall and confident, with long brown hair; her dark dress and boots were cut to fit; the silver bangles on her wrists were as slender and polished as she was. She offered to show me the city, and I agreed to let her. In the bedroom she gave me, I changed out of my driving clothes and into the Sevens, Energie, and Asics Tiger stuff that Kate had sent me off with for my lunch with Deveny. The clothing was brand-new, the labels pulled off in the room.

"I know you're pissed he's making you come up here," Danielle said as she led me through the midday crowd when we went out half an hour later. "But he's done a lot for you, so do the route until you get it down, then dole it out to one of your drivers. As long as he makes his money, he'll never know the difference. And that's all that matters, right?

"Have you spent any real time in the city?" she asked as we ducked into a cab.

"A few magazine editors took me out to lunch up here in a life I once lived."

"Did you enjoy that?"

"Of course I did."

"Then you already know," she said as she dabbed on lip gloss.

She was single, didn't have any kids, didn't want any. She described her business to me over drinks at a basement place in the West Village. It was early afternoon, no one else was there. We took off our jackets, sat in our sweaters in a velvet booth. Soon we were on our second bottle of Prosecco.

"I'm just a broker right now," Danielle explained in that quiet bar, "but what I used to do when I had real fun with it was come across Lake Erie in the summers with my brothers. Speedboats, runabouts—you'd stay in traffic, same as on the highway. Our stuff was always BC bud they'd brought all the way across from Vancouver. We'd island-hop down toward Sandusky, tie up with the buyers, take the money back. I did it in my bikini. My oldest brother made the contacts while he was playing in a band in Cleveland. Then he came home to Ontario, pulled the rest of us into it. Seven, eight grand for one day of work."

"How much would you carry?"

"My senior year of high school, I once carried a hundred pounds. But then I had this dumb idea I wanted a future away from the business. I went to Tallahassee for the climate, paid for college with what I saved doing Lake Erie. I met Eric when he came up after his discharge. When we had trust, my brothers started coming down and picking up haze from him. Eric was still getting himself established, but you could already tell he was going to be a superstar. The 'Superstar.' So fucking arrogant, right? I met his parents once. Conservative types. Salt of the earth. They didn't seem too pleased with him. 'Where did we go wrong,' you know? Eric was totally insane from Iraq, it made it easy for him to push around the competition. Plus, he knew what he was doing from growing up in Miami. Plus, he had his brother. You have to have people with you if you want to go anywhere, right? By the time he joined his frat, he was all set. So what about you? You're still brand-new in this, aren't you?"

"Brand-new? Not so much brand-new. My wife and I got hit by the economy. The opportunity fell in our laps, we took it. Now I manage half a dozen people."

"And you guys are all working interstate?"

"California to Florida. All the way across the country."

"Looping the money back?"

"Twice a month like clockwork."

"Who helped you set that up?"

"I built it all myself."

"Got any muscle?"

"I'm the muscle."

"And now you're in Manhattan."

"It feels almost as good as the first time I was here."

Danielle explained how she laundered her money, made even more by doing it. She leased apartments, furnished them, advertised them on Craigslist, let them out by the day to European tourists. A cash business, easy to say the places were rented when they weren't, then she'd slide her crooked money onto the straight books. She had a tax guy who had no idea what she really did. Because what she really did was flip fifty, sixty, seventy pounds a month for her brothers to white-collar dealers all over the city, Connecticut, and Long Island. BC bud, Miami haze, and, most recently, some Cali kush.

"I like to think I'm big, but what I move is a joke. This city puffs away a thousand pounds an hour. Imagine the scale of it. There's plenty of room to grow, but you have to have a reliable and cost-effective source. Tell me something, James. Everyone's always in the market for talented people. If we could clear it with Eric and you had the free time, would you want to do some interesting side work for me?"

She had this idea, a way to slip around suppliers, cut costs. "The Niagara River. The border between Ontario and New York State. There are places where it's narrow enough to navigate in a kayak. State parks, frontage roads. We'd have to do it at night because they run patrols. Maybe we could even shoot an arrow across."

"An arrow?"

"Yeah, an arrow," she said and started laughing, her champagne flute raised in her hand like she was making a toast. "With a string tied to the fletching. We'd pull the weed across in waterproof bags. Sounds silly, right? People jump out of airplanes. They parachute across the border with hundred-pound bales strapped to their backs. People four-wheel for days through the woods, they don't even know where they are. And what about the Mexicans and their tunnels? So why not get creative, right?"

I swallowed another mouthful of bubbly, thought about the pantyhose. The pantyhose had certainly worked for me.

"We should go up there, check it out. Cruise along the river, find the perfect spot. Stay somewhere nice, somewhere expensive. You'd do the driving, right?"

Then she said, "What about your wife, James? Does she know much about what you do out there?"

"Kate doesn't know anything about what I do."

Danielle said, "In my other life, nobody knows anything either. People I'm close to. People I'd like to be closer to. Then we reach the point where that's all they're ever going to know about me."

When we left the bar, it was evening. Danielle offered me her arm. As we walked across town on Houston, I felt that people were looking at us. Looking at me, looking at how beautiful she was beside me. The wind kept us close together. Shouldn't we hop in a cab? I asked. She said, Isn't it nice to walk? To be with someone you don't have to lie to?

There was a Moroccan place she hadn't been to in a while on the other side of NYU, should we go there? Sure. When we got there, it was shuttered. Okay, she said, there was a place for hand-pulled noodles not far away, somewhere on Bond, Mercer. When we stood in front of it a few minutes later, we saw it was out of business. We went back to Houston and Danielle put up her hand for a cab. She said as she did, "Do they expect us to fucking cook?"

At BLT Fish, we had oysters at the bar—Bluepoints, Fanny Bays, Yaquinas—and drank Bombay martinis, one after the other. The place was noisy and packed; the economy hadn't forced its way in here yet. Danielle and I had to sit close to each other the whole time because of the crowd. When Kate texted me, "where are you?" I texted back, "motel in sac."

"kids miss u. I miss u."

"home in 2 days."

"call before bed?"

"ok."

"That her?" Danielle asked when she saw me texting. I nodded, slipped the phone in my pocket, turned it off as I did. She rolled her eyes and said, "I wouldn't get married if they paid me."

"When you fall in love, they don't have to."

"Do you really love your wife?"

"Most of the time."

"And the other times?"

I was quiet. Then I said, "I wonder why she lets me do it."

I looked at myself in the mirror behind the bar. Was that what I looked like? My hair short? My face lean and innocent-looking? Even handsome? I knew it was the booze working its magic. Still, it felt grand. Danielle said, "Work stressing you out right now, James?"

"Work always stresses me out, Danielle."

"Ever think about taking a break?"

"All the time. But then I wonder what's left for me to do."

"Because of the money?"

"Because of the money."

"Then maybe this is what you were meant to do. Aren't you glad it found you? I can't believe I ever wanted to get out. I wouldn't give it up for anything anymore."

When I glanced at our hands on the bar, I saw she was letting me caress her fingers. If I was ever going to leave this place, I knew I had to do it now. Instead I put my hand up for another round. I said, "Do you really want to know how stressed out I've been?"

She said, "Tell me."

"My beard's been falling out. Almost two years. It started when we lost our jobs. It won't grow back no matter how much money I put away."

She took my chin in her hand, turned it up to the light. She stroked the bare places beneath it with her fingertips. She said, "Your skin feels so smooth where it's missing."

"It fucking embarrasses me."

"Don't be embarrassed. I wouldn't have noticed if you hadn't told me.

"You know what?" she said eagerly as she waved to the bartender for the tab. "I might have something at my place that will fix it."

The thing she had at her place was the Baby Quasar, a small handheld device of LED lights that looked like a ray gun from the future, lying on the marble counter in her white-tiled bathroom. Then I was sitting on a stool in front of her huge lighted mirror drinking a Red Stripe from the six-pack at my feet I'd pulled from her fridge as she smoked a Newport and switched on the Baby Quasar. Blue light shot from it like a laser beam. "They didn't say when I bought it that it would make hair grow back," she said as she turned the beam toward my face, "but I paid too much for it not to." Then she stopped and squinted at me in the mirror. She let out a puff of smoke and said, "You're going to have to take off your shirt."

"What's my shirt got to do with it?"

"Would you relax and trust me already? Or do you not want your beard to grow back?" She lit another Newport, tapped the ash casually to the floor. She was so fucking cool. I knew someone would come and clean up the ash in the morning, someone who wouldn't be her. Because someone else had come while we'd been out, had taken away the suitcases and left behind a gym bag stuffed with cash. I pulled off my T-shirt, tossed it on the floor. Danielle looked at my body in the mirror in that bright room. She ran her hands along my shoulders, then down the sides of my chest. She tapped her ash on the floor and said, "You'd look even better with a few tattoos."

The light of the Baby Quasar felt warm against my skin. I grew drowsy, closed my eyes, didn't notice it anymore. Danielle took a break to open her medicine cabinet, brought out a small, dark vial. I knew what it was right away. She tapped a line onto the counter beside the sink, tucked her long hair behind her ear to clear her face, and snorted it. Then it was my turn to snort a line. Would I? I did. Then it was her turn again. Then mine. We sniffed, pinched our noses, looked at ourselves in the mirror together. I knew I shouldn't be there, shouldn't have done anything I'd already done that day. At the same time, I didn't care. The aspirin flavor was dripping in the back of my throat. I could finally breathe again. When was the last time I'd done blow? A couple of years ago? No, more. Because I'd married, had kids. God, remember them? Danielle turned on the Baby Quasar; now it pulsed like a strobe light. She worked it slowly over my face, stuck Newport after Newport in the corner of her mouth as she did. When I reached down for another Red Stripe, I found that they were all empty. I closed my eyes, rolled my head in a circle, and she called on her cell for more beer.

"What do you think of my place, James?"

"I think it's pretty fucking great."

"Did you know the park's private? You have to have a key to get in."

"That's pretty fucking cool."

And somebody did bring more beer. But who? When? Because then there were Stellas on ice in the sink when only a second before there hadn't been. There was cash on the counter now, too, crumpled dollar bills.

"Who brought up the beer?" I leered at my shirtless self in the mirror and laughed.

Danielle laughed. She said, "You didn't see that kid?"

"Oh yeah. He looked scared."

"He was scared."

"Where was he from?"

"Some country. Hey, why did you tell him what you did?"

"What did I tell him?"

"'Drive fast and swerve a lot.'"

"Did I tell him that?"

"Yeah. You even made him say it. What is that?"

"That's rule number one."

"What's rule number one?"

"Don't get caught."

"Eric taught you that?"

"Other people taught me that."

"What other people?"

"My people out in Cali."

"Who are your people out in Cali?"

"I can never tell you."

"Then that must be a rule, too."

"That's not a rule. That's how you stay alive."

Danielle said, "What's your favorite place to run through?"

I didn't have to think about it. I said, "Northern Arizona. From the moment you cross the Cali border. You leave the desert, go up into these forested hills. Snow deep into the spring. Sometimes elk on the side of the road. The Grand Canyon somewhere just to the left of you. It's like that all the way across to Flagstaff. Then you've got the San Francisco Mountains. Beautiful fucking mountains. Like pyramids. Then you're in Indian territory. Hopis and Navajos. I used to worry when I was a kid that all the Indians were dead. But there are plenty of them out there. They even work in the gas stations."

"You know what I used to worry about? That all the panda bears would die. Isn't it dumb all the things we worry about when we're kids?"

"Now I worry about all this other shit."

"Now I worry about getting cancer."

"You're not going to get cancer."

"How do you know that? Everybody gets cancer all the time. I want to make enough money to buy my way out of it. The Mayo Clinic. Nuclear medicine."

"Why don't you quit smoking?"

"Then how are you supposed to deal with life, you know?"

"I can really hear the Canada in you now."

"It's 'cause I'm high." She dumped more coke on the counter, cut more lines with her fingernail. "We have to shoot an arrow across that river. Or else scuba-dive. You want to do that with me?"

"How are you going to get me away from Eric?"

"I'll buy you."

"You'll buy me?"

"Yeah, man. Don't you know you're a commodity?"

She turned off the Baby Quasar at last. She set her warm face on my bare shoulder and we looked at ourselves together in the mirror. "Can you feel it growing back yet?"

"I can't feel a fucking thing."

Her cell phone started vibrating, then she was talking to people. Then we were out in the night in a cab. What time was it? I asked. Something in the morning, she said. I hadn't called my wife to say good night. Jesus Christ, she said, so call her now, who cared? I patted the pockets of my jeans. My phone wasn't in them. Where the hell had I left it? But I knew there wasn't any number on it but Kate's. Would Kate be mad I hadn't called? I'd make something up. I was good at that.

Then we were in the East Village, in one of those bars. Everyone was laughing, talking, going in and out to smoke. Then Danielle and I were making out up against the brick wall outside. I couldn't feel the cold. Later, we were with all these people in a dingy lounge in Alphabet City, and one of the guys was a comedian everyone was supposed to know. I didn't know him.

Everything started spinning; I had to flop on a couch beside a Sikh in a black turban. His beard was neatly folded and tied up under his chin. What if I could grow a beard like that? What did he do? I asked him. Software something, he said. What did I do? he asked me. I was a drug runner, I told him. Oh, really? Now that was very interesting. How was I holding up in this market? I was holding up fine. How was he doing? Pins and needles. Pins and needles. People were losing their jobs.

Then Danielle and I were in a bathroom stall, bumping blow off our fists. Graffiti and tattered handbills were around us everywhere: *Instant CASH!!!* She turned and hiked up her dress, I unbuckled my jeans, we started having sex in there. The toilet was broken, running and running. I couldn't believe I was doing this. God, it felt horrible. God, it felt good to be free. Then she said, "Stop! Just stop! This is too disgusting." We went out again, drank more. I wasn't even sure if that had just happened. Then we were making out in a cab. Back at her

place, we snorted more lines off her coffee table on our knees.
I said to her, "You always keep so much coke around here?"

"Only when you bring it up to me."

"I've been bringing you coke?"

"God, you're dumb. Yeah, man. You've been bringing me a
little coke every time."

Coke? Fucking coke! How many years could I get for that!

"Who cares, right? Just ask him for more money."

Then I was riding her so hard on the Turkish carpet in her
library that I was frightening myself. I threw her up against a
chair.

"You want to own me?"

"Yeah, yeah."

"What if I owned you?"

I blinked my eyes awake in the morning. Where was I? Then
the wretched night began reeling in.

Danielle was there in a gray dress. I was on the bed, naked.
She glanced back at me through the full-length mirror where
she was slipping on her earrings. Did I want a line to pick me
up? I shook my head. Did I want her to leave the key to the
park before she headed out? I shook my head again.

"See you in a couple weeks?"

"Yeah."

"Drive fast and swerve a lot."

Down in Tallahassee, in Deveny's den, I shouted, "Coke! Are
you fucking insane!"

He laughed. "Give me your connection."

I unzipped the gym bag, whipped the bundles of money
at him one by one. As I stormed out, he called after me in a
happy voice, "Hey, my man, what about my lunch?"

. . .

Around that time, Darren Rudd began calling, just like Billy had warned me he would, texting and calling in the evening almost every day. He wanted to come and see me, inspect my setup, give me his insights on how I was running my loop. He'd had to hop over to Thailand without explaining every last detail of the business to me, he was saying now. And he'd felt really bad about that.

When I'd bother to take his calls, I'd tell him, "I've been doing this for a year, Darren. I've been managing fine without you."

"But you haven't been doing everything right, James."

"Yeah? Like what? Tell me one thing I haven't done right."

"I can't tell you on the phone. I'll tell you when I get there."

"Aren't you happy with the money I've been sending you, man?"

"This isn't about that. This is about doing everything right so you can make even more. For years and years to come. For the rest of your life. Give me your address and I'll just show up and knock on your door."

I could hear the urgency in his voice, knew better than to ask about his real estate and financial problems, reveal that Billy had told me about the trouble he'd had in Thailand. "I'm not giving you my address over the phone, Darren."

"Then mail it to me. So what? Why do you keep putting me off like this?"

"Let me think about it," I'd said the first dozen times he'd called. When he kept hammering away, I finally told him, "I'm going to have to talk to my wife."

You want Darren to come out here? I asked Kate one day when she came home from early Christmas shopping with Cristina and the kids. What did Darren want to come out here for? she asked me as she set her many colorfully wrapped packages on the kitchen counter.

"He says he has things he wants to explain to me about the business."

Kate didn't even look at me as she shook her head. She said, "No way. He wants to meet Eric and cut you out. Tell him I said we have the babies to think about now. Tell him I don't want drug dealers around my kids."

I called Darren back, gladly told him that. He was pissed right away. He said, "What the fuck are you supposed to be then, James?"

"I'm supposed to be Kate's husband."

"Oh yeah? Why don't you ask Kate what would happen if I cut off your flow?"

"What would happen is you'd lose as much money as I would."

"I came back from Thailand especially to see you."

"I didn't ask you to do that."

"Don't you want to know all the things I have to tell you?"

"I got four hundred Gs banked telling me I already know a lot."

Darren started whining. "Come on, James. I'll stay in a hotel. What's the big problem? I've been wanting to visit Florida since the day I got back."

"Great, man. Be my guest. It's a really big state. Go see St. Augustine, drive down to Key West. You're welcome to visit every inch of the place. But the one place you can't come is here."

"After everything I've done for you. How can you even think about doing this to me?"

I didn't say anything at first. Then I decided I wasn't afraid of him. I said in a calm voice, "Do you really have to ask?"

The next time I talked to Billy, he said, "What the fuck did you say to Darren?"

"I told him he can't come here. He says he has all this shit he wants to tell me. I told him I don't want to know it."

"Did you mention anything about Thailand?"

"I wouldn't do that to you."

Billy sniffed. "The dude's riding around in a rage. About you. About Thailand. About the money he's lost and everything. Things are getting fucking gnarly out here."

I was sitting on my patio that day, two weeks before Christmas, looking at my flowering trees and tropical yard. Out on the grass, Kate and Cristina sat on a checkered picnic blanket blowing bubbles with the children. Blowing fucking bubbles. They didn't know anything about what I was dealing with now. They didn't know what had happened in New York or that I felt like slime. As I looked at them, I said to Billy, "You know what? Darren can cut me out if he wants to. I'm not sure I'd even care."

"He would if he could. But now he can't afford it. Still, I'm supposed to talk to Jerome and cut as much away from you as possible."

"Do whatever you have to do." Then I said, "Why did you tell me all that stuff about Darren anyway?"

Billy was quiet. Then: "You know what I'm looking at right now? Big rafts of clouds scudding in over Bodega Bay. The beach, my dogs running on it. It's beautiful. It's a fucking dream. This is all I ever wanted out of this. But it's come with so much more. I don't know why I tell you anything, James. I like you. You're decent. I've enjoyed sitting down with you and talking about our kids. I'd even like to work for someone like you, if someone like you needed someone like me to do work for him one day."

"I'm not going to be in the business much longer, Billy."

"I'd come out there for you if you were," he said. "Take care of yourself, especially if you're going to try to get out. Your

family? Your kids? Put them first. And always, always drive fast
and swerve a lot."

"Same to you, bro."

Just before Christmas, I ran weight up to New York again.
Was I carrying coke? I'd asked Deveny at his house when I'd
dropped off the Cali load, picked up the suitcases. What if I
was? he'd smiled and said. I'd said, "Then I want more fucking
money."

When I reached that building in New York the following
afternoon, Danielle opened her door. "Coming in?" she said.

"I asked the car to wait."

"Yeah, I have some company over anyway."

She took the suitcases inside, came back with a heavy gym
bag. She said, "See you in two weeks?"

"You know you will."

"The Capital Cities Connection, right?"

"That's what we named it."

"Drive fast and swerve a lot?"

"That's what we say."

I took the elevator to the lobby, jogged down the steps to
the waiting car. It was snowing, a winter's day. This time, the
city felt as cold and dead around me as I did inside. What had
Danielle been thinking about it all? Did she feel as disgusted
with herself as I did? Her laser beam had not made my beard
grow back. Of course it hadn't been meant for that.

"Surprised to see you here so soon," Deveny said, wink-
ing, when I walked into his house two mornings later with the
money. We went out to Z. Bardhi's for lunch: zuppa de mare,
filetto di manzo. He was happy, eating with gusto, stabbing the
air with his knife as he rubbed in his victory over me. He said,
"I knew you wouldn't be able to keep your hands off her. That

sick dime? And that's before she opens her mouth. I know you, my man. You've been thinking this whole time you're above all this. That you don't do it for the same reasons as me. But every time I look up, you're sitting across one of these tables, coming back for more. Do you know what that's called, James? It's called greed. Want to know something that will make you happy? I've never touched Danielle. It's always been strictly business between us. So pin your medal on your chest and enjoy yourself up there."

"She told you?"

"She tells me everything. She told me something else. She said there's a dark streak inside of you. She said you broke a couple of her antique chairs—it was an expensive night up there. But I already knew that about you, didn't I?" He winked again. "Hand-to-fucking-hand, right, my man?"

Eric beckoned the waiter for another bottle of wine. "The Briolo?" the waiter asked. "The Barone," Eric said. He cocked his eyebrow at me. "So, how long did you have it planned?"

"I didn't plan it. We started drinking. All of a sudden the lines came out."

He shook his head. "That's it? That's all you have to say about it? No way are you getting off that easy. Because it wasn't just anyone, was it? You could've had a girl up here anytime. But you didn't want a girl up here. Remember that? You? Danielle was good enough for you. You started talking to her and she told you all the things she's done. She told you all about her front and her big plans. Then she started to talk about your place in it, and you began to think about it. You couldn't help yourself. Because you're like me. Nothing will ever be enough for you. Isn't that right, James?"

I didn't say anything.

"Keep lying to yourself. If you're sitting here with me, you're like me. You know something else? You've always been exactly who you are. Even before you got born in my house. You couldn't have got born in my house if you hadn't already been conceived. Too late — now you've got to keep it from your wife. But you're used to keeping things from your wife, aren't you?" He smiled, shook his head, sat back from the table. "I'm proud of you. Danielle? Mad tight, right? Complete package? Not cheap sex at all. Nothing base for my man. That's how I knew it had to be her. For once in my life, I envy you. Did you think you'd come so far so fast?"

"I don't know what I thought."

"Did you think you'd do as well as you have?"

"I've only ever thought about the work."

"Just a simple mule?"

"If that's what you want to call it."

"That's what I have to call it, James. That's what it's called."

He said, "You remember the night we met? That party? How you came out of nowhere? Blasted that kid off his ass? Blew my mind away with the possibilities? A California source fallen right in my fucking lap? Do you remember what I said to you out there that night?"

"'What kind of sign are we standing under?'"

"That's right. And here we are again. Do you have any idea how many rules I broke for you? You could have been anybody. You could have been coming to put pain on me. But I had to take that chance. And then there you were, waiting like any of us to put your hands on the money."

"Money, money, money."

"That's where we're at. Don't you know we're going to do so much work together? Don't you know we're going to know each other for a long time? Anyway, enjoy yourself up there. You deserve it. I'm bumping up your weight after New Year's."

It was then that a woman came to our table, tall, blond, attractive, in a sheer black dress. Eric had cocked his chin to

point her out to me when we'd been seated. She'd been dining alone, drinking wine alone, had started glancing at him
from across the room as soon as we sat down. Her glances had
grown more insistent after every glass she polished off. She
stumbled once in her heels as she made her way over to us,
laughed it away, steadied herself with her fingers on the edge
of our table. French manicure. I looked up: delicate curves,
silky hair. There was no one else in the dining room but the
three of us. "I hope this doesn't embarrass you," she said, "but
weren't you in some kind of movie?"

She was talking to him, of course. Eric shot me a look like he
couldn't believe it, when we both knew he could. "Superstar,"
I whispered, sitting back from the table to give them room to
work. She tousled the ends of her hair in case he hadn't already
figured it out. "I was supposed to meet somebody here," she
said and shrugged. "Apparently somebody wasn't aware of
that."

Eric looked her up and down. He said, "Then somebody's
out of his fucking mind. I'd invite you to join us, but I'm stuck
in a business thing with my man right here."

"Hi," she said without looking at me. Then she said, "I'm
here for business myself. They upgraded me at the Governors.
I have the Jacuzzi suite. Looks like it's going to go to waste
before I have to leave town forever."

"Leave town forever?"

"I'm only here for the day."

Eric pulled out a cell, took her number.

"So what was that movie?" she said.

He grinned. "I'll tell you about it later."

After she left, Eric and I looked at each other. He said, "I
love spending time with you, my man. Nice things always fall
in my lap whenever I do." He stood to leave. "Had enough yet,
James? Want to give me your connection?"

Could I give it to him? Would he let me go if I did?

I shook my head. "No."

"See you in two weeks. Kiss your pretty wife for me."

Deveny was right about one thing at that lunch: my wife in fact was pretty. But what about the other things he'd said?

Out there on the road, going home from New York the day after what I'd done with Danielle, as I ground out the miles, I imagined I'd be able to find a way to make it feel like the night hadn't really happened. But as the miles went on and on, the only thing I knew was that it really had happened. Had I enjoyed it? Had it felt good? I thought of Danielle's naked body—yeah, I'd enjoyed it; yes, it had felt good. But wasn't it also the worst thing I'd ever done? Far, far beyond anything else? Yes, it was also that.

And was this how people felt after they'd done something like that? I'd asked myself on the road. Yeah, this was how they felt. And was this also how they had to continue with their lives afterward? Yes, this was how they had to do that, too. Find a place deep inside to bury it, always keep it there. Did I have a hole in me deep enough? There was no choice any longer; there would have to be.

Had Kate been suspicious of me when I'd come home the following day? Kate hadn't suspected a thing. She'd been trying on clothes in our bedroom when I'd walked in, had wanted to know how I thought she looked in them. My daughter had run to me, grabbed my leg; my son had been cooing in his mittens on a blanket on the bed. For once in our lives, there we'd all been, my family together in the room.

"Notice anything different about me, James?" my wife had asked as she'd twirled for me in her outfit. It had been a pair of denims and a powder-blue blouse. Didn't she always wear things like that?

I'd said, "Your hair's longer. Or else you've had it trimmed."

She'd shaken her head, disappointed by me again. "I'm back to my normal weight. I've been working really hard at it. That's okay, I shouldn't have asked. I know what you're like when you've just walked in from work."

Wait! something in me had wanted to cry out to her. But she'd already turned away. "Everything going okay out there?"

"Everything's fine."

We'd been quiet then, Kate taking off her new outfit in the room with the children, me in the walk-in closet alone, stripping off my driving clothes, tossing them into the hamper. "What are we doing for New Year's, James?" Kate had called in to me. "I can party this year, you know? Cristina's already made plans with one of those beach volleyball guys she's been kicking it with. I talked to your mom. She said she'd watch the kids for us."

In the closet, I'd had the gym bag with me, in it the money I'd earned driving, and having drugs driven, around the country. The dirty clothes I'd been wearing when I'd cheated on my wife two nights before were in there, too. I'd crouched, listened for Kate, then lifted out those clothes and smelled them. They'd smelled like smoke and beer, made me feel like an asshole all over again. I'd buried them in the bottom of the hamper like the evidence against me that they were. In my motel room in Savannah the night before, I'd showered and showered: it hadn't done anything to make me feel clean. I hadn't gotten any sleep in that room either, beating myself up in my mind for the awful thing I'd done.

Then I'd called out to Kate, "What are people doing for New Year's this year? Are they even going to celebrate? If the Ritz is doing something, we can do that. Or we can go out on one of those boats out of St. Pete. What about your friends, Kate? Don't you want to do something with them?" Then I'd looked up. Kate had been standing before me, her long legs bare, her hair over her shoulders, hiding her breasts with her folded arms. How long had she been standing there? Had she seen me hiding those clothes? Then she'd closed the door behind her against the children.

"Hey," she'd said to me in her quiet voice.

I'd stood up. I'd been naked, too. "Hey."

"My name is Kate. It's nice to meet you."

Had I been willing to go along with it? I had. "My name is James."

"Maybe we could get together sometime. What do you think about that? Maybe spend the rest of our lives together."

"I think I'd like that."

"Maybe we could have a couple of kids."

"I think I'd like that, too."

"Just two, though, okay? I've heard they're a lot of work."

"I've heard that about kids, too."

"They say it can be good if both the mother and father are there. But I wouldn't know, you know? My parents are drunks."

"Yeah, my dad was a workaholic."

"I'd want to do it differently."

"I would, too."

We'd looked at each other then, my wife and I. The moment had come upon us at last. Kate had said, "I've been missing you."

"I've been missing you, too."

"There's something I want you to do now."

"What's that?"

"I want you to make it stop."

In bed that night, I'd said to Kate, "Have you thought about where you'll take the kids?"

Kate had said, "I haven't wanted to think about it. I guess I've always had the idea we'd stay right here with you."

"You can't stay here. You have to take the kids and go. You can't even stop to look back for me. You have to trust I'll follow you."

"I've thought about the cabin, but we can't go there, can we? And I know we can't go back to Austin. Where can we go where we can be safe? Where can I take the kids where you'll know how to find us?"

"We'll have to go someplace we both love. We may have to stay there for a long time."

"There's one place I've been thinking of, James. It's a place I think both of us loved, a place where we were in love. Do you remember the place I'm talking about?"

"It's in Europe."

"Yes, in Europe."

"Near the mountains by that beautiful lake."

"Do you remember the name of the little hotel?"

"Bellagio something, wasn't it?"

"Do you think you could find it again?"

"Of course."

"We have to get Evan a passport."

"We'll do the express application tomorrow."

"I'll get an international driver's license this time, too."

I'd smiled at her in the dark and said, "Yeah, you will. The only thing I know for certain is once we get there, I'm not doing any driving."

For New Year's 2009, we stayed home with our kids. It was what we both wanted.

6

Mule to the Slaughter

THE END CAME LIKE this: On Wednesday, January 14, 2009, the Interagency Narcotics Task Force in Siskiyou County pulled the trigger on its five-and-a-half-month investigation. One hundred heavily armed law enforcement officers, deployed in tactical teams across the rugged, sprawling mountain county, stormed their targets at first light.

It went down just like it does in the movies. They busted in the doors of trailers, apartments, houses, places of business. They surprised people sleeping in their beds, sitting on their toilets, showering, getting their kids dressed for school, jogging, smoking weed, weighing weed, getting money together to buy weed, putting weed in plastic bags for sale. They pulled over people as they drove to work, nailed people at their workplaces. They had dogs, percussion grenades. They had assault weapons and Tasers. They were coordinated from a central location by radio and cell phone; they used laptop computers and GPS. They'd done mock runs of the takedown for weeks at their secret practice locations. When the moment had finally come, they were amped up and ready. Their work was the same to them as ours was to us: Exciting. Deliberate. Methodical. Dangerous.

When the smoke began to clear on the operation at midday, the teams had searched dozens of properties, including the two high schools. They'd found heavy weights of ecstasy, hashish, and psilocybin, all packaged and ready for distribution. They'd also scored twenty-eight pounds of kush: people's orders brought aboveground for shipment. They'd confiscated guns, money, phones, computers, properties, vehicles, animals, and children. They'd made thirty-three arrests, including that fifty-three-year-old Mount Shasta city councilman, who had arranged to sell a pound of kush to the undercover agent. They had him on wiretaps and a video. Even better for them, they'd found two guns at his place and a sawed-off shotgun with the safety removed behind the door of another dealer's home. Most of the weed belonged to Darren's organization. Some of it had been intended for the Capital Cities Connection.

The story and its details would run on the front page of papers up and down California the following day, including the *Los Angeles Times*, where I'd eventually read it online. But that's not how I first found out about it. I found out about it because I received a phone call while it was going down. Neither the caller nor I had any idea yet of what was really happening up there.

What was that morning like for me? It was one like any other. I did some pushups in the bedroom, ate breakfast standing up in the kitchen, oatmeal and blueberries, simple food for my nervous stomach. Cristina and Kate were out at the mall with the kids. It was a cool day for Sarasota, down in the fifties. The sky outside was a flat, gray slate.

I took a shower, dressed, watched television—the Weather

Channel for a change. Jerome would be leaving Sacramento two days later, Emma would be coming into Tallahassee on Monday, I'd be heading up to New York the day after that. Snow was a problem for us at this time of year; I wanted to know what I could expect out there. I was tired, nodded off a few times on the couch. I hadn't been sleeping well because of Evan's nighttime feedings. After fighting it off for half an hour, I let myself roll away into the darkened womb of sleep.

On the glass coffee table were the disposable phones I was currently using: one for Deveny, one for Billy and Darren, three more for everyone else. The one I used for Billy began to vibrate on the glass, made a sound like coins shaken in a can, startled me awake. I checked the time before I answered it, to see how long I'd been down. Kate wanted me to meet them for lunch at noon, and fear shot through me that I'd overslept. I'd been trying to be extremely nice to her, to make up for the things I'd done that she didn't even know I had. But the phone said that it was only eleven A.M. Why would Billy be calling from Cali this early?

"Yo, Billy," I said into the phone.

"Billy's going down." It was Darren Rudd.

I sat up slowly in the middle of that shrinking room. I thought I'd be prepared for a call like this, realized now I still wasn't ready. How could I be? How could anyone? "What do you mean, Billy's going down?"

"He got stopped a few minutes ago on the I-5 near Dunsmuir. He texted. He was dirty. There were a couple units behind him, coming out with a K-9 right away. He hasn't texted since."

Running the K-9 right away? I said, "Were they tipped?"

"Of course they were tipped."

"Who would've done that?"

"You think if we knew, they would've had the chance? For all I know, it was you. He was coming down with your shit anyway."

"You think I would've done something like that?"

"Why not, James? It's not like we really know you. The way you've been acting? The attitude you've had with me? How am I supposed to know what's been going on out there with you?"

"Nothing's been going on out here. It wasn't anyone on my end."

"It better not have been. You know I'll find out if it was."

I shook the threat away with my head. "What's going to happen now?"

"Besides losing one of my best fucking guys? Nothing's going to happen. We've shut it down. Isolated it. We'll pick him up, set him up with counsel. It will drag on for a year or two and then he'll be all right. But he's going to have to find other work. Don't worry about Billy. He's retired now and that's it. Get your people up on new lines. You have a McKinleyville address you were working with? Overnight me a number there. Put it in a couple of envelopes, sign across the seals a few times."

"That's it?"

"That's it. Stay calm. Stay professional. Get back to work. You'll get everything you need on time. This line is dead. I'll be waiting for that number." Then Darren hung up.

Maybe if Darren had had any idea what was really happening in Siskiyou County at that moment, he would have done things differently. Head for the airport without calling me or anyone else, carrying as many hundred-dollar bills strapped to his body as he could, enough money to start a new life somewhere, a life he would have to live quietly forever. Open a sleepy beachfront bar on the coast of Nicaragua, a hole-in-the-wall flophouse for backpackers way out in Mozambique. By early afternoon California time, they'd already be up on him, beginning to freeze his remaining assets, starting what would become a RICO investigation, later evolving into a Continuing Criminal Enterprise or "Kingpin Statute" case with the possibility of capital punishment. People were already flipping on him. In the backs of squad cars, in the interrogation rooms of jails even before they'd been processed. Everybody had been caught dirty for a change. And nobody wanted to go to prison, especially when someone else could.

All I knew was that I had to get that load to Deveny. That though I had to get out of the business now, I hadn't figured out exactly how to do it. Not in a way that wouldn't endanger my family. Not in a way that would let me feel certain I'd go on living among them. I had to send a new number to Darren so he could get the load to Jerome. I had to play the game the way I'd been playing it so that no one could make a move on me before I could make a move on them.

As I sat at the coffee table and looked at those silent cell phones, I began to think about all these other things. That maybe the cops were coming for me now. That maybe Billy would give me up and that they were about to knock on the door. I mean, I knew Billy wouldn't give me up. But still there was the thought of it. That a fuse was being lit out there that would race across the country and reach me here. Why had I done what I'd been doing? Why had I done it over and over?

I sent out texts to Jerome, Emma, Nick, all of them: "dump the phones." Texts began to come back right away: "whats wrong?" "everything cool?" "f ing hassle."

Then I did the other things I had to do. I gathered up my TracFones, smashed them under my heel in the kitchen, put the jumbled pieces in two plastic bags, drove across the bridge to the McDonald's on the Trail, threw one bag in a garbage can in the lot there, threw the other one away down the street at the Taco Bell. Nobody saw me do it.

I drove to Wal-Mart, bought half a dozen new phones, charged them up in the lot with the cards, then drove to the post office. I wrote the phone numbers on slips of paper, stuffed them in the security envelopes I'd brought with me, wrote "Don't Open This, Pig" across the sealed flaps. I stuffed those envelopes inside Express Mail envelopes, sealed those, and sent them overnight to all those people under fake return addresses, half a dozen of which I'd long since learned by heart. Then I drove to the 8th Street house, handed a phone to Nick.

"Anything wrong?"

"No."

"Want to hang out?"

"Way too busy."

I went and met my wife and kids at Patrick's on Main Street, where they were running a "Great Recession" lunch special. That's what they were calling it now. Now it had a name. Cristina and my mother were there, too. Could any of them see what was happening on my face? I knew they could not. I sat between my son in his car seat and my daughter in her highchair, ordered a cheeseburger, because you still had to eat, tried to have as fine a time with them as I could.

My mother gave me a look and said, "Shouldn't you be working on the boats?"

"Too cold."

"Don't they heat the warehouse?"

God, my mom. "They don't want to spend the money right now."

"How is Stewart and his new wife?"

Stewart was a friend at work whom I'd made up and mentioned to her once. She'd never forgotten it. "Stewart and his wife are fine."

"Did they enjoy their honeymoon?"

"They had a wonderful time."

Did I want to take the kids to the Mote Aquarium with all of them? they asked. I told them I couldn't—errands. "He's like his father," my mother said, tossing her napkin on her plate.

As we left, I slipped a new phone into Kate's pocket, told her the number I'd already texted to it was one of mine, asked her to give it to my mother and Cristina, too. Kate sensed something was wrong. She grabbed my elbow at the door, said quietly so no one else could hear, "Is everything going okay out there?"

I told her, "Everything's going just fine." Then I stopped, shook my head. "Do you really want to know?"

"Of course I do. I always have."

"Billy got busted a couple hours ago."

"How do you know that?"

"Darren called."

"Did they catch him with anything?"

I nodded.

"Is he going to turn us in?"

What could I say? I said, "My guess is no. But I don't really know."

"What are we supposed to do?"

"There isn't anything we can do."

"Should we get away with the kids?"

"We can't come back if we do."

Kate was quiet as we loaded the kids in the car, that beautiful Subaru we'd bought with our drug money. The backseat was packed with children, their toys, their mess. "This is not going to turn into a grimy kiddie wagon," Kate had told me the day she'd sped us away from the dealership in it. Of course it long since had.

My mother drove by in her Sentra with Cristina. They waved at us; they'd be waiting at the aquarium to help Kate get the kids out of the car. There, my daughter would run around and look at the fish while the adults took turns pushing Evan in his stroller, talking about things the way normal people did, as though the lives we lived were normal ones.

But our lives weren't normal ones. "I want to stay with you," Kate pleaded with me outside the car. "I don't want us to be separated."

"You have to go on like usual."

"How am I supposed to act like nothing's happening?"

"You pretend. You've done it before. You're good at it. This is what we have to do. This is how we pay for it."

"I feel sick."

"I do, too."

"I wish we hadn't done it."

"I'm sorry if I made you."

"I'm sorry if I made you feel like you had to."

"I'm sorry about all of it, Kate."

Just before she pulled away, I tapped on her window. Kate powered it down. "Be nice to my mother."

"I always am."

"We may never see her again."

Kate looked at me a long time. Then she began to cry.

"Put on your sunglasses."

"You know I will."

"Don't let the kids see you crying."

"You know I won't."

Did I sleep that night? How could I? I paced the living room, fed Evan when he cried, consoled Romana on my shoulder when she called from her crib for me. How gentle children seem when they're that small. But then they grow up to be all these people. People just like we were.

In the kitchen, I started to salve my worry with vodka but poured the glass down the sink. There was no one I could call, no way to get more information. When I went out on the patio to smoke, the world around me was calm. It seemed like an average night, *was* an average night for most of the billions of people in the world. But it wasn't an average night for me; my nights hadn't been average for a long time. Would there be any way out of it now? What would that way be? Had we exchanged selfishness for the balance of whatever had been good in our lives? The love Kate and I had for each other? Our children as expressions of that love in the world? Had we really needed to risk losing everything to realize all we'd had from the start? What could we salvage out of it, if we were given the chance?

For example, would we be willing to give up the money if we could get out of this for free? I asked myself as I looked at the night. The stars glittered above me, and the answer that came to me was: I still wanted the money. I was a coward. I was too afraid to live life without the money.

When I finally went in and lay beside Kate, I whispered, "Are you sleeping?"

"No."

"But are you trying to sleep?"

"I've got this nightmare running through my mind."

I had to tell her about what had happened in New York. I said, "I've got all that same stuff running through my head, too. I hope there'll be a day when we don't have to think about it."

Kate said, "Will there ever be a day like that? We're always going to have to think about it. Maybe it won't feel like it does right now. But the things we've done can't just be put away."

"Putting the children at risk, right?"

"That's it. And being as greedy as we've been. There were other things we could have done. But we didn't even try. When we look back, we're going to say, Why didn't we just deal with the hard times like everyone else had to? We're going to have to hear them talk about how they struggled through. Then we're going to feel ashamed."

"Kate? What if I had something to tell you? What if I told you about all the bad things I've done out there?"

Kate turned and looked at me in the dark. I could feel the caution that came into her. She said, "What are all the bad things you've done out there?"

"I've done things I'm always going to have to live with. I've done things I'm always going to regret."

Kate thought about that. She said, "I know you'd never hurt anyone. I know you're not like that."

"I have something to tell you."

She sat up in bed.

I said, "I don't know what I'm going to tell you."

"Did you hurt someone?"

"Yeah, I hurt someone."

"Who did you hurt?"

I didn't say anything.

"What did you do? You're frightening me."

"Kate, there's only one person I could ever truly hurt."

She didn't say anything. Then she said, "Me?"

"Yeah."

"You hurt me?"

"Yeah. I hurt you."

She was shaking her head. "But I asked you. You said you'd never do that. I asked you never to lie to me, and you said you wouldn't."

I was quiet for the longest time.

She said, "Did you lie to me?"

Time and time and time and time. Breathing and not wanting to say it. So long a time that I knew she knew the answer was yes. Then I told her about all the runs to New York that she hadn't known about, that a person had been waiting at the end of those runs for me.

"Who was that person?" Kate said in a quiet voice.

"It was a woman."

She was quiet, thinking. Then she said, "It was the night you didn't call."

"It was that night."

"What did you do?"

"I cheated on you."

"You cheated on me?"

"Yeah."

The passage of time. Time and time and time.

"You cheated on me with that person?"

"Yeah."

The passage of time.

"Why did you cheat on me with that person?"

"I don't know why."

Now it was Kate's turn to control the passage of time. To make me wait. To make me know that there had been a consequence. Finally she said, "You don't love me, do you?"

"Yes, I do."

"But you did that."

"Yes."

"Because you didn't love me at that time?"

"I don't know why."

"Why didn't you love me at that time?"

"I don't know."

"Yes, you do know. Tell me why."

"Because."

"Because why?"

"Because you let me do the drives."

Silence. Time. The birth of a chasm.

"Because I let you do what you wanted to do?"

"Because you let me take those risks."

"Because I let you do what you wanted to do."

"Because you didn't make me stop."

A sundering. A mitosis. The division of a continent.

"This isn't my fault."

"I know that."

"I've never felt as awful as I do right now."

"I've been sorry every moment since."

We lay there a long time. Time did not make it better.

Finally Kate said, "Maybe we rushed into this. Maybe we didn't really know each other. And now we have these kids. How could we have done this to them? My heart is broken. Completely, completely broken. One of us has to leave. One of us has to leave right now."

"I'm the one who will leave."

"I don't know that I'll ever want you to come back."

"I'll do whatever you say."

I dressed in my driving clothes in the dark. I looked at my sleeping children, kissed them, touched them as though for the very last time. I took three bundles of money from the tea-pot on the stove, gathered my car keys, my wallet, my phones. Then I left the house.

I drove across town and checked into the Ritz, because a motel would have depressed me more than I already was. I hadn't dared go to the 8th Street house because that would have been even worse: the pictures on the walls there of when we'd been happy. Kate and I in Austin. Kate and I in the cabin with our new baby. Those people we'd once been who would condemn me now. Still, that plush room at the Ritz might as well have been a cell. What was Kate going through? I texted her where I was staying. She did not text back.

Should I have told her what I had done? I did not know. Had it made me feel any better about myself? It had not.

How could I have done this?

Should I wait to call her? Hadn't I hurt her enough already?

I snatched up the phone, called. It went directly to her voice mail. What could I say but, "I'm sorry. I'm so sorry. I'll do anything. I love you." And it went to her voice mail the dozens of times I called after that.

I chain-smoked on the balcony. When dawn broke over the city at last, I called room service for oatmeal, put a cigarette out in it when it finally came. Would the TracFones ever start ringing? At eleven A.M., the first one did: Eric Deveny.

"Got your new line, my man. Prudent, prudent. Still seeing you on Tuesday?"

"On time as always."

"Then you're going up to see your girlfriend?"

"Yeah."

"You ever hit that shit again?"

"You know I haven't."

"Yeah, that's what I think I heard about it. Anyway, once is better than never, right?"

"That's right."

In the afternoon, the second one rang: Darren Rudd.

"Did you read the news?"

"What news?"

"Front page of the *L.A. Times*. Half of Siskiyou County taken down."

"Are you kidding?"

"When they took down Billy, they were taking down three dozen other people, too. They have my name on their list."

"What are you talking about?"

"Got a computer? Google 'City Councilman Arrested in Mount Shasta.'"

"What would it say if I did?"

"It would say that I'm in a lot of trouble."

"What kind of trouble?"

"RICO. Do you know what that is? Or else CCE. You don't know what that is either, do you?"

"I know RICO. I don't know CCE. Letters aren't good, Darren."

"These ones are the worst of all. They mean I'm going to have to lie low. Real fucking low. It means I'm going to have to get my hands on a new identity."

"You going to leave the country?"

"They've locked me in."

"Am I going to get my load on time?"

"You have to. Now I need the money like you wouldn't fucking believe."

I set him up with Jerome's number, called Jerome, told him someone besides Billy would be making the switch with him this time.

"What happened to Billy?"

"Billy's on vacation."

"On vacation to where?"

"Timbuktu. How the fuck am I supposed to know? You think I give a shit about where anyone goes on vacation?"

"Man, chill out. However it has to get done, I'll do it."

"Drive fast and swerve a lot."

As I sat in that room that interminable weekend, the only thing I knew for certain was that the load coming from Cali would be the last. The last no matter how it turned out. Even if Darren Rudd could somehow get me more, I was done. I wasn't going to do it anymore. I killed those desolate days by smoking, staring at the TV, missing my family, thinking about my life. Every time I thought about Kate, my heart broke all over again. This is what my acts had led to, a destruction of everything important to me. I felt as empty and alone in that room as though I were locked up already. A quiet came into me, an acceptance. Was this how people felt when they were finally tossed into prison?

I read about the Siskiyou County bust in the hotel's business center, about the city councilman and the charges he faced, the reactions of the people around him who hadn't known. Who hadn't had any idea. They were shocked, amazed, all the things you'd expect. The message boards after the articles were filled with comments from stoners about the injustice of the marijuana laws when alcohol and tobacco killed so many people. The simple fucking stoners didn't know.

Monday came and I was on the road. When I pulled off the interstate in Tallahassee that evening, Emma was waiting by her rental, a white Mustang, in the lot of the Motel 6. She passed me a keycard, told me the load was in the room.

"Where's JoJo Bear?" I asked her. The evening was cool and quiet, no one else around.

Emma didn't say anything. Suddenly I knew something was wrong.

"JoJo's in the room, James. JoJo's in the room with the guy in there."

"There's a guy in there?"

"He came with Jerome. He put a gun on me. He took away my phones. He put his gun on Mason in Dallas. He pointed his gun at Bayleigh. He told Mason he'd kill me if he called you. There was nothing we could do. What does he want? Who is he?"

I looked at the door of the room. I knew right away. I told her, "He's somebody who's in a lot of trouble."

"What kind of trouble?"

"You know what kind of trouble."

Emma thought about it. She said, "What's he doing here?"

"I'm not sure."

"I couldn't stop him. There was nothing I could do. Once he pointed the gun at Bayleigh, I didn't even think about trying. It was the worst two days of my life."

"I'm sorry."

Emma said, "Are you going in that room?"

"I have to go in that room."

"I don't think you should."

I looked at the door of the room. The room I would have to go into now. I knew that if I didn't, things would only get worse. The person in there knew too much about me.

"It's all over," I said. "You know that, right?"

"It ended for me when he got in my car."

We looked across the lot at the door. The door someone was waiting behind for me. Emma said, "Remember when I saved your ass in San Angelo? I never told Mason about that. I'd never seen anyone as shattered as you. If I hadn't come out and got you, you'd be in prison."

"I know."

"Can't there be a way out of this?"

"I don't know."

"What am I supposed to do?"

I looked at her. She wouldn't be standing here if it wasn't for me. I said, "You're supposed to get in your car and leave."

"Leave you behind?"

"Yeah. And go home. This is something I have to deal with for fucking around in all of this."

"You'd better have a plan, James," Emma said. She looked around the darkening lot. She hugged me. "Be careful." Then she hopped in her car and was gone.

Was it time to text Kate "Emergency"? Would I ever see her again if I did? When I opened the door of the room to get my answer, I said to the man in it, "Hi, Darren."

"Hi, James."

Darren Rudd was sitting on the edge of the bed in his calf-skin jacket, looking at a basketball game on the TV. He seemed calm, maybe bored, his yellow hair shaved close to his head like a pelt. The black duffel bags were beside him. Seated on top of one of the bags was JoJo Bear.

"I caught a lift with your people," Darren told me as I closed the door on us. "Figured it was finally time to come and see Florida, visit your operation. You'd better keep your eye on that Sacramento guy. All he wanted to talk about was how to cut you out. The girl is much better. I'd hire her myself."

"Where's Billy?"

Darren looked at the game with his angular face. He said, "Billy made bail on Friday. Then he disappeared like he had to."

"Where'd he go?"

"He has a cabin in the woods. Way back of beyond. He kept it stocked with provisions in case of something like this. Billy can stay up there till infinity if he wants to. We may not ever hear from him again."

I knew right then, Billy was dead. I said, "Why'd he have to disappear? Because he could take you down?"

"He's one of them. But you're one of them, too."

"And the rest?"

"None of them have anything on me like Billy did. Nothing even close. As long as Billy stays away, maybe I'll go back and face it. Even if they manage to make a couple things stick, without him, they can't CCE."

"The Kingpin Statute."

"You read up on it?"

"Death penalty for the top guys if they pin bodies on the organization."

Darren looked at me. "But they don't have any bodies to pin on it, do they?"

I sat down in a chair, stared at the game with him. Who was playing? Lakers and Bulls. Billy was dead. Darren had killed him. Or had him killed. A profound coldness settled into me. I glanced at Darren. I could see he was thinner than when I'd known him up in Siskiyou, tired-looking. Was it fatigue from the long crossing? Or was it because of everything else? I was surprised at how familiar he looked, as though no time had passed at all. But there was something more to it: as he sat there in those lean lines of his, he looked like an animal, a leopard, one of the great predator cats.

"What happens now, Darren?"

"All that money I let you make? It's time you paid me back. You're going to help me keep my head down. Put me somewhere safe, put me in touch with your guy. Then we'll all be back in business before anyone's even noticed."

"You don't have anywhere else to go, do you?"

"I have a million other places to go."

"How do you know I won't just leave you in this room?"

"You know you're in too deep for that."

"You're in a lot of fucking trouble, Darren."

"You're going to help me get out of it."

"Why did you have to bring your trouble to me?"

"You're the only one whose name they don't have on their list."

I had my answer. It was time to text Kate "Emergency." Would she do it? Get on a plane with the kids and go? Everything just like we'd planned? Or had everything changed for her now? Darren showed me he was wearing his gun, let his jacket fall back over it. "Give me your phones."

"Come on, Darren."

"Give me your phones."

I pulled out my phones, tossed them to him, sat back in my chair, looked at the game. Then I thought of something. Could he use a beer? I asked him, because I sure knew I could. Yeah, that was what the doctor ordered, he said, just give him my car keys and he'd run out and get some.

"Let me do it," I said. "You've got to be tired from the trip."

"I'm not that fucking tired."

"What if I take off while you're gone?"

He didn't bother to look at me. "I make a phone call. I'll tell them your name, everything about you. I'll make shit up. I'm your responsibility now as long as I'm out here."

While I waited for him to come back, I kept looking over at the landline phone on the nightstand. It felt like the thing was mocking me: I had no idea what Kate's cell phone number was. Fifteen minutes later, Darren and I were sitting across the room from each other, drinking bottles of Pabst. He was talking about the bust, about how so many other people had done so many things wrong. But had he done anything wrong? I asked him at last. Maybe he'd worked with too many people in the end, he told me. But how else was he supposed to make any money?

"It was that goddamn city councilman," Darren explained. "When they figured him out, they went huge on it—they love getting politicians. You can't play both sides of the game. If you want to be straight, be straight. But don't deal out the back door of your house and still want to be on the fucking city council."

"You don't think lots of people do that?"

"They're smarter about it. They keep their operations at a remove. They don't set up a deal with a high school kid. And they don't keep the shit in their own goddamn house and have all their different businesses under the same fucking name."

Darren began to relax, get friendly. Had Kate and I figured out how we were going to clean up our money? he asked me. I told him we hadn't thought about it yet. We should open a hair salon, he said. Get a small-business loan, make the government chip in the seed money. Then we could say the place was hopping even when it wasn't. The only trick would be to find someone to babysit it who could both stand the boredom and also chop hair. Sooner or later some joker always walked in who really did want a fucking haircut.

"Now, what you and I are going to do," Darren told me, "is you're going to put me in touch with this big fish of yours. Then he and I are going to work something out. I have to keep my head down, stay behind the action. You are going to be my main guy now. You're going to have to set up a safe house for me, or else I'm going to bunk with your fucking kids."

When the morning seeped in around the edges of the curtains, I was under my jacket on the floor, where I'd passed out sometime during the night. I rubbed my eyes, sat up, looked around. Was it still happening? Yeah, it still was happening. Darren Rudd was there in his leather jacket, lying awake on the bed. He was watching an episode of *Cops*.

"You watch this shit?" I said.

He said, "I like the takedowns."

I had to hustle across town and make the drop, I told him, had to run some stuff up to New York for a couple days after that. Because I was working all over the place now. Because that was what my big fish had decided to make me do. When that was done, I would come back and take care of him, figure out where to hide him. But for right now he would have to stay in this room.

"That's not how it's going to work," Darren said, glaring at me. "How it's going to work is, you're going to take me with you and introduce me to all your people."

I shook my head. "These people are heavy, Darren. If I show up at the drop with you in the car, they're not going to open the door. And at that point, we wouldn't want them to. Because at that point, we'd both be dead."

Darren rubbed his head. "I didn't think you'd be working with people like that."

"Why not? I've been working with you, haven't I?"

"You're not leaving this room without me."

"You're not coming with me."

Darren drew his gun, pointed it at me. I knew if he pulled the trigger, he wouldn't miss. Then he'd drive away in my car. "You want to shoot me, Darren? Go ahead. That won't get you out of this room. I'm not going to abandon you. I'll be back in a couple of days. You're going to have to sit here until I'm finished with my run."

He held the gun on me, a black little snub-nosed sidearm. He said, "I'll pin so much shit on you. I'll say you were there for everything."

"You're not going to have to."

"I'll tell them to look at your credit card, give them the dates. Fucking bush league. You never stopped using it, did you?"

I told him, "You have to be patient while I'm gone. You can't freak out or anything. It's going to take me a day and a half to get up there. Then a day and a half to get back. I'll check in on the phone, let you know where I'm at. I'll be back before you know it and then I'll figure out how to put you in touch with my guy."

Darren looked at me a long time. His whole world was fucked and he knew it. Would he really take me down if he went down? I had no doubt about that. He clenched his teeth so his jaw muscles flexed. He said, "If you don't come back, I make that call."

"I understand."

"You won't see your kids again."

"I know how it works."

He holstered his gun, began tossing me my phones.

How much money did he have on him? I asked. Fifty-six thousand dollars, he told me, most of it was the cash I'd sent out for the run. Any other money anywhere he could get his hands on? Everything else was frozen. Did he want to hole up somewhere better than this? Yeah, someplace with a pool would be nice. Then he added, "You know, you're a documented accomplice as soon as you book me in, right?"

I loaded the duffel bags into the back of the old Forester, then waved to Darren to come to the car. If I thought he'd run across the lot with his head down, he didn't. He walked with confidence, looked around at the day with his chin stuck out like he was daring them to take him down. On the way to the Marriott, I stopped for gas. Did he want something to eat from inside? Only if it was vegetarian. Would a couple bananas do the trick? Bananas would be fine, even if they weren't organic.

"How was everything over at your farm?" I asked when we were on the road again. He looked at the city, the passing cars, told me, "Everything in Thailand is always fine. Nicest people in the world." A few moments later, he added, "You're lucky with Kate, you know that, right?"

I booked him in at the Marriott under my own name, settled him into the room. He should go down in the mornings for the buffet, I told him, swim if they could scare him up a suit. Otherwise he should stay put, order room service. Then I asked him for JoJo Bear.

"This thing?" Darren said and squeezed the bear's belly.

JoJo Bear said, as if pleading for help, "I love you."

Darren said, "I'll hang on to it. It's gotten me this far, hasn't it?"

In the elevator, on the way down to the car, I took out the phone with Kate's number on it. What should I do? Text her "Emergency" right now? Or should I drive home first, beg her on my knees to let us leave the country together? I thought about it all the way to Eric Deveny's.

When I pulled up to his house, I texted Eric that I was there, took a deep breath, and carried the duffel bags in through the unlocked side door. The kitchen was clean and quiet. The den was like that, too. If the assault rifle was in there anywhere, I couldn't see it. I stood around a minute; the place remained silent. Then Eric came down the steps in his white boxer shorts. His hair was messy. He was yawning, his face bloated from sleep. I'd never been there this early. I'd never caught him like this.

"Got my weight?"

"Right here."

"Heading up to NYC?"

"Right now."

He unzipped the duffel bags, sorted through the kush as though it was any other weed and any other day I'd made a drop there. But these were the last pounds that would ever come to him from California, and this was the last day I would ever bring weight to him. I also wasn't going to New York. Eric didn't know that. If he had, I would have already lost my value. Where would I dump his shit on my way home? My heart was pounding as hard as the first day I'd been there as he picked out the bags he thought would be going up on the run, put them in the open suitcases on the floor that were already full of pounds of haze, smaller packages wound with brown tape that I knew were cocaine.

"Going back to bed, my man. Crazy fucking night, you know? I'll be waiting for my lunch when you get back. You'll get your money then."

He was halfway up the stairs.

"Eric."

He stopped, turned around.

"I'm not going to New York."

"What did you say?"

"I'm not going to New York. I'm giving you these pounds for free. I'll never say a word about you to anyone. I'll give you the connection as soon as I know my family is safe. Then I want you to let me go."

His face did all these things. Hard things with his eyes. Grinding things with his mouth. It was like a mask was coming off. What was underneath it was in so much pain. Then he got control of that. He said, "You think you're done?"

"I am done."

"Get the fuck out of my house."

I ran out to the car, peeled away.

About six blocks from his house, I pulled into the lot of the Greek place we'd eaten at before: Pegasus. Everything on me was shaking. I looked in the rearview mirror; no one was behind me. I called Kate. Would she answer? She didn't. The message I left was "Please do it exactly like we planned."

Then I texted her: "Emergency!!!"

I'd have three full days on Darren Rudd. Three full days to get out of the country before he picked up a phone. But really, I'd only have an hour, maybe less, on Eric Deveny. Was he going to come after me? At least Kate and the kids would be gone. Wouldn't they? All I had left to do was grab the money, my passport, and my mother.

One of the TracFones rang as I sped down the 75 through Gainesville. It was Mason. "You okay?"

"Yeah."

"Who is that motherfucker?"

"That motherfucker is the motherfucking source."

"What's the source doing out there?"

"He's busted. He wants me to take care of him."

"Are you going to take care of him?"

"What do you think I'm going to do?"

"I think you're going to leave the country."

I didn't say anything.

"Are we ever going to see you guys again?"

"I don't know what's going to happen."

Mason was quiet on the line. Then he said, "I'm always going to regret what I did that night."

I saw the redhead running in the moonlight. I saw the moonlight on the cotton. I saw her tumbling down. There were so many things I wanted to say to him. What I said to him was "Take care of your girls."

Was Kate at the house when I got there? Nobody was—the car was gone. But had they really left? Were their clothes in the closets? In the drawers? When I ran into the bedrooms to check, there were their clothes.

Where the fuck was Kate?

I texted her: "answer." She didn't answer. I texted her: "fucking answer right now!!" She didn't.

I jumped in the car, peeled out, called Cristina.

"Where's Kate?"

"Kate? I don't know. Isn't she at home? She was there with the kids when I left."

"Did she tell you anything about what's happening?"

"What's happening?"

"Where are you right now?"

"At the beach."

"Don't make a fucking move until I call you and tell you what to do."

"Okay."

I texted Nick: "stay away from the house."

A few minutes later, he texted back: "why??"

I texted him: "raided. go away." Then I turned off that phone.

I drove to the Vault to get my passport, the money. When I got there, I sat outside in the car. Kate had the keys.

I pounded on the steering wheel over and over. Then I sat and looked out at the day. Somehow the day was still going on. How had I forgotten about the keys? I'd have to go to Kate's friends' place and find them. Then I'd have to come back here and get the money. I was wasting so much time! Where had we agreed she'd hide them? The downstairs toilet tank. And this new thought came to me: I'd find out at her friends' place if my wife still loved me. If the keys were there, maybe she did. And if the keys weren't, she didn't.

One of my phones rang. Kate.

It wasn't Kate. It was my mother.

"James? You have to come over right now. There's a detective here. He wants to talk to you. What have you been doing?"

"A detective?" Tell him I'm out of town, I thought to tell my mother. But I knew my mother wouldn't tell him that. I began the drive to my mother's on the Trail. Up to this point, time had been frenetic. Now it slowed, became dreamlike. Where were all these people going in these cars? Did any of them know how good life was? The sky so blue, the world so beautiful. Why had I given up on that? What if I didn't go to my mother's? Would I be on the run? Would they freeze our documents? Would they keep Kate and the kids from getting on the plane? I couldn't do that to them.

I thought all these things as I hurried up the Trail: Maybe they were just going to ask me questions. Maybe they didn't really know. Maybe it was about something else. Maybe they wouldn't arrest me.

But as I drove through the bright afternoon, I knew none

of that was going to happen. Soon I would be in handcuffs, and then in the cage in a cruiser. Wasn't it a relief? That it was finally over? That even though I'd never hold my children again, the police would be responsible for my family's safety now? After all the miles I'd done? To show up right now? I'd give them Darren. I'd give them Deveny. I'd take whatever deal they gave me. Then I'd be in prison.

A black Crown Victoria Interceptor with tinted windows was sitting in the driveway of my mother's house when I pulled up. Unmarked. A narc car. I knew as I walked past it I was taking my last free steps.

I saw them talking in the doorway, the plainclothes cop and my mother. He was burly, tall, in a white collared shirt and khaki slacks: a detective. My mother looked past him when she saw me. I'd never seen that kind of worry on her face. It made me feel so ashamed I had to glance away. When I looked back, the detective had turned around. His face was covered with acne scars.

"James," Eric's guy Manuel said to me, "you're supposed to be on your way to New York." I hadn't seen him in a year, but had no problem recognizing him. From sitting on Eric's couch that first day. That first nerve-racking day when Eric had had his muscle with him and I hadn't even known he had. Not until now. Now I understood that Manuel was Eric's muscle.

He grabbed my arm, started marching me down the walkway. Behind me, my mother was saying, "What have you been doing? What were you supposed to be doing in New York?"

I said to him, "Don't shoot me in front of her."

He said, "Shut the fuck up. And get in the car. You drive. I know you're good at it."

He sat in back, had a gun on me. I reversed the Interceptor out of the driveway.

"Where we going?"

"You know where we're going."

"I won't give him anything."

"What if he tortures you?"

I made the obvious plan. I would crash us into a tree. I would wrestle the gun from him. Before I could do that, Manuel said, "Circle the block."

I hooked a left, began to do that through the neighborhood of small houses. There was no one around. He tossed a manila envelope on the seat beside me. "Special delivery."

I opened the envelope with one hand as I drove us slowly up the street, shook out whatever was in it. There were pictures, black-and-white pictures of Danielle and me. Danielle and me naked on the bed, the telltale upper arm; she'd taken the pictures herself. I was passed out, she was sweaty, her hair plastered across her brow. It was obvious what we'd just done.

"Get back to work," Manuel told me. "Otherwise she texts those pictures to your wife. To your wife's phone. And if your wife doesn't have that phone anymore, they'll go in the mail. To that little house. To that bigger house. Don't make me come down here again. I'll kill your mother. I'll kill your wife. I'll kill your kids. Then I'll dead-check all of them. You think I like killing women and children? You think I've never done it before?"

Back at my car, Manuel put the gun away, popped the trunk on the Interceptor. The suitcases were in there; I loaded them into my Forester. Before he drove away, Manuel said, "Don't fuck around. If I have to come back down here, I'll shoot your mother. Don't ever make me drive weight around for you again. That's not my job, it's yours."

I got on the road. Clarity began entering into me. Eric Deveny thought he knew me, thought he had something on me that would always keep me working for him. But I'd already told my wife. He didn't have anything on me at all. Was Kate gone? Did it matter now? He'd played all his cards and he had nothing. I knew what I had to do to end this.

To end this, I needed something I didn't have right now, the thing that had gotten me into it in the first place: I needed the money.

One of my phones began blowing up: my mother.

"James? What's going on?"

"There's something I haven't been telling you, Ma. There's something I've been lying to you about for months."

"What is it?"

"The yacht-detailing crew."

"What about the yacht-detailing crew?"

"It isn't really about detailing yachts."

"It's not?"

"It's about stealing them."

"Stealing them?"

"Stripping off the serial numbers and sending them somewhere else."

"Why would you have gotten involved in that?"

"I needed the money."

"Did Kate know what you were doing?"

"Yeah, Kate knew."

"Why would Kate have let you do that?"

"Kate knew we needed the money."

"Are you going to jail?"

"I'm not sure."

"I can't believe you did this."

Neither of us said anything. Then she said, "I don't really know you, do I?"

"No, you don't."

"I let him push you too hard."

"It wasn't you. It wasn't him. It was always just me."

I told her, "You have to do something now whether you like it or not. You have to leave your house. You have to stay in a hotel until I call you. It doesn't matter where, any hotel. It may take a few days. Be patient. Don't worry about the money. Take your cell phone, leave it on. Don't call the police if you want your grandchildren to have parents. I love you." Then I hung up.

I called Cristina. "The money in the teapot on the stove—there's two thousand dollars left, take it all. Get your shit together, don't leave anything behind. Take a taxi to the airport, get a one-way rental car to Tallahassee. Drive up there as fast as you can, drop off the car at the airport. Take a shuttle downtown. Get a room at the Governors. Stay in the room until I call you and tell you what to do next. I'll be there as soon as I can. I'm working on getting your money."

"Okay, James. I'm leaving right now."

Then I called Eric Deveny.

"A few facts," Eric told me when he picked up. "Fact number one: you came to me. Fact number two: that mess we took care of for you can and will come back up. Fact number three: your wife will get those pictures. Fact number four: you can shut this down and get back to work. You're the one who came crawling to me. You're the one who wanted it."

"I want those fucking pictures to disappear."

"Give me your connection."

"Then I'm giving it to you. But you have to help me with something first."

"Tell me what it is, I'll tell you if I will."

I hustled to New York. Drove through the night. Would this be the last time I would ever have to carry weight? Or would the cops catch me at last? The road was long and empty. The cops did not catch me.

I parked at Newark, grabbed a taxi to the city. It was a clear, cold morning. The city stood before me in its solemn length as the driver took me in.

At her place, Danielle came to the door with the gym bag. Was she frightened to see me? She was not. She was wearing a T-shirt and jeans, looked like she was taking the day off.

"I saw the pictures," I said.

She smiled. "What did you think of them? I mean, I never studied photography or anything like that. But I think I did a pretty good job. You know what? You should have gotten better at this before you got in over your head. See you in two weeks? I hope so. Where will you be if you aren't here, you know?"

"How much did he pay you?"

She shut her door on me.

Back in my car at Newark, I quickly counted the money in the gym bag: $181,000 in thousand-dollar bundles. Sixty-two of the bundles belonged to me. But right now that wasn't the point. The point was: now I had the money.

I got on the road. The road went on before me. Should I stop in Savannah and get some sleep? I did not stop. There would be time for that later. Right now I had a lot to do. Everything I had to do, I had to do in Tallahassee.

In the room at the Marriott the next morning, Darren Rudd was pacing like a trapped tiger. Had what had happened to him begun to settle in while I'd been away? He threw JoJo Bear at me when I opened the door. He said, "You know how many fucking times I almost picked up the phone? You know how many fucking times I almost took you down? It's time for you to start taking care of this situation. It's time for me to meet your guy and get back on my feet."

"Relax," I said. "Everything's okay. We're going to go and meet him right now. I hope you'll remember how I helped you when the two of you decide what to do with me."

"Fucking middle man," Darren said.

"Isn't that how it works? Cut out who you can, get all the money?"

He sniffed, put his hands in the pockets of his leather jacket. He said, "I never tried to do that to you."

"I never gave you the chance."

We went down to the car. I began to drive him across Tallahassee. What did he think of Florida? I asked him. Piece of shit place, he told me. Too flat, too commercial, nothing compared to the Siskiyou Mountains. Had he ever dreamed of Mount Shasta? I asked him. Dreaming of the mountain was for moonbeams, he told me, not for people who had been born up there. How long had Billy worked for him? I asked. Billy had worked for him for almost eight years, he said. What kind of work was Billy going to do now? I asked. Whatever the fuck kind of work he wanted to, Darren said, because now Billy was a free fucking man.

"They're not going to charge him?"

Darren didn't even glance at me. He said, "Oh yeah. I meant free from the business."

When we pulled up to the garage with the pond beside it, it was a beautiful day. The pond was flat and reflected the sky. The wind moved quietly through the pine trees all around us.

"Let's go," I told him. "My guy's waiting in there."

Darren looked at the closed door of the garage for a long time. Was he having second thoughts about meeting Deveny? Or was he just being cautious? He opened the door of the car, stepped out, put his hands in the pockets of his jacket, and started walking down the gravel drive.

"We're going to have to work with a few different networks

at first," Darren told me. "You're going to have to start carrying heavier weight. You'll have to go and check on things for me, see which of my bunkers are still up, which ones they've taken down. People are probably thinking they can fuck around out there, but I'll work out some kind of muscle with this guy, then we'll send you all out there together. You're going to make a shit ton of money now, James. Much more than before. Nobody is going to cut you out."

I turned the knob of the metal door at the side of the building, opened it for my new boss, guided him gently in with my hand. He was still yammering away about the business when I shut the door behind him and began sprinting away. Then the shots rang out.

When the shooting stopped, Eric Deveny poked his head out the door. "All clear, my man," he called over to where I was crouched beside the car. "I just solved your problem."

I walked along the gravel drive. Did I want to see what had happened in that garage? No. Was I going to have to see it? Yes.

Inside, Darren was crumpled against the wall as though a great wind had blown him there, his gun on the floor a dozen feet away. But I knew it hadn't been a great wind; it had been fourteen or fifteen bullets from the assault rifle in Eric Deveny's hands. I'd wondered in Eric's kitchen, the first time I'd seen it, if there were bullets in it, and what would have happened if I had picked it up and pulled the trigger. What would have happened was a whole lot of bullets would have sprayed out.

Eric was dressed in white, holding that rifle, a big smile on his face. His brother with his messy beard was standing beside the worktable with the Skilsaw. The two of them were there because I'd told Eric on the phone two days before that if he wanted to have my Cali connection, he had to help me with a problem.

"What's the problem?"

"One of my mules."

"What's he doing?"

"He's blackmailing me."

"What's he got on you?"

"You know what he's got on me. You're the one who cleaned it up."

"Fifty thousand dollars."

"Done."

Now Eric said, "Little fucker got a shot off. Can you believe that? This was not your average mule. Good thing you took care of him now."

I walked across to Darren's torn and bloody body. Had he really been as small as that? He'd seemed so much bigger in life. I pushed his tongue into his mouth, shut his eyes. What could he and Eric have done together if they'd ever had the chance to meet? After they'd cut me out? After they'd put me at the bottom of the pond where Darren was going now? I felt in the back of his waistband, found the heavy envelopes, tossed all three of them to Eric. "Here's the money. Asshole carried it in himself. I know there's extra in it. Give it to your brother for a tip." As though to say thanks, Eric's brother started up the Skilsaw.

I grabbed JoJo Bear out of the pocket of Darren's ruined jacket. Did JoJo have any of that blood on him? He didn't. "I'm sorry about what I've put you through," I whispered to him. When I pressed his belly, he whispered back, "I love you."

Eric set the rifle down on the workbench, then he and I left the fluorescent-lit garage. Outside, he said, "What about that other thing you owe me, James?"

"The connection?"

"The connection."

"How do I know those pictures will go away?"

"When have I not played straight with you?"

At the car, I passed him his share of the New York money out of the gym bag, bundle by bundle. He needed both hands to hold it all. Would I make it out of here alive once I gave him the phone? He would have to drop the pile of money to kill me. I knew he would not drop the pile of money.

I looked around at the day. At the beautiful day. I said to him, "Are there fish in that pond?"

He said, "All kinds. Bass, crappie, bluegill. Hungry fish. They all work for me, too."

I took a TracFone out of my pocket, set it on top of the money in his arms. I said, "Here's the connection."

Eric looked at the phone, made a face at it. Was it smaller than he'd imagined? Less complex? He said, "This really it?"

"That's really it. The only number on it. Now that you have it, I can't get it back. So don't lose it. If you lose it, you'll lose the connection forever. Don't forget about the time zones. It's only eight A.M. out there."

"Too early to call?"

"You can try it."

"What's your connection's name?"

"His name is Darren Rudd."

I hopped in my car. Eric started back toward the garage. He wasn't going to shoot me this time? Why not? Did he want to wait until he was certain the connection was true? That's what I would have done. I wouldn't have trusted me anymore. Not after seeing me run away. Not after knowing I wanted out. As I was driving away from there, Eric Deveny did make that call to California. A few moments after that, a TracFone began to ring in the jacket pocket of the guy he'd just killed.

I wasn't half a mile down the road when one of my phones began to vibrate. I knew which one. "You're dead," Eric said when I picked up.

"I'm not dead."

"My people are already on their way down there."

"My people are already gone."

"I'll hunt you for years. I'll enjoy it."

"Why bother? You're never going to see me again."

Then I hung up.

I was on the road. Was I afraid? Yes. At the same time, Eric Deveny didn't have a police force, couldn't put out an APB on me. I drove to the Tallahassee airport, rented a car, a one-way rental. It was a silver Buick Lucerne, a pretty car. I sat in it, started it, drove around the airport, turned into the short-term lot, parked the Lucerne beside my Forester, and hopped back in my car.

I left the airport on Capital Circle, turned onto Springhill Road, drove southwest, not far, and entered the Apalachicola National Forest. I turned off the paved road onto a dirt road, drove into the trees until the forest closed around me. The forest was pine, with small lakes and ponds all through it. I turned off the car, took out a phone, called Cristina.

"Where are you?"

"I'm in a room at the Governors. Where are you?"

"I'm here. I'm ready. I have the money. Book the room now. Text him tonight. Let me know what happens. Go to the hotel tomorrow at three."

"I'm scared."

"Don't be scared."

I waited until night fell. I started the car, reversed through the trees, got back on the road, drove into the city, and asked a gas station attendant how to get to a Wal-Mart. At the Wal-Mart I bought rope.

"Gonna tie someone up?" the checkout girl asked me when she took my money.

"Maybe," I said.

"That sounds pretty fun," she said, gave me that ancient look.

I put the rope in my jacket pocket, walked out to my car, drove back to the forest, hid in the trees. JoJo Bear was with me. When I pressed his belly, he said, "I love you." I slowly sawed the rope to the length I needed with the car key against my thigh. It took awhile. And passed the time. When the rope was cut, I threw the long remainder out the window onto the forest floor. I tried to sleep in the car, but couldn't. I thought about Kate and the children all night.

The dawn broke. Small brown birds flitted about in the woods. I did not know what kind of birds they were. The pine forest around me looked like a gray mist with the canopy green and dark above it. The tops of the trees swayed in the wind. I smoked cigarettes.

At noon, Cristina called. She said, "He said okay."

"Thank fucking God."

"I can't do it."

"You can do it."

After I hung up with her, I took a slip of paper out of my wallet. There was a phone number written on it; I called the number. When the receptionist answered the phone, I told her to make a note on my reservation that a friend would be arriving before me. I wanted my friend to be let into the room.

"Thank you, sir," the receptionist said.

At three, Cristina called again. She said, "The guy here wants to talk to you."

I talked to him; he was also a receptionist. He wanted information from me. I took another slip of paper out of my wallet, read him the information that was written on it. When I'd finished, he told me, "Have a nice trip. We'll see you when you get here."

I started the car, sped into the city. Cristina was standing on the corner outside the hotel, wearing a baseball hat and sunglasses. Her hair was tucked up inside the hat. I powered down the passenger-side window; she handed me a keycard. She said, "You look exhausted."

"I am exhausted."

"I'm so fucking scared."

"Don't be scared."

I drove back to the woods. Evening settled upon the land. I thought of my family.

Then it was night. A text message came in on one of my phones. It read, "He's here."

I started the car, sped into the city. Then I was downtown. I pulled into the parking garage off College Avenue. I left the gym bag on the floor of the passenger seat. I locked the car because there was $62,000 in the gym bag. Then I ran the three blocks over to the high-rise Capital Hotel.

I entered the lobby in a small crowd of people, business-people, and stepped into an elevator with them. I rode up to the seventh floor, stepped out, walked down the hall. At the door to the room, I put my car keys in my mouth, wound the rope around my hands. In my jacket pocket was the keycard. I took it out, slid it in the slot. The light flashed green, the door unlocked. I could enter the room if I wanted.

I did want to enter the room, just like I'd wanted to enter all of them. I had to enter the room; the end of it was in there.

I slowly turned the handle, went in. The lamp on the dresser was lit. The people on the bed were lit in the light of it. The two people on the bed were naked. The two people on the bed were Cristina Freeman and Eric Deveny.

I spit my car keys on the floor, was on him in five running steps. He didn't have a chance to see who I was before I had the rope around his neck. I pulled it so tight it began to cut into my hands. What Cristina was doing, I didn't care.

Cristina had once told my wife and me that if there was ever anything she could do for us, all we had to do was ask. So I'd asked. Asked her to come to a restaurant where I'd be having lunch with a man.

"Who's the man?"

"Someone I'm afraid of."

She'd been sitting alone in the restaurant when we'd walked in. At the end of our meal, she'd come to our table, asked him if he'd been in a movie, tousled her hair, gave him her number, and later that night she'd let him into her suite at the Governors Inn. She'd had sex with him. While he'd been in the bathroom afterward, she'd opened his wallet. Part of why she'd done those things was because she cared about my wife and children. The other part was because I'd paid her.

Two days later, she'd been sitting with me in my car at Siesta Beach. She'd opened her purse, pulled out a slip of paper: a sheet from a Governors Inn notepad. On it was written a credit card number, an expiration date, the security code from the back of the card. Below that was a driver's license number. All of it belonged to Eric Deveny.

"You think you have to do this?"

"I'll give him every last chance."

"I don't want to have to see it."

"Just get me in the room."

And now, in the room, she was dressing as fast as she could, picking up the car keys. She was walking down the hall, leaving the hotel, running in her high heels down the street. She was looking for my car in the parking garage, finding it, getting in. She was opening the gym bag, staring at her money. And now she was driving away.

For part of the time she was doing those things, Eric Deveny was dying. And the rest of the time she was doing those things, Eric Deveny was dead.

What a beautiful body Eric Deveny had on the floor of that room. Except for his bleeding neck. I had pulled the rope so tight. I had fucking hated him.

The room was like any other hotel room in the world. But now it was the one where Eric Deveny had died. As I recovered my breath on the edge of the bed, I took JoJo Bear out of the pocket of my jacket. When I pressed his belly, JoJo Bear said, "I love you."

My hands had bled onto the rope. So I could not leave the rope behind. So I took the bag out of the garbage can and put the rope in that. Then I took off my driving clothes for the last time, put them in the bag as well. I tied the bag shut, dressed in Eric Deveny's white clothes. They would think I was him on the video as I left. They would not think to look for me; they'd only see him. A waitress had once said to us, "You two look like brothers." Our hearts had been similar in many ways. But now our hearts were also different. Mine was the one still beating.

I took a towel from the bathroom, wiped the door handles clean, put the keycard in my pocket with his wallet and phone. I rode the elevator down to his Mercedes, got in it, and drove through town in the night. The phone and keycard I wiped on my shirt and threw out the window. The wallet I wiped and slid under the seat. I pulled into the McDonald's by the Governor's Square Mall, dumped the bag I'd brought with me in a garbage can in the lot. Then I opened the Mercedes' trunk, looked at the assault rifle inside.

I drove to Eric Deveny's house, lifted out the rifle, walked to the side door. I didn't care if the door was locked or not because I also had his keys.

I entered the dark kitchen, went down the dark hall. I stepped into the den, pointed the rifle at the two men on the couch, who were playing a video game.

I could not hear the shooting in the video game. They stopped playing when they saw me. I pulled the trigger. The rifle did not fire because the safety was on. The two men and I looked at one another. I dropped the rifle and snatched up the handgun from the coffee table. Then I shot them both with it. I wiped the guns clean with a cloth from the kitchen. I wiped the doorknobs clean.

I drove to the airport, parked in the long-term lot, wiped the Mercedes, left the keys and cloth on the seat, and walked through the lots to my rental car. Then I did what I'd always done. I got back on the road.

All there was now was the road. My life was ruined and my life might always be ruined and maybe always had been ruined. And I did not want to go to prison and I did not want to lose my family; I did not care if I went to prison and I did not care if I lost my family. And I did not care if I lived and I did not care if I died; I did not care if I did not live and I did not care if I did not die. But there was the road. I got myself on the road and the stripes of the roadway flashed in the headlights. And I felt hunted and I did not feel hunted. And there was the money. And I was a rich man and I was a poor man and I was a good man and I was a bad man; I was a not rich man and I was a not poor man and I was a not good man and I was a not bad man. And there was the recession and there was not the recession and there was the fear from the recession and there was not the fear from the recession. And there was America and there was not America and there was me and there was not me.

But there was the road. And I was on the road.

Acknowledgments

First, thanks to my wife, Jessyka Lee, partner in crime, who helped me write this book. To my banditos, Gwendolyn and Rohan, we love you so much. To Granny, Nana, Sis, Jerry, Bud, Catherine, and both our families. Good times!

Thanks to the John Simon Guggenheim Memorial Foundation and the Japan–United States Friendship Commission/ NEA Creative Artists Exchange for the generous fellowships.

My editor, Jenna Johnson, gave me line-by-line Maxwell Perkins–caliber direction. Thanks for rolling the dice on me. This book would not exist without you. Thanks to Johnathan Wilber for the fine insights, Larry Cooper for catching everything else, and everyone at Houghton Mifflin Harcourt. Thanks to Liz Darhansoff and Michele Mortimer at the agency, for pushing me hard.

To our friends in Austin—#1 JWB, Meredith, KK, Amelia, Nate & Matt, Lindz, Lisa, & Mr. Moustache. In our beloved NorCal: Guthrie, thanks for the sense of humor. BW, "drive fast 'n' swerve a lot." Joel Dunsany "The Cosmic Man," Penn, Cathy & Jack, the Dunsmuir Writers, Kathryn, Paul, Brian, Frank & Kazumi, the Coopers, Robb, Charlie, everyone at the *Mount Shasta Herald*, Steve & Marcella, Skye, Jeff, Susan. Lance, thanks for the cabin. Helen, thanks for finding it for us.

In Sac: R, TJ, Mayah & Shar. In Tally, the inimitable TS, thanks for the opportunity. Bob Shacochis, whose voodoo made this book possible. Southwest Florida: Tierney & Alex, Tim, Josh, the Infantis. Breanna, who gave me a line from her poem "Swish," Amanda, Whitney, Chris & Stella. Mumbai: Uncle Cipri & family. Patnem: Sarika, who took good care of Sissy and Bubby while their parents wrote. Joe Pedo in NYC, the Elliotts of Brattleboro, VT, the extended Martins, & Stewart Cummings of Calgary, AB.

To my writing support: Barry Spacks, Brian Weinberg, Matt Walsh, Eric Trethewey.

Last, thanks to Jeff B. and all my anonymous friends.

In loving memory of Mouse and Dad. We miss you.